HAT DANCE

DANCE

Michael A. Thomas

WITHDRAWN

UNIVERSITY OF NEW MEXICO PRESS
ALBUQUERQUE

Library of Congress Cataloging-in-Publication Data

Thomas, Michael A.
Hat dance / Michael A. Thomas.— 1st ed.
p. cm.
ISBN 0-8263-3134-3 (alk. paper)
1. Americans—Mexico—Fiction. 2. Indians, Treatment of—Fiction.
3. Indians of Mexico—Fiction. 4. Journalists—Fiction.
5. Festivals—Fiction. I. Title.
PS3570.H5739H37 2004
813'.54—dc22

2003023790

10 09 08 07 06 05 04   1 2 3 4 5 6 7

Printed and bound in the USA by Sheridan Printers, Inc. Typeset in
Sabon 10.5/13. Display text set in Pompeia Inline and Mambo Initials.
Design and composition: Robyn Mundy. Production: Maya Allen-Gallegos

To My Wife, Minda Stillings, and my friend,
Enrique Lamadrid, *por todo el cariño*
y apoyo que me han dado en esto,
mil gracias

Acknowledgments

Many Thanks to:

Dustin Cole, Gena Coldwell, Catron Allred, Laura Fashing, Robbie Edwards, Lee Pfiefer, Sharret Rose, Jamie Barr, Jennifer Hengen, Deborah Thompson, and two anonymous readers at the University of New Mexico Press: They read the book at one juncture or another and then told me how to make it better.

Carolyn Meyer, who gave me two packed pages of priceless, worth-its-weight-in-gold, advice when I really needed it.

Minda Stillings, my wife, who was there for every word of every draft, which is saying a mouthful. Her advice is invariably accurate and astute.

Enrique Lamadrid, my friend and companion in a seemingly endless series of Mexican adventures and misadventures.

Rosalie Otero, director of the University Honors Program at UNM, a patient, supportive boss.

Margo Chávez-Charles, a fellow traveler on these same roads.

My step-daughters Laura Fashing and Jamie Barr and my daughter Alexa Thomas for their various perspectives on the Father-daughter relationship.

Mexico, the land, the mountains, rivers, deserts and most of all, the people. Mexico has been my *naco* zen master, my mentor, my truth serum. I hope I do it justice.

One

"... *Nacieron todas las flooooores*. ..."

Something bumped. Water whined in the pipes, loud and surprising. A faraway voice was singing, muffled and distorted by walls. Other voices joined in. Finally, the song faded into laughter. People were drunk. They hesitated, gave a hoot or two, and restarted the song.

Lee White awakened without knowledge of his whereabouts. He could see nothing and dreaded the prospect of moving. "The drunken bastards!" He said aloud. He lay still, anger heating the pillow.

At length, he resigned himself to the noise, a rhythmic, recurring pulse. Recurring pulse or no, there were no helicopters and He was not in Vietnam. The smell was wrong, no mildew . . . good. The pillow cooled and neck muscles began to relax with a strangely intense sense of relief. He listened closely. There was, actually, quite a cheery quality to the noise, the unmistakable sound of happy drunks. He recognized the song, "*Las Mañanitas.*" Now he knew. He was in a hotel somewhere in Mexico. It was someone's birthday and the water was a surprise. Not being in Vietnam was a bonus he still appreciated. Not being in the U.S. was pretty good too.

He lay there gloating. He was, after all, Lee White, a pretty cagey guy. It's always cheering to be in Mexico and know it. By degrees he recalled his agenda for the day that would shortly dawn. He'd make calls, collect debts, avoid creditors, tie up loose ends, and then shag it on over to Mexico City. He rolled over, intending to get up, and make an early day of it.

Rolling over turned out to be an adventure. Pain in his gut stabbed, sudden and merciless, taking control. The pain was like the ringing of a thousand telephones. It surged up and then subsided gradually, as though one by one the callers had concluded that no one was home and hung up.

As the pain subsided, Lee tried to remember: The city, was it Tepic? Seemed like it, but Mexico is a big country. He'd have to check. For now, it'd be best to stay in bed, and try that moving business again later.

He congratulated himself on one point. At least he was alone. He smiled. All the Mexicans regarded him with pity.

"Poor man, to be so alone."

That's what Minerva always said.

Minerva was Checo's newly estranged wife. Lee partnered with Checo on magazine projects. Lee provided the text and Checo took the photos. Lee wondered if Minerva felt any pity for poor Checo. Highly doubtful. Lee had long observed that Mexican women are among the most vengeful creatures on the planet. American women, he'd concluded, are often more destructive, but only because they have more to work with.

Yes, it was lucky that he was alone. Not that it was luck—not in the sense of random good fortune. No. For good or ill, Lee's solitude was the fruit of effort and expense. And just look at the issue. There he was in his predawn repose, summoning the courage to meet the day. He was sick, hurting, and perplexed in a country he did not understand.

Once again he'd eaten food that'd made him sick? He was certain it was *tacos*, chicken *tacos* he'd ordered in an expensive but empty restaurant. The *tacos* had waited for who knows how many eons with their lurking multitudes of bacteria. Twenty years of intermittent life in Mexico and he'd learned nothing? What a way to work his parcel of eternity!

Of course things would change. Courtney was coming and his precious solitude would be gone. Courtney, Lee's second daughter, could not possibly be as angry with Lee as Hannah, her mother. That was the most optimistic spin he could manage regarding the imminent visit. He loved and struggled with his daughters with an intensity that often surprised him, caught him off guard.

Eventually, as the day dawned, drunks and birds quieted their songs, and Lee got back to sleep. As he slept, the pain cycled, now acute, now almost tolerable.

The geriatric telephone rang several times before Lee recognized the harsh noise as distinct from his cramping, distending innards.

"*Bueno?*" Lee missed the comfortably noncommittal "Hello" that English offered.

"Daddy?"

Christ, it was Courtney!

"Yo, Towanda."

He could hear Courtney deciding to let it go. She drew a deep breath and slowly exhaled.

"You sound funny, are you OK?"

"Yeah, I'm fine, great. I mean, I think I'm sick. I can't tell. I'm still in bed."

He prodded at his belly, which gurgled loudly.

"Well, now that we have that cleared up, you are where? Tepic? The phone code seems to be for Tepic."

"Yeah, Tepic. At least I think so. Let me look, there have to be some hotel matches around, or an ashtray. Here, I've got it. Hotel Fray Junípero Serra, Tepic, Nayarit. Now, what was it you were calling about? How'd you get the number?"

There was a pause.

"Now I know it's early, Daddy, but cast your mind back and you'll remember that you left the number on my answering machine. By the way, where is Tepic? I can't find it on the map."

"It's a bit north and a bit west of Guadalajara."

"No wonder I couldn't find it. I was thinking you'd be within fifty miles of Mexico City. What on earth are you doing in fucking Tepic? I thought we were meeting in Mexico City this afternoon!"

Lee could picture Courtney sitting at her desk, her back erect, her pointy nose threatening to pin him to the wall. She was a big, healthy,

American beauty, this girl he'd fathered. But her edges were sharp, her limbs restless. The image was irksome.

"Sweetheart, that tone is unpleasant, accusatory, and I don't appreciate the vulgar talk. It puts me in mind of your mother. Now why don't we just fall back and regroup, just start over . . . Yo, Towanda."

Regretting the words as they left his mouth, Lee heard Courtney catch her breath. Her stamina was gone.

"Can't you just call me by my name?"

"You know . . . it's . . ."

"No I don't 'know.' All I 'know' is that it's an odd name and it annoys Mama. It was kind of fun when I was little. Now it just seems immature. I'm sick of it and you know it."

Lee could not find the discipline required to make an apology and get beyond the argument he'd provoked.

"You think 'Courtney' isn't an odd name?"

"No, of course not. There were a whole bunch of 'Courtneys' at my school."

"Along with all of the 'Tiffanys,' 'Brittanys,' and 'Chelseas,' right? Your school could have used couple of 'Krystals' or 'Towandas.'"

Courtney sniffed.

Lee did not like being sniffed at. Women always felt they had the right to sniff at him. His head was swimming. He could not remember how he'd gotten into this conversation. Predictably, but against all reason, he blamed Hannah, his ex. With effort, he ignored the sniff and pressed on.

"It's like this, Court. It was a miracle Hannah and I stayed married long enough to produce children to fight over. Agreeing on names was beyond us. Your mother named you and I decided to call you whatever suited me. I came up with 'Towanda.' It annoyed Hannah and I actually liked it. It sounded African-American to me and Hannah is the whitest person on the planet. I still like it. I thought you liked it too."

In fact, Lee knew very well that Courtney hadn't liked her pet name since she was sixteen. For at least nine years, then, he'd used the name to annoy both Hannah and Courtney. Why? Annoying Hannah was one thing, she had it coming, but Courtney? There was really no excuse.

"You know better, Dad, so just knock it off. Think of other ways to bug Mama."

"OK, that shouldn't be hard."

Courtney, showing more discipline than her father, let the crack pass.

"So why'd you call?"

"Oh, I just wanted to let you know that I won't be at the airport in D.F. to meet you. I'll never make it by 5:47."

"Well, that's just terrific. We're bringing a bunch of cameras and video equipment and have to go through Mexican customs. We were counting on your Spanish."

"Doesn't Kevin speak Spanish?"

"Nope, his parents never spoke Spanish in the home."

"Tell me about Kevin. I mean he's your techie . . . but I'm picking up on something . . . You met his parents?"

"No, Daddy. We've mainly worked together but we have been kind of an 'item' lately."

"An 'item,' eh? You better keep some boundaries in your professional relationships, Court. Things get messy."

"You should know. Kevin's just very lovable, sweet. It's not to the point of having to either hang it up or quit working together, but I am aware that such a point exists."

"Well, in that case, you're smarter than most of the filmmakers I know. Anyway, the 'García' threw me. I figured he spoke Spanish. Don't worry, though, I'll have Checo meet you. I'll tell him to come to your gate and hold sign that says: '*Bienvenidos, Courtney y Kevin.*' Checo is small, about 5'6", dark, and very skinny. His posture is poor. He'll probably be wearing slacks and a short sleeved *guayabera* shirt that'll give the impression of a leisure suit. He's balding and does a comb over that does not quite work. You really can't miss him "

Lee smiled, as he pictured Checo with the sign, uptight and glancing at his watch every thirty seconds.

"Checo's English, despite years of study, deteriorates in situations of stress, like airports. But he'll know what to do. He's related to almost everyone in Mexico City, all the bureaucrats anyway. I've got your flight information. I'll call Checo and set it up. I'll get back to confirm that he'll be there. You'll love Checo."

"I'd be happier if you could be there. I'm beginning to wonder if this film project is a good idea . . . I'm used to a lot of control in my projects."

"I'll bet. . . . It's a little late for misgivings, Court. But don't worry, the film's in your able hands and yours alone. I don't know Jack about films and neither does Checo."

"That's not altogether comforting, you know."

"Honey, you just worry all you need to. Worry is fundamental going into something like this. I'm not worried because I've survived so many disastrous projects and assignments. I've lost the capacity. You go ahead, though. Worry and worry, it's really your job right now."

Courtney laughed. "Well, I'm giving it my best shot. Just like my old man."

"That's my daughter!"

Lee smiled and felt a wave of warmth suffuse his troubled tummy. Despite the sharp edges, Courtney's sweetness came through. Lee, despite his habit of disappearing at crucial times, was a fond father.

They made their goodbyes and hung up. Lee's stomach seemed better but he was still queasy. He lay on the bed, and decided to sleep a bit more.

When he awoke at the civilized hour of nine, the pain was mostly gone and had taken the heaviness, the sense of malaise along with it. The tag ends of intestinal distress and muscle pain were bearable. Shedding his underwear, he made his way to the bathroom, flipped on the light and, out of habit rather than optimism, turned on the "caliente" tap to run while he took a leak.

Pissing, he looked out the bathroom window and over Tepic to the mountain-framed horizon beyond. Something moved across his field of vision. What was it, there on the window frame? . . . a beetle, a furry beetle . . . no, it was a mouse, a ball of fur the size of a walnut on the frame, not more than a foot in front of him. He started back astonished, then recovered. He stared and the mouse stared back—its small, shiny black eyes scrutinizing the dark giant that suddenly loomed.

Lee felt a smile move across his face.

"Well, aren't you a surprise?"

The mouse stood still, meeting Lee's gaze and betraying no emotion.

"Jesus, you're little. Don't you know this is a four star hotel? I mean, one call to the lobby and they'd be on you with everything short of nukes. So just mind your manners, sport, and look away while I pee. You've never seen a man pee before?"

The mouse cocked its tiny head as though assessing Lee and the sounds he made.

"Okay, whatever. I give up. I was on my way out anyway. With your leave I just plan to freeze my ass for about thirty seconds in the shower and then I'll be gone. You have my best wishes for a long prosperous life. May your tribe increase, good Master Mouse. Or is Madam Mouse? Or is it Miss Mouse? Can I take you on my knee, Miss Mouse? Will you marry me, Miss Mouse?"

He gave the mouse a courtly nod.

The mouse either misunderstood or suddenly had its fill of conversation. In a split second it was gone, vanished down a hole in the window frame that was barely big enough for a pencil to pass through.

Lee smiled. The hotel doubtless spent a bundle on pest control yet the little blighter lived. The tall man closed his eyes and breathed deeply, his spirits lifted by the small indomitable creature. Now for the dreaded shower.

He stepped into the shower stiffening in anticipation of the cold water he'd come to accept in Mexican hotels. The water was hot! Instantly and gloriously hot! What a magnificent omen! Kindly jets of warm water pummeled and invigorated his poor, ill-cared for body. He watched steam rise and condense on his chest hair. He felt hope. His body had some miles on it but it had some left in it, too. He flexed his thighs and enjoyed the response—tight, defined muscles rippled to attention and showed themselves ready for the mountains. He was a big man, standing 6'4", and though he'd thickened a bit in the waist, he could deem himself a pretty fit specimen. He was still very solid in the chest and thighs (where it counted!) and more handsome in his grizzled way than he'd been as a young, raw, whey-faced, curly-headed *gringón*.

"I am fucking irrepressible." he said aloud. "You have to get up pretty God-damned early in the morning to put anything over on the good *Señor* White!"

He wondered how early Courtney had gotten up to make her half sweet, half caustic little communiqué. Early enough to have her

Daddy's number. Mexico, though, would take her down a peg or two. It had certainly taken him down a peg or two when he was her age.

In Mexico, Lee learned early on that the only real sin is taking yourself, and your particular misfortunes, too seriously. He had learned this from at least a hundred different Mexicans, but mainly from Checo. He wondered what the hell had happened to Checo. He was supposed to have called yesterday. It would have been surprising, though, if Checo had actually made the call.

Two

In Mexico City, a holiday, like an election, is a kind of disaster. Checo hoped that Lee would understand. It seemed unlikely. How could he comprehend that anyone would drive to Acapulco, eight to ten miserable hours each way, for a three day weekend? Nobody but a Mexican would believe that tens, maybe hundreds of thousands of people had done just that. But it was the grim truth. Traffic on Sunday night had backed up for more than 100 kilometers, over the mountains and well south of Cuernavaca. Checo had sat in his car with his four year old daughter, two aunts and a cousin for almost six hours. The car was a nine-year-old VW bug without air conditioning. He was witlessly proud it had not broken down. Maybe, he thought, being stuck in a seven-hour traffic jam had actually improved the car, perhaps charged the battery.

At any rate, Checo was glad to get back to D.F., even if it meant enduring the midday meal at his mother's house in San Angel. A true *chilango* is never completely at ease away from the city. Those years at Berkeley, for example. Talk about the hinterlands! What a relief it had been to get back to civilization. He could no longer summon even the fantasy of living somewhere else. It was incomprehensible that Minerva had taken the children and moved to Ciudad Juárez. She had pulled some amazing stunts through the years, but this beat anything.

With *gringos* like Lee, absurdities were forgivable. No one could expect *gringos* to be rational. Lee hated the city, the most beautiful and dynamic city on the planet. He was forever parking himself in Querétaro, Morelia, Guanajuato, Puebla, or some other shabby and inconvenient backwater. Even that wasn't as bad as Cd. Juárez. Now Checo would have to fly to Cd. Juárez to see his children. The idea was appalling.

Checo's parents' San Angel mansion was not quite as grand as the palace at Versailles, but it was not exactly the place you'd want to be if the revolution Checo had always prayed for suddenly broke out. Despite the size, the place always impressed Checo as crowded, bursting at the seams, leaking relatives who were only vaguely familiar from every door and window while servants hovered disapprovingly in the background. Checo's daughter, Marisol, was there, along with a roving pack of six or seven doubtlessly related kids around her age. She'd come on the train with his aunt Gabe, who was also living in Cd. Juárez.

Checo was waiting for things to get quiet enough for him to return Lee's call. Marisol ignored her father and continued to play with her cousins. His mother and Aunt Gabe were watching the kids and shouting at them while they gossiped.

"Willy, Willy, don't hit your brother like that."

"Marisol, keep your dress down."

"Poor thing! She's turned into a real hellcat since her parents separated. Look, Checo, look at your daughter. Aren't you ashamed of yourself?"

The old man had left port and was sailing with resolve into his afternoon Brandies. He was watching a soccer match on one of the many television sets that junked up most of the rooms in the besieged splendor of *Popi's* show house. People—Checo's sisters, sisters-in-law, and grown, dimly familiar cousins—were coming in, grabbing food, and griping about how slow the servants did their work, how the price of groceries, the bare basics, had become insupportable, and how insolent the city's taxi drivers had become.

Checo was tempted to start drinking brandy with the old man. The din was unbelievable. He watched the scene at the table and felt that he could not possibly be related to these people. Surely, he had been secretly adopted. He'd been born in 1957 and had always fantasized that he was the child of impoverished Hungarian refugees who'd had to give him up for adoption. Or, maybe there'd been a mistake at the hospital. The Hungarian community in D.F. had produced some of the most wacked-out people Checo had ever known—extreme, artistic people. Checo was, in his heart, such a person—extreme, artistic, perhaps Hungarian, despite his undeniably brown complexion. Hungarians, though, were often dark, often darker than Checo, and they were seldom the loutish big-boned creatures that Germany and Scandanavia extruded into the world. Slight and fine-boned, Checo felt that he was just the picture of a Magyar, a man with an expressive face that reflected the ravages of artistic ferment.

The house in San Angel had nine phones. Unfortunately, only one of them worked and it was in the kitchen, the center of the noise and hysteria of the daily two o'clock *comida*. The old man had a cell phone he kept in his car, but the car was the old guy's sanctuary. He never let anyone in the family into his car. No chance Checo could use the cell. So he just sat at the table and waited, nursing the fantasy of his Hungarian ancestry while he nibbled at a cup of green Jello.

"So I said to him, I said, 'No sir! On principle I would never pay that price for a cut of meat. If I was a millionaire, I wouldn't pay it!'" Graciela, Checo's mom, addressed a favorite concern.

Checo was beginning to get a headache. His mother was a millionaire, not that it meant much, the *peso* being what it was, but his parents were very well off. Checo took some deep breaths. He worried that he would hyperventilate. Marisol had armed herself with hard, snacking-style garbanzo beans and was throwing them in his direction. Several actually found the mark. That was, evidently, the last straw. However much a father deserved a pelting with garbanzo beans, it was the prerogative of mothers and aunts, not children.

To Checo's immense satisfaction, Aunt Gabe and his mother made the children all go outside to play. To his even greater satisfaction, the women followed to supervise. The first big rush at the *comida* was over. Now, in the eye of the hurricane that was the typical midday meal at Checo's parents' house, Checo had a few minutes to call Lee.

He had the number. God knew where Lee was. The area code was one Checo had never seen. Every time Lee came, he drifted further from the capital. This was annoying but Checo could hardly complain. The money from the magazines had gotten better and better. The new project, a massively photographed interview with an incipient group of guerrillas in the mountains of Teonanaca, looked particularly juicy.

Lee did deliver. He was a wonderful friend. Still, his neurotic avoidance of the only decent city in the western hemisphere made Checo nervous. It was annoying to have to dial the alien area code.

By a miracle, Lee had not left the hotel. By another miracle, he was actually in his room. When Lee got on, Checo began speaking English. English, for Checo, was useful. It kept the conversation confidential. Also, there was always a chance that Checo's father might stroll in for some snack food and hear his son speaking English. The old man always liked to hear Checo speaking English. It probably justified, to some degree, the great expense of Checo's education at Berkeley. Checo was acutely aware of the fact that, in his father's eyes, the expense was not otherwise vindicated. "Lee, so you're there?"

Lee admitted this.

"So where are you? I don't recognize the area code."

"Tepic, I'm in Tepic."

"What are you doing there? Why Tepic of all places? It's the wrong direction. How'll you ever get here in time?"

"Don't worry, we'll be heading to Teonanaca tomorrow morning. You just be sure you have your supplies. I like Tepic and I have some business concerns here. It's great. There are all these vendors that sell juice from raw sugar cane."

"Lee, you can find that stuff anywhere."

"Yeah, but here it's a real thing. The city runs on the stuff. In the morning at ten all the offices empty out. Everyone, all the business types, head for the sugar juice. They load up on this amazingly strong coffee and chase it down with shots of the cane nectar. Then they head back into the offices. Watch out for Tepic, Checo. Give these people a few years and they'll be running the fucking country. Anyway, why are we talking this bullshit, you were supposed to be in touch yesterday?"

"Give me a break, Lee, we just came out of a three day weekend. You know what that means."

Lee grunted.

"I got stuck in a traffic jam on the way back from Acapulco. Don't give me any shit about it, this is Mexico. It's a miracle we've managed to find two phones that work. If you could fly into the city like a rational person I wouldn't have to call you at all."

"OK, Jesús. Let's get on with it. What do you hear from Minerva and the kids? "

"Marisol is here for a week or so. Minerva sounds fine on the phone, but I can't imagine she's doing very well. She's running an optical shop and apparently makes decent money. *Gringos* flock there for cheap glasses. Minerva is being very cordial. She's waiting for me to drop my guard."

"That's probably true, but don't start talking bad about Minerva."

"Who's talking bad?"

"Well, don't start. Oh! Before I forget. I've got a favor to ask."

A new entourage of relatives arrived. Checo could see them taking their places at the table.

"I want you to meet my daughter at the airport later this afternoon. She's coming in with an assistant who also seems to be her boyfriend. You can hook up with them as they leave the international flight area. They'll need your help getting through customs. The flight is TWA #3016 due into the international gates at 5:47. The guy's name is Kevin García. Courtney's last name is Gerard. She's Hannah's girl, you know."

Checo waited, watching with clinical fascination while the new wave of relatives attacked the food.

"Courtney is tall, maybe a meter eighty. She's a big-boned girl but thin. She's twenty-five but probably looks nineteen. Her hair is kind of blond but I have no idea how she's wearing it and I don't really know how she dresses or anything. She probably has fucking tattoos and body piercing, so don't be alarmed if you see an eyebrow ring. I have no idea what Kevin looks like. Hell, just make a sign that says '*Bienvenidos, Courtney y Kevin*' and stand there where the international passengers walk by. Let them find you."

"'Kevin and Courtney'. . . Isn't Kevin an Irish name?"

"He's a *Chicano*. Courtney's going to be making a film and the guy is her technical support person. We'll see that she gets good footage. She has some backing and a good chance to come up with a documentary that'll run in a fairly big venue, like Discovery Channel. Her ideas aren't too refined and she doesn't even speak Spanish . . . and neither does the guy."

Lee was talking fast and breathing hard, obviously wanting Checo to absorb this information with as little discussion as possible. His voice was pinched, irritated as though Checo were to blame for Courtney not knowing Spanish.

Checo laughed edgily.

"Do they know how to wipe themselves?"

"Checo, they're talented. Courtney got a prize from the Syracuse film festival for 'Chili-dog.' They're paying their way, too. Courtney has grant money."

Checo sighted over his thumbnail pretending it was a rifle sight. Bang! bang! Obnoxious in-laws and nondescript cousins fell bleeding onto the table of his imagination.

"Did you know that the Irish used to fuck horses as part of their religion?"

"I don't think Kevin's Irish. I told you that."

"Good, maybe the horses of Teonanaca are safe."

Lee laughed.

"Listen, wise guy, we're in the catbird seat."

"What on earth are you talking about? English is difficult enough without 'catbird seats.' I am living with insanity all around me. I am standing in my mother's kitchen with servants and relatives dancing around me as if I were the fucking maypole. Please, I beg you, spare me the 'catbird seat' and say what you mean in plain language."

Lee laughed. "Patience, Checo. What's the good of knowing a language if you miss the poetry? I meant that our work will be easy. The articles will practically write themselves. My contacts are the best imaginable, *compadres* of mine, Felipe and Elena Piñeda. Thinking ahead, I also bought a pump for the village well. It's a nice one, and the village needs a new pump. It'll create good will. People will cooperate, talk to us. . . . Naturally, I'm eager to spend time with my daughter."

Checo said nothing. It wasn't the first time family concerns had complicated a project. It was, however, the first time it'd been Lee's family.

Lee kept explaining. "The village celebrates the *fiesta* of Santiago Apóstol. Courtney will get video footage of the *fiesta*. She's got grant money to pay you for doing the story-board stills."

"All she needs, then, is a story." Checo was aware of the fact that he'd been on the phone for quite a while. Graciela was coming into the kitchen every minute or two and drawing a pointedly deep breath to remind Checo of the high cost of long distance calls. "Seriously, Lee, this has the smell of disaster."

"Checo, it'll be something new. I mean, what is life without novelty? Besides, I've already spent all of the out-front money from 'Dominion Quarterly.' I already emailed the nuns at a convent down the road from the village. They're expecting us, they'll get us up to speed on the background of this rebellion."

The fact that Lee had already spent all of the per diem money did not upset Checo. Lee had lots of *movidas* going and was forever taking money out of one to prop up another. It was very Mexican, a custom Lee had readily adopted.

"Seriously Lee, I have reservations. We're not so strapped that we have to have your daughter's grant money."

"No, but we might as well. . . . They will be with us."

Checo groaned. "And you can't even meet the plane. Do they have a place to stay?"

"Let them stay at your apartment for God's sake. Show them around. They'll probably need to do some last minute shopping. Or, if you want to be a jerk, you can park them at a hotel."

"Why are you on my case? I am doing this for you in the face of all reason. Look, I know you like Minerva, but I am not the bad guy. I wasn't with the *putas*."

"Whoa! Checo! Calm down. What does Minerva have to do with anything? I just want you to put Courtney and Kevin in your apartment for one damned night."

"OK, so how soon are you going to be able to tear yourself away from the cane nectar?"

"I'll come in tonight, but it'll be late. I have to buy a hat. We'll leave tomorrow morning. We need to be in Huatepec, ready to go Saturday morning. I've got a van reserved at the Hertz just down the street from the Latin American Tower. Courtney's an early riser, so let's meet for an eight o'clock breakfast at the downtown Sanborn's, you know, the 'Casa de Los Azulejos.'"

"Yeah, the Latin American Tower is going to fall on it any minute."

"Don't be a wimp, Checo. Pancho Villa and Emiliano Zapata had breakfast at the Casa de los Azulejos in 1916, did you know that?"

Checo doubted the story but did not argue the point. He was too distressed about having to drive into the center of the city at eight in the morning.

"Make it nine,"

"Nine it is. You got your cameras ready? Bought the film you'll need?"

"Yes." Checo lied. He would be ready, though, so he wasn't really lying, "How the hell does a *Chicano* get a name like Kevin?"

"See you at Sanborn's. We'll eat, get the van, and then swing by the apartment for the suitcases and equipment."

"Nine?"

"Nine. Give my regards to your Mother."

"OK, bye."

"Ciao."

Three

An airplane came in low, ready to land, casting shadow images of itself onto the inert village. Felipe watched. His jaw tightened and his lower lip bulged as the plane swept out over the vast void of the *barranca*, turned and headed back towards the little landing strip on the lip of the *barranca*. Who would be on that plane? Someone sinister, someone with plans, someone with guns, drugs, death? No, the irregular drone was unmistakable. It was the milk run flight, full of old ladies who'd been to the Monday market at Ixtlán. For years the sound of the plane had been rough, as though each flight was certain to be the last. Felipe smiled a strained smile. The plane was hours late.

He noted that Elena, much against her inclination, was keeping her mouth shut. Appreciating the effort his wife was making to allow him his sour mood, he smiled again. "Maybe I should take the milk run to Ixtlán and pay their chiseling prices."

Throwing her plaits over her shoulders, the woman bustled, clearing dishes from the table. "Get the fireworks from Donaldo Sabino. The misers at Ixtlán can get along without your dollars."

"I suppose we could make do with Donaldo's lousy poppers, but Don Mateo needs me to take a deposit for the band. He's worried. Without a deposit they might not show up."

"I know, I know, I know . . . and with a deposit they'll show up hammered on rot-gut. . . . Anyway, eat. You haven't eaten enough to keep a Sparrow alive."

Elena hung her apron on a nail and joined Felipe at the door. He shook his head and resisted the temptation to gripe about the sardine salad. "I'm worried. Lee left a message at the Maldonado store. He's on his way and he's bringing his daughter. He could be here any day and he's got the new pump."

Elena clapped her hands in delight and did an impromptu little jig across the room. "No more bending over the stream for clothes washing, husband. The women can say goodbye to their backaches!"

Felipe blinked and rubbed his head. Time to let the boot fall. "The bad news is that Lee wants to meet with 'the ones in the hills.'"

Elena continued to caper about.

Felipe pressed on, tightening his jaw. "The soldiers have that checkpoint . . . "

Elena stopped and stared, beaming out the window. "They have had that checkpoint and will have it. What would Lee care for their stupid checkpoint?"

Felipe ignored the comment and continued. Lee was driving in and would not let a small inconvenience like an Army checkpoint long hinder him. Elena had an exaggerated view of Lee's powers but in this case she was right. Still, the situation was worrisome and Felipe wanted to defend his right to worry. "Another thing, Lee sent an email to the nuns at San Lucas. It's all well and good to cut your capers, but things could get . . . complicated."

Elena rolled her eyes. A smile skittered across her face. "With or without emails, Lee's on his way, isn't he? There's nothing in these mountains he can't handle. I can't wait to see his daughter. I wonder what kind of hat he'll have this time. I'll never forget that goofy red baseball cap. I hope they get here in time for the *fiesta*."

Felipe frowned. "I shouldn't have asked him to bring the pump. The ones in the hills will be envious and I worry about him emailing those nuns. What's that about?"

Elena shook her head dismissively. "Why not email the nuns? They're sweet girls. As for the pump, the village needs the pump. That's obvious. Why shouldn't our *compadre* bring it? You asked him and you deserve the credit." She put a hand on her hip and turned, waving a large wooden spoon. For Felipe, Elena's beauty was a perfect expression of her avidity, her way of brimming over with life. Her black eyes flashed and matched the sheen of her scrupulously plaited hair.

She stood straight, erect, and fierce—her smooth skin shimmering with zest, ambition, and certainty in her opinions. Her bright, beribboned *huipil* found resonance in the rainbow dazzle of teeth, eye, hair, and skin. Wielding her spoon, she projected authority, the regal air of a youthful queen, a short queen with a hint of sensuality. Felipe smiled with happy understanding of the emphatic nature of the heat that smoldered beneath the peasant reserve that the aprons, pleats, and multiple petticoats created. He'd married a fireball, an implacable person who tended to put herself and her family forward a bit more than she ought.

"Listen," he said, "Boasting about that pump, taking credit like that. . . . It'll bring spite, envy. It'd be better for Dzul and the others to get the credit."

Swinging her spoon she continued. "Envy? I incite envy by having a husband with brains enough to stay away from 'Subcomandante' Dzul. I'll tell you one thing, Felipe, the wives of the morons in Dzul's little *pendejada* in the hills have about had it. If you started such foolishness, I would do you like I did the dog when he began eating Nazario's precious chickens. Just try it, husband. I'll bring you to your senses. I'll tie you to the damned tree. I swear it!"

Elena lifted the spoon over her shoulder as though to strike him. Felipe feigned a dodge and laughed, giving her a small swat on the fanny. She was a treat, so young and voluptuous in her pleated dress and ribbons.

"'Precious chickens?'"

"I meant Nazario's chickens, the way they improved when our dog began eating them. It was in March while you were in Chicago washing dishes. I wish you had seen the stricken look on Nazario's mug. I truly thought he would weep for those chickens and I'll tell you those were the skinniest, sorriest chickens that ever emerged cackling from eggs. I swear, when he began to talk about those miserable wretches, it would have brought tears to your eyes.

Elena glared over the wall at Nazario's disreputable hut. Felipe convulsed with laughter. She continued. "Our dog is the most useless animal imaginable. How he even managed to catch those chickens is beyond me. Look at him! He is so lazy that he won't even stand up to bark."

Felipe gave up. Even though Elena would not take his concerns seriously, at least she'd pulled him out of his grim mood. He decided to drop by Maldonado's store. Perhaps there was news of the soldiers and their checkpoint. If he had a beer, or a glass of *aguardiente*, who could blame him? "I'm off, woman. I need some kerosene, and Miriam Maldonado may know something more about the Army."

Elena cast a skeptical glance at her beloved but let him go without protest. He looked so nice in his white straw hat and jeans that she'd indulge him anything. He always characterized himself as the most ordinary of men, 'neither tall nor short, fat nor skinny, dark nor light, handsome nor ugly,' etc. She knew better. Compact and contained, he was a handsome man with an open smile, honest penetrating eyes, and muscled limbs that just made her melt!

He could go! He'd be back with bells on! Her man wasn't like the wasters that buzzed like flies around Maldonado's while their families went hungry and their *milpas* disgraced the town. He might have a thimbleful of *aguardiente*, but he knew where he lived. . . . And didn't she know a trick or two to keep him eager for his own house and thinking of his *petate?* Damned right she did! As he walked away, Elena heard the milk run revving up. Almost dusk and a storm was brewing. That plane should have been and gone by midday. If only Lee were on that plane!

The spongers outside Maldonado's store hovered like buzzards in the seldom realized hope that one of Miriam's customers would be in a festive, generous mood. Felipe did not mind buying rounds when two or three fellow villagers, upstanding peasants, happened to be there drinking. That was expected and reciprocal. The spongers, however, had no money, no credit, and no standing in the village. Buying drinks for them was like pouring good alcohol into a pile of gravel.

Felipe bought a liter of kerosene. He'd visit for a while and then have his dram of *aguardiente*. He was exchanging idle pleasantries with Miriam Maldonado when Efraím Estrada came in. Ignoring the bleating spongers, Efraím made no pretense about his intentions. "I want an *aguardiente*. . . . Felipe?"

Felipe nodded. Miriam took two plastic cups and half filled them with *aguardiente.* "Orange?" She asked.

The men nodded. She opened two Orange Crush sodas. Felipe took a big drink of the Orange Crush. He then poured the aguardiente into the bottle, gave it a shake to mix and then poured a bit of the mixed liquid back into the plastic cup. He took a sip. Nice.

Efraím downed the *aguardiente* in one gulp, grimaced and then knocked back better than half the soda. Raising one finger, he petitioned Miriam for a second portion of the rot-gut. This he mixed with the soda as Felipe had done.

Felipe was alarmed. Efraím was one of the stingiest men he knew. In fact, Efraím was notorious as a man who was abstemious through thrift. What had prompted this breech of custom? As a decorous man, Felipe did not ask. He would know in good time what had prompted this astounding behavior.

The men chatted for some time, a pleasant, unhurried peasant conversation covering the obligatory topics: the weather, births and deaths (both human and animal), and preparations for the upcoming *fiesta.* Outside, it began to rain, a storm with plenty of thunder and lightning. Easing by degrees into touchier topics, Felipe asked if Efraím knew anything about the Army. Efraím knew exactly what Felipe and everyone else in the village knew: the Army had just that week come in and set up a checkpoint below the village.

Now Felipe ordered a round. Miriam measured the rot-gut and opened more sodas.

Efraím mixed his poison and moved away from the counter, motioning to Felipe to follow. He spoke in hushed tones. "'The ones in the hills,' I am told they are now armed."

Felipe smiled for a moment. Everyone knew that Efraím was one of "the ones in the hills." As Elena had pointed out on several occasions, the affectations of secrecy were ridiculous, the comings and goings of everyone in the village were known to everyone else. Efraím was one of the ones who, by dark of night, met with his compatriots to plot revenge against landowner Don Esteban Castellano. The villagers had wanted Castellano to loan them the money to buy a new pump for the village cistern. Don Esteban, a man much given to brandy, was drunk and had refused outright. Later, an outbuilding on his rancho mysteriously burned. The original timid request for a loan had become a list of demands.

Efraím, with his habit of allowing drooping pants to reveal the crack in his ass, had been acting the part of a guerrilla. He'd just told Felipe that they were armed. His behavior showed that he was nervous. Felipe, nervous himself, pressed for details and was relieved to hear that Efraím "had been told" that the guerillas had come into possession of a twenty-two caliber pistol and an entire box (one hundred rounds) of bullets.

The relief was short lived. Even as pitifully "armed" as the "guerillas" were, something very ugly could result. With the upcoming *fiesta* of Santiago, things could lurch out of control. Oceans of alcohol would be flowing through the village. Lee might be arriving at just the wrong time. The situation was beginning to give Felipe a gut ache. Maybe the *aguardiente* was responsible to some degree. He was, perhaps, a little drunk.

Efraím, looking a bit dyspeptic himself, wanted more *aguardiente*. Apparently, however, he did not want any more company. He had Miriam pour him a pop bottle full. He paid for it, bid Felipe good bye, and slid into the murkiness of the twilight.

Felipe stayed put and nursed his "orange." The shower had ended but clouds had settled in, creating a thick fog. The sun had set.

Miriam lit a couple of kerosene lanterns so prospective customers could see the merchandise. She had a white gas lantern behind the counter so she could see the money, every *centavo*. The store was a box of light in a world that had become very close, wet, and opaque. The village was obscure. Few villagers used their electric lights, except maybe on Sunday evenings and important *fiesta* days. The spongers had fled when the rain began. The street was deserted. Felipe declined Miriam's offer of yet another *copita* of *aguardiente*. He'd had enough.

As he stepped out of the store, Felipe could hear the sound of an automobile, seemingly close by. Suddenly the vehicle loomed out of the fog. It was an Army jeep. Startled, Felipe put up a hand to shield his eyes from the intense headlights. As he moved, he tread on a rock that gave way in the mud. He managed to stay on his feet but the kerosene went flying. It hit the jeep on the front driver's side fender, fell to the ground and broke with a shattering crash. The jeep slammed to a halt. Two soldiers with rifles climbed out of the jeep followed by a third with a holstered pistol. Felipe walked carefully away from the jeep as though nothing had happened.

"You there," shouted one of the soldiers, "halt."

Felipe stopped. He did not answer. He did not move in their direction. He simply froze.

The soldiers approached, bearing their weapons with casual insolence. One of them inspected the broken bottle. He picked up some of the shards and cut his finger.

"Son-of-a-bitch," he said and began to wrap his bleeding finger in his handkerchief. "It's kerosene."

The soldier with the pistol wore riding trousers with puffed legs stuffed into tall boots. His hat was a camo-colored baseball cap. He walked with an air of authority, a swagger. This was the much gossiped-over Lieutenant Campos. By Huatepec standards, he was tall, perhaps an inch taller than Felipe's five-seven. As the officer approached, Felipe took off his hat in a gesture of deference. The Lieutenant looked Felipe up and down. "We have ways of dealing with those who would bomb our vehicles."

Felipe was aware of the hair on the back of his neck. He was suddenly very cold. "It was kerosene, sir, for my lantern. I tripped and dropped it. I apologize. I did not mean to drop the bottle in front of your jeep."

"Where did you 'mean' to drop it? Through the windshield? Hoping to immolate government property and burn soldiers alive?"

The officer lit a cigarette and threw the spent match at Felipe's face. Felipe looked down at the hat in his hands but noticed with some relief that the two soldiers were smiling. "No sir, the headlights were bright and I tripped. The bottle got away from me, that's all. It was no bomb, nothing, just a busted bottle and a spill."

"Empty your pockets."

He did so. One of the enlisted men took the stuff into the headlight so Campos could inspect. There were matches, a comb, a pocket knife, Lee White's business card, two small padlock keys, some coins, twelve *pesos* and the fifty-seven dollars that he was planning to use for Mateo's fireworks and the deposit for the band.

"So," Lieutenant Campos said, "you are one of these worms, these nits, these insects who've caused all the trouble up here, right? You know, I do not like having to come into your pathetic village, *Señor* Worm. It makes me angry. It makes me grouchy with my troops and that's not like me. Why do I take it out on my troops? It's because of having to deal with this infestation of worms. So tell me, *Señor* Worm, where are you wiggling tonight?"

"Nowhere. My house, my *milpa*."

"What's that I smell on your breath, *Señor* Worm, alcohol? Did you have to pump yourself up with Dutch courage to do your assassin's work?"

"No, I tell you I went to the store to get kerosene for my lantern. I wet my whistle with a drop or two of *aguardiente*. I meant no harm. I tripped."

"Well, *Señor* Worm, we see that you can trip. I wonder, though, if you can run. Would you like show us how you can run?"

The two soldiers pulled at their weapons. Felipe could hear the click of the bullets sliding into the firing chambers. He pictured his two or three running steps before the inevitable *"ley fuga"* hail of bullets. "No," he said, "I'm certain we can find a way to work out this misunderstanding. I live nearby and hold the office of policeman in this village."

The two enlisted soldiers burst out laughing.

The officer hissed. "Stop braying, you *burros*. *Señor* Worm here will get the idea that he is a comedian. Are you a comedian, *Señor* Worm?"

"No sir, I am not. I am a simple peasant of the village but I do hold the office of policeman. To be a policeman in this village is not much. If someone gets drunk and beats his wife, I lock him up overnight in the schoolhouse."

"What happens when you beat your wife? Do you lock yourself up in your stinking schoolhouse?"

"I do not beat my wife."

"Well, listen to this, boys, he does not beat his wife. He is a saint. Saint Worm. Tell me, Saint Worm, when is your feast day?"

The enlisted men laughed again. This time there was no

admonition. Felipe felt the situation shift. He kept quiet.

"Well," Campos said, "everyone knows that policemen are too lazy and too busy taking bribes to run. Anyway, I am enjoying our conversation, aren't you?"

"To tell the truth, sir, I am finding it difficult."

Now the two enlisted men began to laugh uncontrollably.

'Well, pardon me," said the lieutenant, "but we always make great efforts to cooperate with the local police and authorities. Here I am, going out of my way to be cordial to a policeman, and this is the gratitude I get. I think maybe you should enjoy our conversation. Either run along, and right smartly now, or show some gratitude."

Felipe grasped at straws. "Thank you, sir," he said," for having the decency to talk to me. I regret breaking my bottle of kerosene and apologize for startling you. I know it is difficult for you, given the problems that have arisen in this village."

The officer listened. Felipe couldn't think of anything else to say. He felt a small release of muscle tension in his chest. They weren't going to kill him. He had to be patient, let them take the time they wanted for their sport. He would endure.

The Lieutenant inspected Lee White's business card. "Tell me about this *gringo*. Is he providing support for your little nest of worms? Did he pay you to assassinate us? The card says he is a journalist and a cultural worker. Now what the hell is that? Is he an instigator, like those priests and nuns that are the instigators for the worms in Chiapas?"

"No, he buys things for stores in the United States. Things like baskets, textiles, blankets, pots. I guess he calls himself a cultural worker because those are cultural art products."

"Are you sure that it's not drugs he buys for export, mushrooms in honey, *yerba mala*, heroin?"

"I'm sure."

"The dollars, he gave them to you. What? He bought a basket?"

"No, I earned those dollars washing dishes at a restaurant in Chicago. I was going to use them to buy things and pay for a band for the *fiesta* de Santiago."

"I thought you said you were a policeman. It's a poor policeman who betrays the republic to suck up to the *gringos*."

"I needed the money. I have heavy obligations to my *compadre*.

I have a *compadre* who is a *carguero*, responsible for the expenses for the *fiesta* of Santiago. It is my obligation to use my dollars to help him. That's why I have the dollars . . . to pay a deposit for the band."

"Well Saint-Officer-Policeman-worm, it looks like you have had a stroke of luck. It just so happens that when you stumbled and broke your kerosene, you stumbled over the musicians you need."

The two enlisted men howled with laughter.

"Listen to them bray! Who would know that they are the finest musicians you'll find anywhere? Ignacio there, for example, is as stupid as sack of marbles. But he has an instrument, does he ever, and he practices on that instrument every day. All he thinks about is the music he can coax out of that reed. Jesús is the other one, even more ignorant than Ignacio. He also, however, has an instrument. He does his finest playing, though, on Ignacio's flute. Me, I am a virtuoso on trombone."

Campos then swiveled his hips and to the delight of his subordinates, ripped off a huge, bellowing fart.

"As you see, hear, and smell, there is no finer *conjunto* in the state. *Señor* Worm, you've hired your band."

He took the wad of dollars, gave two to each enlisted man and put the remainder into his pocket.

"Look for us," he said, "to make some music for your *fiesta*. Come on, boys, let's leave this policeman to make his rounds. I will keep this *gringo's* business card. It's hard to tell when a man like me might need some cultural work. Goodnight, *Señor*-Saint-Policeman-Worm. I think you'll agree that this has been a lucky night for you. Before we leave this *municipio,* we'll bring good fortune to the worm population. I guarantee that!"

The men got back into the jeep, which had stood with its engine running during the entire interchange. One of the enlisted men took the driver's seat and began to rev the vehicle. The officer spoke one last time, now shouting. "Surely, friend worm, you will express your gratitude?"

"Thanks," said Felipe. "Thanks very much."

The jeep moved and disappeared wraithlike into the fog.

Felipe closed his eyes, took a long, deep breath, and began to weep quietly. The shame of the situation, he thought, was that he actually did feel grateful.

Four

Standing in a Mictlán *abarrotes* store, Checo wondered why it had been his misfortune to be born in such a country. This line of inquiry was far from new. It was, in fact, a habitual thought, a thought that Checo revisited on a daily basis. Mexico had infinite ways to annoy and vex. Checo was forever encountering new ones, especially outside the *periférico*, the "ring road" that encircled Mexico City.

Mictlán was on one of the main two-lanes that connected Ciudad Guzmán, the provincial capital of Teonanaca, to the freeways that led to Mexico City and, in Checo's mind, reality. He found Mictlán graceless, a subnormal town seemingly devoted to sugar processing. Here the Dodge van would turn east to climb on dirt roads to Huatepec, their destination, some eighty difficult kilometers into the mountains. Checo figured that Mictlán was the last outpost of civilization. He decided that he should take advantage of the amenities, such as they were. Lee and the others were taking a break from the road to explore the dreary town.

Larga distancia, long distance, was a service commonly offered by small stores in the *afueras* and in poorer sections of all Mexican cities. Most such places installed a couple of phones in small, quasi-private booths, separated by partitions. The customer would come in and give the number to the person at the register, who'd complete the call. The customer would take the call in one of the booths and then pay a fee, the cost of the call plus a surcharge for the service. It was a simple, effective way to provide long distance service to the poor who could not afford phones. At least it ought to have been simple.

Checo had decided to call Minerva at her work in Cd. Juárez. Lee had been working on Checo ever since they'd left D.F. He was right, of course. Minerva was a fine woman and the problems, however perplexing, were not insoluble.

"She has your attention." Lee had said, "Listen to what she has to say."

Checo did appreciate this astounding advice. He'd assumed, probably inaccurately, that Minerva had learned about the weekend in Oaxtepec with Rocio and her psychotic gynecologist. He supposed that he ought to tell Lee about Rocio. His protestation about not having been with the putas was maybe not 100% true, even if it was true in the ways that mattered.

So he'd decided to call Minerva from Mictlán. Phones in the Sierra Nacoteca might be chancy. Courtney and Kevin were walking around enchanted with the dump. Kevin had a guidebook that said that the town went way back to pre-Hispanic times and was a place where there were temples to the planet Venus. Lee was content to sit like a dope in the town plaza, a peaceful place tiled in blue and yellow, shaded by locust's trees and bougainvilleas. He was wearing the hat he bought in Tepic, an absurd straw cowboy-type hat that must have been a meter across. The sight of Lee's hat gave Checo a sinking feeling. Existence was obviously senseless and struggle futile.

Thus prepared, he descended into a hot, close suburb of hell disguised as an *abarrotes* store. Examining the place, he wondered how a town like Mictlán could consume the thousands of cans of sardines that lined the shelves.

He decided to sneak a call to Rocio. Rocio would flirt and tease. It'd help him get up for dealing with Minerva.

He could imagine Rocio. She would be sitting in her apartment, eating chocolate while she waited for the lottery numbers of the day. He pictured her looking at the cosmetic ads she'd posed for six weeks earlier. Rocio had the smoothest, roundest and most enjoyable ass in Mexico. God, how he loved to knead those twin loaves. It was worth anything. It was even worth listening to Rocio talk about the movie she was going to be in that they'd be shooting in Cancún in a couple of weeks. The movie would be horrible. It was the type of movie that Checo called a *"nalgada,"* certain to expose Rocio's luscious ass to the view of millions.

At first the phone call went well. Sure enough, Rocio flirted, teased, and shrieked "Ay Checo" several times, very gratifying. By the time Checo hung-up, however, he'd decided that the call was a huge mistake. In a little spasm of heedless self-disclosure, He'd told Rocio about the project and even named the village. Astoundingly, Rocio knew where the village was and even knew that the village had air service of some sort. Now she was threatening to fly in for the *fiesta* of Santiago. The terrible truth was that she would probably do it. All of the shitty little villages in the Sierra Nacoteca apparently had air service. The mountains were so rough that it was easier to get in and out by plane. Rocio had been in the sierras just a year before, shooting a twisted beer commercial at a remote waterfall that was only a few kilometers from Huatepec.

He hung up and bought a pop to compose himself. He'd call Minerva at work. He decided to make the call person to person. He gave the woman at the store the name and number. "My wife," he said.

The woman at the store was like a clothes hamper with ears—a stout, imperious little woman with long black hair, piercing black eyes and a formidable sense of dignity. Small as she was, maybe 5'1", she threw back her head and looked down her nose at Checo.

"Have you no shame whatsoever?" she asked.

Startled, Checo had no reply. What on earth was this?

"Do you think I run a whorehouse?" she continued.

Checo began to have a hunted feeling. He got a knot in his throat.

"I'm calling my wife," he said, ashamed to note a whining tone creep into his voice.

"Oh, I don't doubt it, poor woman that your wife is. Just tell me what you expect to say to your poor wife."

Checo took a deep breath. The woman was seething. Her nostrils were dilated, her jaw tight.

"I don't see that it's your business," he finally said, feeling that he had no control of the circumstances of his life.

"It's exactly my business," she said, "and my business is not the business of a whorehouse. I don't run this *larga distancia* for men to make dates with their *putas* and excuses for their wives. We're decent people here."

Checo realized that the woman had listened in on his call to Rocio.

"Look," he said, "you can get in trouble for listening in on calls. Anyway, I wasn't making a date. I'm trying to distance myself from that woman. Now will you please dial that number?"

"I certainly will not. Do you expect me to stand here while you lie to your wife? No, *Señor*, I will not."

"I'm not calling my wife to lie to her. I'm calling to tell her to come to Mexico City to pick up our child. I want to meet with her, talk to her."

"Ay Checo," the woman mimicked Rocio's voice. "Why don't you come over? I'm lonely. I'm bored. I'm in my bed. Come over and take some pictures of me."

"She's a model," Checo explained, wondering why. "I'm a photographer. She always wants me to take pictures. Now for the love of God, make the call for me."

Checo was amazed. He was pleading with this busybody, this snoop.

"What are you going to tell her?"

"I already told you that. I'm going to ask her to fly to Mexico City to pick up our little girl. Then I'm going to ask her about getting back together."

"Well, just this once. But don't think you can come in here, into my store, and use my phones to deceive your poor wife."

"I'm not deceiving her!"

"Does she know about this one? The one who stays in bed until noon urging you to come take her picture? Don't you dare lie to me."

"Of course my wife knows I have clients. She knows I do commercials. Now please . . . "

Checo felt that he would die if he had to talk any longer to this woman. Why had he let Lee talk him into calling Minerva? It was going to take his last shred of energy, evidently, just to make the call. He took another deep breath. He said nothing.

The woman dialed the number.

"Person to person call for Minerva Rodríguez Rivera."

She motioned to Checo to get into the booth.

"Hello, hello Minerva. It's Checo. I'm calling from Mictlán."

"Where?" Minerva's voice was a bit strident, high and clipped, but it was purest music to Checo.

"Mictlán, south of Puebla. I'm with Lee. Listen Minerva, when it's time for Marisol to . . . "

"My God! You don't have her with you?"

"No, of course not. I'm working. Now let me finish. I want you to come to Mexico next week. You can pick up Marisol. I don't want to put her back on that rattletrap train with Gabe."

"So why don't you fly with her? You bring her. . . . You come. I miss you."

Checo could see the reflection of the clothes hamper woman behind the counter. He felt as though suddenly his bones were turning to water.

"OK," he said, horrified at what he was saying. "I'll come. I love you. I want to see you. I want us to be together. I want to hear what has made you so unhappy."

Now he could hear his wife crying. Checo could not recall ever feeling less in control of his life.

"Oh Checo," she said, "why couldn't you have said that six months ago?"

Checo pressed his lips together.

"Look, I'll call you when we get down from the sierra."

Checo felt his breath sending oxygen to his clamoring cells. Maybe, just maybe, he could convince her then to come to D.F. Maybe, despite what he'd just said, he wouldn't have to go to that stinking pit on the border.

"Ok," she said. "I was afraid you were never going to make this call. Oh Checo, Checo, how did it ever get this far?"

"I don't . . . Uh . . . I need to go. I'm calling from a damned *abarrotes* store."

He looked up and met the inevitable reflected glare.

"I'll call, I promise. We'll talk. I'll listen."

"Goodbye, Checo."

"Goodbye, my love."

Minerva hung up. Checo started to do likewise, but the Mexico City Domestic Long Distance operator came on the line.

"Sir."

"Yes?"

"I just wanted to say that I hope it works out for you. Don't give up on her now even if you have to go to Cd. Juárez. Just think of what she is going through in a place like that. She may not realize it now but she is a lucky woman. The world is full of women who are sitting by their phones with their prayer beads just yearning for the phone call that your wife just got."

Checo listened in horror as the operator seemed to break down. She snuffled and choked back a pained sob that became a squawk, an animal sound! She continued.

"So I just had to tell you that you have my very best wishes and I will pray for you."

Checo thanked her and hung up the receiver. He felt light-headed, wondering how many others had listened in. God only knew the routing and how many people had the option to monitor the traffic. He looked around. The woman with the clothes hamper shape was regarding him with the disinterested vigilance she'd no doubt accord to a neighborhood teenager she suspected of shoplifting.

Checo paid for the calls and left the store. Outside it was blistering hot. Sure, it would rain later. The clouds would come, they had to. The look of the place, though, gave no indication that it would ever rain again. A hint of gardenias lingered in the motionless air but provided no promise of better times. The blast of light and heat gave Checo an instant headache. No matter. It was such a relief to escape the woman in the store that Checo practically welcomed the headache. It gave a focus to misery that, until that moment, had been general. He thought of that animal sound that the operator had made. Only in Mexico could such a thing occur! That horrible sound! No wonder he had a headache.

Lee indicated with a nod of the head that Kevin should sit. They watched Courtney cover ground, heading over to the bus station and the restroom rumored to be inside.

Courtney looked great. She wore khaki shorts, a white cotton blouse, Teva sandals and a practical but fashionable straw hat.

Moving, she was all grace, she inhabited her body comfortably, her angular nature seemed to dissolve into soft, round undulations as she walked. Lee could barely believe he'd spawned such a wonder. Kevin, dark and smiling, leaned back on the bench and crossed his legs.

Lee looked him up and down, as though making an appraisal. A bit on the soft, pudgy side, the boy carried himself well and met Lee's gaze without wavering. His eyes were greenish hazel, pretty, pleasant eyes. Lee was pleased that Courtney had chosen a soft, obviously comfort-loving man. He wore basketball shoes, a purple tee shirt and cut-off overalls that were probably not quite the height of youthful fashion: good!

"So you're my daughter's techie."

Lee dreaded this first "solo" conversation with Kevin but he didn't know any way to get out of it. Kevin stiffened in the heat. His face tightened and his eyes fastened on Lee's for a moment and then shifted away. He nodded to acknowledge the question and indicate that yes, indeed, as Lee well knew from weeks and weeks, he was Courtney's techie.

"Are you sleeping with her or is the relationship professional?"

Kevin rubbed his head. He wore a close-cropped crew cut and an earring. These probably were the height of fashion, oh well! He took a deep breath.

"Is that an either/or?"

"You're damned right it is."

Lee smiled. He didn't need to bludgeon. Right out of the gate and he'd got his elbow into Kevin's solar plexus! Good, the boy was intact.

Anticipating this encounter, Kevin had boned up, read several of Lee's articles, especially the series that got the Pulitzer nomination. He told Lee that he admired his courage in blowing the whistle on museum complicity in the traffic in looted artifacts. He went on to say that he enjoyed Lee's pleasant, forthright writing style. It seemed so natural and easy that it had to have been a lot of work.

Lee was pleased; Kevin had survival skills.

"How about Checo? My Pulitzer nomination was a fluke. Checo is the real artist and he's the one who makes the partnership work."

"I didn't know anything about Checo until he picked us up at the airport. I suppose Court mentioned him, but . . . anyway, last night

I went out to a bookstore and bought all his coffee table books. I looked them over before we left. The images are deceptively simple and forthright, like your writing style. I couldn't read the text."

"Did it occur to you that Checo and I might just be a couple of simpletons?"

Kevin laughed. It was a merry laugh that bubbled out of his soft belly, no guile to it. "I guess I'll fit right in."

"Well get ready for discomfort. Doesn't it feel a little weird, here you are in Mexico, a *Chicano* film type, and you can't speak the language?"

Kevin shifted, his jaw tightened. Lee had finally hit the quick.

"It's painful. I remember my *abuela* when I was a little kid. She spoke almost no English. My parents . . . "

"Tried their damnedest to spare you pain. That's the gift of their generation. Too bad it robbed you of the language. It's a great language . . . awful hard to learn as an adult."

Checo lurched out the door of the *abarrotes* store across the street. Jesus, he looked terrible. The designer denims that seemed so smart in D.F. looked sprung. They hung off of him and made him look like he'd been sleeping in a boxcar. The business with Minerva was taking a toll. He was wearing his shades and looked like a down at the heels pimp, a pseudo-hipster, Mexican style. He crossed the street shakily, collapsed, looking ten years older than he had ten minutes earlier.

The van was near the bench where Kevin and Lee were sitting. Lee went and opened the two front doors. It was siesta time and the plaza was practically deserted. Checo went straight to the bench and sat heavily down.

"Checo, you look like hell."

"Thanks a million. It's the heat. It's insupportable. I have a headache."

"Listen to this."

Lee put a cassette tape into the van's tape player.

"This is a *bolero*, Kevin. It's a trio style *bolero*. These were really something back in the forties and fifties. This one's *El Farolero*, 'the Lighthouse Keeper.' Like most of them, it's about loneliness and misery."

"En cambio tú, me ves y nada,
y pasa un día y pasa un mes,
Es que la suerte estaba echada,
las cosas salen al revés.
¿Y ya lo ves?, pasan los años
dejando huellas al pasar,
Nuestro amor es imposible;
yo soy pez del río, tú eres pez del mar."

Lee translated.

"The years pass by leaving traces as they flee, Our love is impossible, I'm a fish of the river . . . you're a fish of the sea. . . . "

"How on earth do you find that shit?" Checo yawned.

"A guy over by the market had twenty or thirty cassettes spread out on a card table. This was one, six *pesos*. Beautiful, no?"

Checo put his middle finger between his eyebrows, closed his eyes and began to massage.

"I can't believe it. I ended up promising Minerva that I'd bring Marisol to Cd. Juárez."

"Well, bravo, old friend. That's what I call progress."

"That's what I call a lapse in sanity. I only hope I'll be able to talk her into coming to D.F. instead. If I go to Cd. Juárez I'll probably end up crossing the border as a *mojado*. I'll get caught up in the spirit of the place and end up doing your roof in Santa Fe, no doubt listening to that damned *bolero* drifting up among the fumes."

Lee smiled. The image of Checo working with a crew of *mojados* on his roof was pretty rich. "So, did Minerva ream you out? When you crossed the street, I didn't know if you were going to make it or not."

"It's simply the horror of the thought of having to get off an airplane in Cd. Juárez . . . and the sun. I expect the sun in Cd. Juárez is more relentless than here, if that is possible. I'm a *pez del lago*, friend—the great invisible lake of Tenochtitlán. How did I ever let you talk me into this project just as my world collapses. To think of Minerva there, measuring glasses frames for thrifty *gringos*. My God, Lee, why don't I just cut my throat?"

"It's always the end of somebody's world," Lee grinned. "Yours, mine too, in good time. Right Kevin?"

"What does that mean . . . 'in good time?'" Checo sounded cross. He had not acknowledged Kevin. "If you're going to be morbid, my friend, at least speak plainly. I told you I have a headache. Let's get in the van and get the air conditioner on. And take off that ridiculous hat. It looks like a mushroom on a pile of horseshit."

Kevin bobbed his head, attempting to make eye contact with Checo.

"Basically," he said, struggling to connect, "'in good time,' means 'later' with the implication that things happen when the time is ripe."

Checo looked up, meeting Kevin's earnest gaze with a quizzical, pinched expression. He continued to massage his head.

"So to you *gringos,* time is a watermelon you thump to see if it's 'ripe.'"

Lee laughed, but neither Checo nor Kevin joined him.

"I'm not a *gringo.*"

"No?!? You look like a *gringo,* you talk like a *gringo,* you dress like *gringo* (or a clown), and you keep constant company with *gringos.* You'll excuse an ignorant Mexican for drawing conclusions."

Kevin's eyes softened and Lee marked the wound.

"I'm a Mexican too, a *Chicano.*" Kevin said. "One of the reasons I'm here is to connect with my Mexican roots."

Checo looked Kevin up and down, peering at him over imaginary glasses. "Lee, I finally understand why you need me on this project. You figured you'd need an actual Mexican to help you endure the dull hours with Mister *Chicano*-Power, English-only, Boy-Wonder, Daughter-Boner here . . . Kevin *Jodido* Spielberg of the Mexican roots, overalls, and puppy enthusiasms."

Checo's sudden nastiness startled Lee, leaving him sad and mute. He'd maybe not appreciated the impact of the separation in Checo's existence.

Checo continued, furious and serene, like a matador, Lee thought, with poor Kevin as the bull—Kevin with his boyish load of innocent passion.

"Listen *Señor* Kevin García . . . I guess you'll spend your vacation looking around down here to see who you are. Just remember: Mexicans don't give a shit about your identity. If you want to be a Mexican, you'll soon learn that being Mexican is being chained to an ox. It's big, it's stupid, it drags you through the brush and down the canyons until you're flayed alive. Being Mexican is having *gringos* associate your fatherland with diarrhea. I say you are a *gringo,* which is your good fortune and none of mine."

Kevin had allowed his mouth to fall open. Wilting, he seemed exposed, humiliated, vulnerable, and near tears. Lee could barely believe Checo was being such an asshole.

"Whoa, take it easy, pard. I don't mind you insulting my new hat but this is getting a bit dense for my taste. That 'being chained to an ox' business is pretty good . . . I can't imagine, though, how *Chicanos* have done you much harm."

"You're right, the sun is getting to me. I'm begging you, let's get in the van and get the cooler on! Listen Kevin, It's annoying to hear about your Mexican roots. I apologize. I just had an experience that's left me weakened. If you want to know something of the pain of being Mexican, go into that *abarrotes* store and spend some 'quality time' with the proprietress."

Lee got into the van, started the engine, and turned on the air conditioner.

"Kevin, you look almost as bad as '*señor* congeniality' here. Why don't you go find Courtney? I'm beginning to worry that she fell into one of those big sewer holes."

Kevin nodded and managed a strained smile. He looked pretty hangdog, though, schlepping off towards the bus station.

Checo and Lee waited in the cool comfort of the van.

"So what, are they working on the sewers?"

Checo's eyes bugged with mock incredulity.

"Not exactly. I was here two years ago and they had the holes dug then. They got that far and then stopped."

Checo smiled, the refrigerated air was working its magic.

"They probably started the repairs just before the last local election. They'll get back to them in another four years."

"What a cynic."

"Just a *chingado* realist, Lee, another of Cuahuatémoc's savvy children."

"Well, what in the hell do you have against Kevin? I thought you were beyond the Mexican prejudice against *Chicanos,* no?"

"I don't know. These Mexican wannabes . . . "

"Come on Checo, it's part of the maturation process."

"Yeah, so is shitting your diapers. I don't have to like the smell."

"Oh come on, Checo. It's nice to be with young people. It'll give us a fresh perspective. Just notice how excited Kevin is to be in Mexico, just to take it all in. Even the heat is fresh, new, exciting."

Checo had nothing to say. He moved his head into the stream of refrigerated air.

The hot air Checo chose to avoid moved languidly through the town and gathered in a thermal column over a baseball field. Turkey vultures spiraled effortlessly up six thousand, nine thousand, eleven thousand feet above the valley and then launched out to glide the vast heights. Lee watched them. They scanned the exposed surface of the planet in an unending quest for dead flesh. Perhaps the *zopilotes* would reap the ultimate benefit of the rebellion in the Sierra Nacoteca . . . along with the journalists.

Five

As the first light of the coming day began to dilute the blackness of the departing night, Elena had moved silently away from her sleeping husband. She stood up and stretched, popping her elbows and back. She smiled. That randy husband of hers had a surprise when he hit the *petate* the night before. He'd given her a midnight gallop and it had sure felt good. There was something about it, though, that she did not quite like. There had been a frenzy to it, a desperation that seemed almost fearful.

She went outside to her lean-to kitchen. She built a fire in the charcoal under the *comal*. She blew into it. She filled a pot with water and set it on the two-burner gas stove. She located a small pot of cold beans and put it on the other burner. She got out a *piloncillo* of crude sugar and took a big bite out of it. The rest she put into the water she was heating. She sat on a chair in the yard-compound beside the lean-to kitchen. She let the sugar work inside her and waited for the *comal* to warm. She enjoyed the little moment of repose. Roosters were going off all over the town and soon everyone would be awake. Licking her thumb she tested the *comal*. Just about ready. She removed the cloth wrapper from around the ball of *masa* she'd ground and mixed the day before and began to make *tortillas*, patting them into shape with her hands.

The sound of the pat-pat-pat of *tortilla* building must have awakened Felipe, who'd spent a restless night. He got up and walked outside. His hair was sticking out in all directions, as though alarmed and attempting to escape from his head. A big fond smile bloomed across Elena's face.

"Good morning my husband."

Felipe nodded.

"You were eager last night. I swear you almost got that thing of yours into places where it doesn't belong. Why were you in such a haste?" She smiled broadly, jesting but still wanting an answer.

He told her of the incident with Campos and the soldiers outside Maldonado's store. Her throat tightened and her pulse quickened as she considered the fate of Indians. A brute's whim had allowed her husband to live.

No wonder the night's sport had seemed so strained. She shivered and her lower lip trembled as she mouthed Nacotec curses and resolved to make Felipe a Benito Juárez amulet for protection. She'd speak to Carolina Carrera. A formal curse might be in order. Mexicans might be able to kill Indians without compunction, but Indians could send dream monsters to feed on the brains of their oppressors and disrupt the cycles of desire and satisfaction. But that was women's business. She addressed her husband. "You are troubled still."

"Yes, and I have to act. The dollars are gone but my obligation is not. What I can sell? Shall I walk the cow, pigs, and goats to the market at San Martín and sell them or shall I take chickens, eggs, and cheese on the milk run to sell on the streets of Ixtlán? Or should I see my other *compadres* to see if they can lend me enough to buy the firecrackers and book the band? There are only four days before the feast day of Santiago."

Elena began to cry. She loved her animals and now luck would perhaps deal them a terrible blow. If the hens had to go, then they had to go. The saint had to have his *fiesta*. Oh, those poor hens, though. She'd had to buy twenty-five chicks to get fourteen hens. She sold a couple of the capons and killed the others one by one for meals. Chiseling Nazario had done her out of two of the hens, leaving a dozen. She hated to lose those hens. They gave a dozen eggs a day! Who knew what kind of stingy, spiteful harpy would buy her hens? Everyone knew that Ixtlán was full of witches, greedy ones, vindictive! Felipe might sell the hens to some miser who hoarded corn. The poor hens would starve, get nervous, and quit laying. Then, because they'd quit laying, the woman would have an excuse to kill and devour them. It was the fate of hens, a hard one that made Elena cry. The only thing worse would be if Felipe took Yolanda, the cow. Yoli was only a fair milker and her farts had driven the family out of the house on many occasions. Still, she was a dear old thing, who shared Elena's distaste for procreation.

"Girls like us," Elena had said many times, "just like the FIRST part of that business."

Yoli's fate could be to march off to San Martín and fall into the hands of some careless girl who'd not know how to ease her mastitis. Elena's tears rained down onto the *comal* where *tortillas* burned. The acrid smell of steaming tears and burning *tortillas* filled the lean-to kitchen and Elena just sobbed.

Felipe stiffened and bit his lip. There was no other remedy. What else could he do? Then, to his astonishment, he thought of the television set that he'd brought from Chicago. How could he have worried for hours and never once thought of the damned television? It took up a lot of space and he had to move it constantly. The rain leaks migrated as though seeking a way to create shorts to electrocute the family. Suddenly, the TV was superfluous. Felipe had no money for electric bills.

"Maybe Miriam Maldonado would want to buy the television set."

Elena quit crying. The television set! Losing it would be bad. Felipe had brought it from 'the other side' and it was the pride and joy of the family. Still, it had caused problems. In the first month that Felipe was back, every one of the kids had come down with whooping cough. Elena suspected that this misfortune was caused by the debilitating effect of the envy that the television set had sparked among their neighbors. Maybe the television should be at Maldonado's store for the drunks and wasters to watch while they got plastered.

"It's your decision, husband. The television set gives neither milk nor eggs. We can't kill it for meat. Perhaps we should keep the animals and let the television go."

Felipe had already decided. Miriam Maldonado was always after him to tell her what had happened on this or that novela. The

Maldonados bled the peasants dry with that store of theirs. They would have sixty or even seventy dollars for the television set. He had bought it at a Chicago Price Club for three hundred dollars and brought it by bus more than three thousand miles to the village. The sum was nothing in Chicago. He'd have it in two weeks when he went back.

"It's all settled," he said. "The television goes. The kids will set up a howl but they'll recover. I must act today. If the Maldonados won't buy it, I'll sell it to the Cosme store. Any store with such a television will attract more customers. Even Mauricio Cosme will be able to understand that."

The mention of Mauricio Cosme drew laughter from Elena, who was still swabbing tears from her eyes. Mauricio was famous for his inability to make correct change and a widely circulated story suggested that a ground squirrel had once bested Mauricio in a contest of wits. His wife was no smarter. Everyone said that the courtship was no more than a simple collision. The two of them bashed into each other, fell down, and ended up married. Recalling this, Elena laughed until she, like Mauricio and his wife, fell down right on the kitchen floor.

A minute or two later, she was able to compose herself. What a start to the day. She'd trembled with fright, mouthed terrifying curses, burned three *tortillas,* cried herself dry, and fallen down laughing in the dirt and chicken shit. She was starving her poor husband! Well, she'd be getting her period soon and all this would pass. The kids were getting up. Elena got serious about breakfast. Soon everybody was eating beans and *tortillas* and drinking the heavy, sweet coffee.

Felipe, however, did not move off to start work in the *milpa* or chores with the animals. He ate his food and waited. The kids were rowdy creatures. They had the spirit of their mother. It was a noisy household, entertaining for a quiet man like Felipe.

After breakfast, Elena ran the children out to 'swarm over the hills and valleys.' They were well-behaved, busy children who had chores to do before play.

"Look at the ragamuffins run!" she said, watching her children scatter to their chores.

"Now husband, what else is preying on your mind?"

Felipe drew a deep sigh.

"If it's not one thing it's another. Now that the selling of the television is settled, I have thoughts of the Army. Efraím is boasting that the "ones in the hills" are armed.

He smiled broadly.

"They have one little pistol is all. Maybe some of the geezers have an old shotgun to blow up and blind them. The Army is here because of Efraím and the others. I came that close."

He held up two fingers.

"I can't get it out of my mind. You had a brush with widowhood. This business has gone too far. I need to go find 'the ones in the hills' and tell them what Campos said. I fear they are fooling themselves about what danger they are calling down on themselves. I will warn them. I may also visit my *compadre* Don Esteban Castellano. I will take him a bottle of Presidente and a box of candy for his servants and their kids. Perhaps he will unbend."

Elena listened, getting angrier with every word, every phrase, every breath. "Why," she said, "does this fall to you? Are you the only man on this mountain with a brain? If that pack of idiots wants to boast about their demands and then face the soldiers with nothing but their farts to blow at their enemy, why should you stop them? Can you out-talk that moron from the soccer team? Why lower yourself? And what about your *compadre Señor* Don Bottle Stopper? Everyone knows that he's like a cork, either on the bottle or on the floor. Just stay here and pour your *Presidente* into Yoli. At least she is not a mean drunk. That man has not drawn a sober breath since his father died. Greedy, blood-sucking maggot! Who can blame the morons of the *mesas* for wanting to blow his pickled brains out?"

Felipe smiled. What a woman! He felt like pouncing on her again.

"You're right, but don't foam at the mouth. Do we want this village to be known as a place of widows? It's a dangerous situation and the Army will kill anyone they please. They were ready to kill me . . . it was, for the moment, more amusing to see me squirm. Next time it might be amusing to see me kick three times, vomit blood and convulse, full of bullets, for an hour or two. No, Elena, it is my fate that this task has come to me."

"Go then, scat! If you must spend the day thus, just get gone. I see that look in your eye! If you stay much longer you'll be wrestling me to the *petate* again and the Army will end up killing everyone in the village. Go. Do your duty for your village first and do your duty to your wife later. I'll keep it warm for you."

Felipe took a gourd full of water, a few *tortillas* and the television set. The Maldonado store was a kilometer down the hill from Felipe's thatch-roofed concrete house. In Huatepec everything was either uphill or downhill. Even the *milpas* angled up the hillsides and everyone joked that Huatepecos were born with one short leg from the generations of working those sloping fields.

A kilometer is a long way to carry a television set—even downhill. Felipe's was a nice big 27" Panasonic. The church bell had just tolled nine and already the spongers were out in front of Maldonado's Store. Several saw Felipe struggling with the TV and raced to help him carry the set the last few meters. The least he could do, by way of gratitude, they figured, was to buy the "helpers" a bracing breakfast jolt of *aguardiente*. Felipe was not in the mood and Miriam Maldonado cast a glance at the sponging society that made them wince. The woman was a lion at the gate!

Miriam Maldonado would have the television. She took the TV, plugged it in, and set it to its highest volume even before she started haggling. A game show was playing. Narciso Maldonado was gone. He was in Hannibal, Missouri copying and boxing motivational tape cassettes for a small company that had a double wide trailer and three employees. He was sending money once a month just as regular, Miriam said, as her menses. It occurred to Felipe that if the people who worked on 'the other side' could get together, they could've easily afforded to buy the village a decent pump. But then, who would be willing to sacrifice the money they hoarded for the huge *fiesta* expenses that everyone expected them, the people with income, to assume? The very thought was heretical. A television for the store, though, that was different. It was the kind of investment that would pay off. Everyone had to use the stores. Who would not prefer to buy sardines, oil, and *aguardiente* from a store with a television they could watch?

The highest sum Miriam would pay for the television was fifty-seven dollars. Felipe agreed with suspicion. The transaction was stacked, fishy. He took the money and asked Miriam how she had heard about his misfortune. Miriam was pleased with her purchase and inclined towards generosity and candor.

"José, Samuel, Isabel, and I were on the roof, above your head, while the soldiers were molesting you. We had the pig."

Felipe started to walk off. He got as far as the door before he turned around. "What do you mean, you had the pig?"

"Ay Felipe, do you think we would let those animals kill you? When you left the store, I climbed the ladder to feed the pig we're fattening on the roof. Just think. The pigs of this village eat shit—shit and garbage. Imagine the difference in the taste of a pig that has eaten corn and powdered milk."

"Yes," he said, "such pork would surely taste heavenly, but . . . "

"Well," Miriam went on, "I heard the soldiers having their sport with you. I woke José."

José was Miriam's and Narciso's eldest son, a dull, spoiled, fat slug of a boy, maybe sixteen years old.

"The two of us lured the porker over to the ledge and kept it quiet with a piece of watermelon. If they had tried their little *ley fuga* business, we were going to push the pig off the roof into the jeep. Just think of the squealing that pig would have made. They would have probably killed each other while you disappeared into the fog. We waited, though. We didn't want to risk breaking the pig's leg unless they were resolved to kill you. We listened closely. I noticed the sum that those animals stole from you and have now had the opportunity to see that it was returned in full."

Miriam, a stout woman who stood perhaps four feet ten in her blue and black pleated wool skirt and beribboned *huipil*, glowed with humanitarianism. Felipe felt obliged to point out that she had the reward of a three hundred dollar television set for her benevolence.

"Yes," she said, "and it goes to show that God, the Saints, and Benito Juárez reward virtue."

Before leaving, Felipe bought a liter bottle of Presidente Brandy and a box of chocolate covered cherries before taking his leave of Santa Miriam. He was down to forty-five dollars, the bare minimum he would need for the firecrackers and the band.

The men of this world, he thought, should just go to the United States and stay. Just look at how Maldonado's store was taking over now that Narciso was not around to disrupt business and squander the profits with his habit of doling out generous drams of *aguardiente* to his numerous *compadres*. Felipe walked along shaking his head in admiration.

He took a pathway into the forested hillsides that towered over the town. Banana trees gave way to huge pines on hillsides too steep for Don Castellano's loggers to exploit. The insurgent "headquarters" was six kilometers above the village where the little spring branch bisected a series of relatively flat meadows. "Headquarters" was not much. As far as Felipe knew, only one person, Jorge Dzul, the elementary teacher/village soccer star, a prissy Mayan from Yucatán, actually occupied the camp full time. A person could stand in the village plaza in front of the church and scan the mountains, and see the clearing, the most obvious spot imaginable for rebel "headquarters."

He found the rebel camp in that annoyingly obvious spot. "Headquarters" was no more than one disreputable hut. Like the village houses, its roof was made of thatched banana leaves. Unlike the village houses, most of which were made of reinforced concrete, the "rebel headquarters" was a flimsy affair made of hastily tied poles of various dimensions. Three occupied hammocks hung from the poles. The earthen floor of the hut was littered with rusting *machetes*. A tiny pistol in an oversized holster hung from one of the bearing poles that defined the tiny space. Sure enough, propped against another pole was a shotgun that might have been a pre-Hispanic artifact. It looked deadly enough, though, to anyone with the poor judgment to try to fire it. The cadre of village guerillas was apparently conserving its energy in the traditional way. They were all fast asleep.

Waking them was no cinch. Felipe stood a discreet distance outside the hut whistling and clearing his throat. Nothing happened. The sleepers slept on and Felipe might well have thought they were dead, surprised in their hammocks and killed by Campos. They provided, however, unmistakable evidence of life. They were snoring like muleskinners.

After a few minutes of futile hawking, Felipe began shouting the men's names. "¡Jorje, Oswaldo, Indalecio!" Still nothing. The snoring actually seemed to get louder. Finally, Felipe approached the hut, went inside, and gave each hammock a vigorous shake.

With resentful reluctance, the slumberous rebels roused themselves from their hammocks.

Felipe spoke to Jorje Dzul, the leader, the *"subcommandante"* of the rebels. Oswaldo quietly started rustling up some breakfast and Indalecio simply walked away in the direction of the village. Jorje Dzul, with a sweep of his hand, welcomed Felipe to "rebel headquarters." Felipe wasted no time. He told Jorje about his encounter with Campos and the soldiers. The situation, Felipe pointed out, was extremely dangerous. He urged Dzul to temporarily disband the group for the safety of the village. He mentioned that Lee White would shortly arrive with a pump.

Jorje Dzul listened. He was wearing a yellow knit shirt, chino trousers, and deck shoes. The clothing was a bit dirty, a bit sprung and wrinkled, but Dzul still managed to look dapper. He was not a peasant. He was in the village to teach school. His father was a bus mechanic in Mérida. He was twenty-eight years old, just a year younger than Felipe.

At length, he spoke.

"Lee White should not stick his nose into this."

Felipe blinked. How could Dzul focus on Lee? Wasn't he listening?

"He's not sticking his nose into anything. I asked him to bring the pump. He's my *compadre.*"

"He's a *gringo,*" said Dzul. "The *gringos* cannot buy us with their pumps."

"It's not like that. Without a pump the women have a tough time. The dispute with Don Castellano goes beyond the issue of the pump and it may take a lot to resolve it. Until then, we need a pump."

Felipe scratched his head and watched Dzul stiffen against the logic.

"Can you name one time in the two hundred year history of the United States when the *gringos* have sided with the poor?"

Dzul began to pace, gesticulating as though to a crowd, as though to his students. "The *gringos* are always on the side of the bosses, the tyrants, the death squads, the torturers. Why should we trust him? Because you had the poor judgment to take him as your *compadre?* How is it that he has such a reputation for benevolence? He organized a crafts cooperative? I say that makes him a thief, exploiting the craftspeople of this village, getting rich off of the labor of the poor."

"That's not true. You don't know him. You weren't even here when he got the crafts cooperative going. Blame me. The pump was my idea. I didn't walk six kilometers to listen to you run down my *compadre.* I came to warn you! Back off for a few weeks. Go back to your school. Send poor Oswaldo back to his pregnant wife before she breaks her back weeding his *milpa.* Send Indalecio back to swill *aguardiente* with the rest of the spongers at Maldonado's store. Don Castellano is my compadre. I will speak to him. Perhaps he will see reason."

Dzul jumped to his feet, ready to launch into condemnation of Don Castellano. Felipe silenced him.

"Let me speak without interruption. Don Castellano is a drunk. He is yellow from drink and will soon die. He is in constant pain from alcohol poisoning and hangovers. Almost every man in the village is his *compadre.* We dealt with him for decades before you arrived."

Felipe took a deep breath and continued, looking into Jorje Dzul's eyes.

"Until Campos goes, you are sitting ducks up here. Go back to your school, your soccer field, and the screened windows of your little house. Why stay here to be massacred like worms?"

Dzul considered Felipe with withering contempt. "You are an enemy of the people." he said, "You and your *compadre,* the *gringo* and the high *hacendado.* You can Kiss Castellano's ass like you have for years! We are taking his ranch."

"You are out of your mind. I told you what happened to me last night."

Dzul snorted in derision and Felipe gave up. He realized that his stroll up the mountain had been futile. His one comfort was that Oswaldo, behind Dzul's back, was rolling his eyes and silently making fun of his *commandante.* The lark with Dzul was obviously a bit stale.

Felipe walked back down the mountain. He had the *Presidente* and the chocolate. He decided to put off the visit to Don Castellano. Don Castellano was an unpleasant man and Felipe had reached his limit with unpleasant men.

Six

"Daddy, isn't it dangerous to pick up hitch-hikers?" Courtney's voice strained as she attempted to manage her anxiety.

Ever since leaving the paved highway at Mictlán, Lee had been picking up riders. He'd not noticed his daughter's reaction.

Everyone except Lee had gone through a little wear and tear in Mictlán. Courtney had run a gauntlet of wolf-whistles, lascivious gestures and shouts of *"güera"* and *"Je, bebé"* between the van and the bus station. She'd been infuriated that the whistles ceased when Kevin showed up.

"Sexist bastards," she'd said and went on to characterize Mexico as a "Retrograde macho culture." She'd called her father's attempt to explain the cultural differences around sex roles "apologist shit."

It had not been Courtney's finest hour and Lee congratulated himself on his forbearance. He had not called her a *"gringa* twit," the words that had come readily to mind. Instead, he tried to be supportive. She was suffering from culture shock.

Now the people hitching rides were getting to her. The men wore huarache sandals and cowboy-style straw hats similar to the one Lee affected. The women wore extravagant embroidered blouses, be-ribboned pleated skirts and rebosos formed into turbans. They smelled, men and women, of sweat, beans, farts, the rot-gut *ponche* that was apparently ubiquitous, tooth decay, and the gardenias and frangipani which they'd either bought or sold.

Lee picked up as many as the van would hold. When several got off at a tiny hamlet, he immediately picked up an equal number who stood at the side of the road apparently waiting for the bus up the mountain.

Greeting the people, Lee had practically glowed with satisfaction. He smiled at Courtney's tight-lipped question and glanced at the rearview mirror for a look at his uptight daughter. She sat straight-backed and rigid, apparently overwhelmed at the continual sensory barrage. Checo, next to Lee in the "shotgun" position, looked as uptight as Courtney.

Lee spoke. "These people are peasants, Court, not hitch-hikers like U.S. hitch-hikers. They flag vehicles down for rides whenever they can. It's faster and cheaper than waiting for the bus. What does it hurt us?"

"Won't it slow us up?"

"Sure, but we're going so slow that it won't make much difference. We'll never make it to Huatepec anyway, not today. There are some cute *cabañas* up the road a bit. We'll spend the night there."

"But . . . "

"You and Checo can both just relax. You don't begrudge these poor people a ride do you?" He winked at his daughter, making eye contact in the rearview mirror.

"Well I just hope that none of our cameras disappear."

She flounced in the seat. She got out the cell phone she'd rented in Mexico City.

"She's right," Checo added in English.

"Oh for Christ's sake, Checo. These people are poor. They aren't thieves. Enjoy them. Drink the *ponche*. We'll see if we can get the guy with the little *Nacoteco* fiddle to play it."

Checo didn't answer. Lee guessed correctly that he was ashamed of the fact that he was terrified of the Indians, the *nacos*.

Courtney used the cell phone to call one of her film instructors in Syracuse. Lee was impressed. Evidently there was plenty of budget, always good news. She asked her mentor what he thought of doing the postproduction on the film at a studio or film lab in Mexico City. Courtney's side of the conversation was limited to a series of "uh-huhs" and "OK's."

The Indians watched Courtney with courteous but avid interest. The phone was so small that it looked like a toy. Lee wondered if the Indians thought they'd hooked up with a madwoman who had pretended conversations on a toy telephone.

Kevin was apparently in heaven. He drank the *ponche,* taking deep drags of the milky orange liquid. He tried to talk to the Indians without much success, but seemed pleased that some of then spoke Spanish as poorly as he did. They were no more than an hour out of Mictlán when he started nodding off. Lee was glad, figuring that it was good the *ponche* put him to sleep before he'd drunk enough to make him sick.

It was later than Lee would have hoped. It'd been five before they got away from Mictlán and it was a good four-hour drive to the *cabañas* where Lee wanted to spend the night. Around 6:30 the sun began to set. Beautiful. Soon it'd get dark, though. Things could get dicey on rural roads at night.

Kevin jerked when the van hit a deep rut in the road. Somehow he managed to bring his foot down on the neck of a live chicken. One of the riders had two full-grown chickens tied together by the feet. She put them under the seat and they migrated a bit via the many bumps and lurches. They ended up underneath Kevin. One chicken silently strangled beneath his foot. When the animal gave what might have been a death shudder, Kevin came awake. He fumbled in the burgeoning darkness and found the chicken. It was limp and unconscious. He assumed that it was dead. It was still tied by the leg to its companion. The owner was dozing herself, ignorant of the bird's plight.

Kevin's guilty instinct was to simply ignore the inert animal. He'd act surprised later when the woman noticed that her hen was dead.

Courtney, unaware of the agony of the throttled chicken and the moral quandary of her boyfriend, had adjusted her attitude a bit. She was pleased that Kevin was awake.

"Kev, she whispered, "while you were asleep, I decided that Checo and my dad are out of their minds. They've been arguing about photography. Checo said that 'color is a whore,' I wish you'd heard it."

"Well," he yawned, nervously eyeing the sleeping woman who owned the strangled chicken. "I can see Checo's point. I mean you've got to draw the line somewhere."

Courtney gave a dry laugh. "I was commenting on how absurd the argument was, not asking you to take sides. Look at Daddy's hat. It's ridiculous. My mother would never let Weldon, my stepfather, wear a hat like that."

Before realizing that he had murdered a hen, Kevin had been in and out of sleep. Fitful and guilty, he'd come to a decision about a "little secret" he'd held. He supposed that he had to tell Courtney. He was a bit fuzzy headed from sleep and maybe even a little drunk from the *ponche*. He straightened himself and drew a deep breath.

"Court . . . I bought a gun in Mexico City."

He flicked nervously at the spot where hair used to fall in his face before he got the crew cut.

Courtney was silent, her body stiffening by degrees.

"Court?"

"I'm hoping there's a punch line."

"There's not. I did it last night when I went to buy Checo's books."

Courtney remembered wondering why Kevin had been so stubborn about doing the errand on his own.

"I helped," he continued, "with the cameras on Danny G's documentary on gun shows. One of the dealers told us he could have any gun delivered to any location in any major city in the world. I called him and set it up before we left. He gave me a phone number in Mexico City. I called the number and a guy brought the package to the bookstore. It was incredibly efficient."

Courtney strained to contain herself. She didn't want to show how shocked she was.

"Isn't the information age wonderful. What on earth made you think you needed a gun for this trip?"

"It's for the rebels; a gift, a show of solidarity. Now I don't think it'd be such a good idea."

Checo and Lee were arguing about the merits of pimping their work to serve the ruling classes. They were enjoying themselves too much to listen. Courtney remembered, however, that Lee had said that some of the Indians might speak English.

"Lower your voice. I can't believe you. It's totally unethical. We're doing a documentary, that's journalism. It's our job to make a film, not support a revolution. Didn't you have an ethics class?"

"Not really . . . my training's been pretty technical. I got all excited. I figured we could make a big impression with a gift like that. Seeing these people made it real for me. The gun could kill everyone in this car in five seconds."

"Jesus, what is it?" Courtney was sitting erect, tense. Even her ears looked angular.

Kevin took a deep breath.

"It's a machine pistol, pretty much a standard machine pistol. The dealer was enthusiastic about it because it's compact. It's a 'Cobray-SWD M-11 9 millimeter,' for all that means to us. The dealer had a photo of it posted on the Internet. I also bought a bunch of ammo. Nine millimeter ammo is easy to find but ammunition of any kind may be hard to get in remote areas."

"You do think ahead . . . what a jerk! Where is it?"

Kevin came up with a thin smile.

"It is compact. I've got it in a camera case, I brought along an extra with the gun in mind."

"What a genius. Can we lock it in the bag? I don't want Daddy to know about it. We've got to get rid of it."

"The dealer would probably buy it back. We'd take a hit on the price, but he was pretty good-natured. I could email him. The case is locked."

"How much did you pay for it?"

Kevin rolled his head on his neck and stretched his back.

"Um. The gun itself cost twenty-five hundred dollars but that included a noise suppressor and all the accessories. The ammunition came to about two hundred and fifty. The delivery cost another eight hundred. All in all, we're out three thousand five hundred and fifty dollars. I expect we can recoup about a thousand or eleven hundred."

Courtney was dumbstruck. She sat there with her mouth open, staring into the fading light. Fireflies were starting to fire up and dart across the path of the van.

"You keep saying, 'we,' Kevin . . . ?"

Kevin drew another deep breath and let out a long sigh.

"I used grant money, the corporate American Express card, actually, the one you gave me to use for the portable Klieg lights and so on . . . the invoice from the gun guy says 'photographic equipment.'"

"Son-of-a-bitch! I ought to fire you. Do you know what falsification of grant accounting is called? It's fraud, Kevin. It's beyond unethical. We can't turn in a faked up receipt, I won't!"

A muscle in Courtney's jaw began to twitch.

"We'll have to pay it out of our own pockets and even then it's going to screw up the accounting. I got that card to use for all the grant purchases, nothing else!"

"Well, I apologize. I got carried away. I was thinking I could help . . . my people."

"You have to pay for it. I can't dock you the money because I'd have to explain why. But you have got to get me the money right out of your paychecks. You are going to sign them over to me as you get them until the money is paid off. Whether you can resell the thing to your dealer is none of my concern."

"Alright. I guess that's only fair. It's going to be a costly lesson, though . . . but maybe you'll save a bundle doing the postproduction down here?"

Courtney leveled a look at Kevin that was concentrated ice. She would not use one dime of grant money to make it easy on him. "Call it tuition. I never would have dreamed that a gun, even a fancy one, would be so expensive."

"The one I wanted was an Uzi ultra. It cost forty-five hundred."

"Aren't you the bargain shopper." She laughed. "Just make sure I never see it. It stays locked in the camera bag, got it?"

Kevin nodded.

"And give me that credit card."

"Now?"

"Yes, now. Who knows what you'll do with it. Gamble? Use it at a whorehouse? God knows you'll be needing an outlet for sex before long."

"Court!?!"

"Don't 'Co-ow-ert' me. You have about twenty years of trust building before you get in my pants again. Now scoot over. I don't want you touching me. I mean it."

She pushed at him. As he crowded against the dozing Indian lady with the chickens, one of them, apparently the one who'd avoided strangulation, began to cackle loudly.

Lee swerved the van. When he regained control, he checked the rear-view and gasped. As he re-checked, he felt the hairs on his neck begin to prickle. Behind them, almost on their bumper, was a dark sport utility vehicle, probably a Grand Cherokee.

He had scant time, however, to react. An uproar had flared. An Indian woman was speaking excitedly in Nacotec. Her baby began to cry. A chicken lay wheezing, gasping, and cackling on the seat. Kevin, stuttering in Spanish, was trying to explain something about having injured the animal. Courtney was laughing. Risking another swerve, Lee looked at the chicken, at Courtney, at the owner of the chicken, and at Kevin. He failed to draw meaning from the tableau, so said nothing. Checo said nothing.

Kevin was getting agitated. His attempts to communicate bore an unfortunate resemblance to the panicky vocalizations of the injured pullet. He offered to buy the chicken but the woman wouldn't respond.

Luckily, the chicken made rapid strides. Weak, hollow croaks became lusty full-voiced squawks. She showed that her strength was not entirely sapped by her ordeal. The baby showed her stuff as well. She was not to be outdone by a chicken.

Poor Kevin was getting nowhere. Along with the Nacotec woman, he was proving that shared ignorance of the Spanish language is a rather poor basis for mutual understanding and effective communication. Finally, taking pity on both Kevin and the poor woman, Lee spoke. "She does not want to sell the chickens, Kev." He cast a worried glance at the rearview mirror. "She bought them as layers."

"Well, what can I do? I want her to know I'm sorry."

The woman began speaking very rapidly in Nacotec. Lee was concerned. How could he help out if the woman truly spoke so little Spanish? As the gravity of the situation became apparent, one of the Nacotec men spoke up in Spanish. "I'll interpret," he said. "I am Mathilde Sandoval at your service."

"I am Lee White. This is Kevin García, Courtney Gerard, and Checo Rivera."

Mathilde Sandoval took a deep breath. "She says She's worried about her chicken."

"Yes," said Lee, "that's understandable. Choking like that cannot be very pleasant. This young man is willing to buy the chicken."

Soon people were talking all at once, engaging the situation in three languages as full night fell on the San Lucas valley.

Courtney smiled in the dark.

"The van of Babel," she said.

Lee laughed.

The woman asked Mathilde what it was that Courtney said. Mathilde asked Checo. Checo didn't understand the word "Babel" in an unfamiliar context. He asked Lee what Courtney had said. Lee told him.

"She made a joke," Checo said in Spanish.

Mathilde Sandoval translated this into Nacotec. To everyone's dismay the Indian woman started crying. Her baby followed suit. The chickens continued to cackle raucously as though sympathetic to the plight of the confused humans.

This was just the kind of situation Checo could not stand. It reminded him of his family. People talking past each other, women crying, great aunts cackling and working up to attacks of hives or asthma. He'd taken it for as long as he could.

"Silence," he shouted. "Why is this woman crying."

Mathilde asked the sobbing woman. Lee explained to Courtney and Kevin, doing an excellent job of simultaneous translation.

"She does not want to sell the chicken because she bought the chickens for eggs. But now she is worried. Gasping like that at the margin of the day when the sun sets, the hen could have gulped up an exhalation from the grave. She is worried that her chicken is ruined and is saddened when white people laugh at her so scornfully."

Lee managed to render this in English. Courtney felt the blood leave her head. She began to weep.

At this point, Lee chilled Checo to the core. In Spanish, he pointed out that a suspicious car had come up behind them. It had dropped back a couple of times and was apparently going to hang rather than pass. Checo turned. The dark S.U.V. reminded him of a shark. Lee pointed out that it was useless to worry and proceeded to deal with the chicken crisis.

It took time, but a solution gradually emerged. Kevin would buy the chicken from the woman and then give it back as a gift. Mathilde explained that the only way to cure the chicken was to give it away. The act of giving had cleansing power. The act would create enough virtue to blast away the effects of gasping an unclean exhalation. A chicken does not provide much of a foothold for evil.

So Kevin would buy the chicken and present it to the Indian woman as a gift. This would cure the chicken, restore it to the woman's care, and leave her several *pesos* to the good. There was, however, still a problem.

The chicken, all agreed, was a fine healthy one, a hearty, thriving cackler that'd defied all *gringo* efforts to strangle the life out of it. It was surely worth ten *pesos*. All Kevin had to pay the woman for the chicken, however, was a twenty *peso* bill. The woman had no change. Indeed, no one had change. Kevin said that he would simply pay twenty *pesos* for the bird.

Mathilde Sandoval replied without even translating the offer to the woman.

"What can she do with a twenty *peso* bill? The most she will ever spend in the stores of San Lucas is three or four *pesos*. The stores don't have change. Besides, she will not want people to think that she has hoarded up twenty *pesos*. It would create envy."

Lee was preoccupied and, he thought, a little slow witted. His mind kept returning, unbidden, to the mysterious vehicle on their tail.

"Look, when we get to the store, we'll have a little *fiesta*. Kevin will spend ten *pesos* on *ponche* and snacks. We'll include the store-owner in the festivities. As our guest, he or she will find a way to change the twenty."

Slow witted or not, Lee felt like a genius. The plan might even help deal with their other problem. Surely the Cherokee would continue on while they had the little *fiesta* at the store. The knot in the middle of Lee's chest loosened a bit.

With the distraction of the chicken issue gone, Lee drove under increasing strain and tension, constantly aware of the Cherokee. Checo, chewing at his lip, was not much better.

"Does the village have electricity?" Checo asked.

"I think so. It's prosperous. If not, the stores will have intensely bright white gas lanterns to attract the night owls who roam the village and drink."

Checo wanted to stop the vehicle in a well-lit place with plenty of people around. Lee agreed.

Kevin and Courtney were, fortunately, unaware of the "tail." No use in worrying them. Courtney, still snuffling, was apparently under more of a strain than Lee had known. He was glad he'd not argued with her about her judgment of Mexico as sexist.

He drove on in silence while the suddenly animated Nacotecs joked and jabbered. For them, tensions had dissipated. Although the moon was due to rise, it was still inky dark and the headlights of the Cherokee a fixed feature in the rearview. Lee had to finally force himself to not look. The next quarter hour passed very quickly for the lighthearted passengers. For Lee and Checo, however, it seemed interminable. Finally, as the van neared the village, Lee told Courtney and Kevin about the Cherokee.

"Look, you may have noticed, but we've got company. The black Cherokee behind us has been there for more than an hour. The Grand Cherokee is the buggy of preference for some very nasty types. It's probably nothing, but we are going to be cautious. If they do anything squirrelly, we may have to improvise. I am going to speed up and put a little real estate between the vehicles."

He yawned and scratched his chin.

"When we stop, I want Kevin and Checo to get out as quickly as possible. I want one of you on one side of the road and one on the other side. Walk away from the van and stand back, in the shadows. We've got enough of a lead that they won't see you get out of the van. Don't do anything to draw attention to yourselves. Just watch the vehicle closely as it passes. Look for logos or painted signs. Also look at the license tags and note any unusual features. Seventy-millimeter turrets, for example.

"I want you, Courtney, out of the car, into the store, and away from the door as fast as you can get there."

Checo felt an odd sense of relaxation suffuse his body. He was ready to act and his task was straightforward. Weakened as he'd been after the situation in the *abarrotes* store in Mictlán, the interminable negotiations about the idiotic, bewitched chicken had taken a heavy toll. Being shadowed by *rateros* was almost a relief. At least he had dealt with *rateros* and had some idea of what kinds of things might happen. He might get robbed and end up with his throat cut, but at least the situation was metaphysically secure.

Courtney's voice became husky. She spoke to Kevin purposely loud enough for Lee and Checo to hear.

"Who does he think he is? I won't do it, Kevin. I am not going to scamper into that store like the girlfriend in a sci-fi movie."

Kevin was alarmed. He shushed and whispered. "Do what he says. He knows more than we do."

"It's sexist bullshit and pure paranoia. Next, he'll be wolf-whistling at women like the machos back in Mictlán. He's spent too much time in this country. I'm not going to hang around to 'inspect' the S.U.V., that is too stupid. But I won't scamper either, I might just twist my little ankle."

Courtney was practically shouting.

Kevin moaned while Lee's blood pressure soared and his temples pounded with anger.

They came up over a ridge. The newly risen moon illuminated the road sloping gradually down to the village, which was situated in the broad San Lucas valley. Two lights and the moonlit squat shapes of huts gave the only clue to the village's presence. Lee put on a tape of *Ranchera* Music for the Indians. The van hurtled towards the quiet, moon-blasted village and added some distance to the margin that the Cherokee maintained.

As they approached the store, Kevin, Checo, and Courtney were poised to leap from the vehicle. Suddenly, however, things got confusing. Checo noted huddled shapes of people were in the street on the opposite side of the road. There were moving lights, the flicker of candles and the shifting probes of flashlights. Some of the marching figures were carrying, what? Weapons? Lee pulled the van to a halt. He looked at Kevin and Checo.

"Okay, go."

Just as they started to pile out, bells started pealing. Next they heard explosions, rat-a-tat, rat-a-tat-tat.

"They're shooting!" Checo shouted to Kevin who stood beside him. "Under the van!"

Kevin did as he was told, hitting the deck and rolling under the vehicle. Courtney followed. Checo crawled under from the front. The bells and explosions continued. The din was overwhelming.

They couldn't see if Lee or any of the Indians had been able to get out of the van. It did not seem likely. In the immensity of time that two or three minutes can be in such circumstances, they waited for whatever would follow. They heard music that increased in amplitude. It was . . . a marching band playing "Santa Catalina." Courtney mouthed the lyrics, which came unsolicited from the depths of the collective unconscious.

> "Twenty-six miles across the sea,
> Santa Catalina is the place for me,
> Santa Catalina is the island of,
> Romance, romance,
> Romance, romance.
> Forty kilometers in a leaky old boat,
> Anything that will stay afloat . . . "

It was the weirdest rendition imaginable, with anomalous rhythms and unexpected clarinet runs. The band played dazzlingly bad but plenty loud.

Anyone could see that the musicians were drunk, all of them. Two, a trombonist and a drummer, were so drunk that they were depending on others, just slightly less drunk, to carry them piggyback as the band lurched along, followed by a knot of drunks who carried a small casket. They had not happened on a pitched battle. They had interrupted a funeral.

Checo, Courtney, and Kevin crawled out into the margins of the chaotic parade. They saw that Lee was slouched against the van, apparently relaxed, gossiping with the passengers, and enjoying the music.

When the trio dove beneath the van, Lee knew what had happened. Unfortunately, he'd long since concluded that there is no way to prepare people for the sudden outbreak of a *fiesta* in rural Mexico. In this case, the cataclysmic *fiesta* was a celebration of death complete with all of the formalities of grief. There was alcohol. There was a band. There was the constant peal of church bells. There was the usual profusion of mind-numbing *cuetones* and the smaller rapid-fire *cuetes*. There had been feasting before the procession filed down the street and there would be more feasting later as people staggered back from the burial. Many of the people in the procession were crying and all of them were drunk, with the exception of the numerous small children.

As the shaken trio dusted themselves off and approached Lee, the Indians headed to the store to wait for the *ponche* Kevin had promised. The woman had assembled her chickens. She stayed close, a discreet distance away, obviously worried that the *gringos* were going to chisel her out of the money they'd promised.

Kevin, Courtney, and Checo stared after the band, now disappearing into the darkness up the street.

"It's a funeral," Lee said. "Big firecrackers."

"Lee," said Checo in English, "while the explosions were going— the artillery, the machine guns—I made myself a promise that if, by some miracle, I lived through this ordeal, I would search you out, destroy that absurd *sombrero,* and end your life. 'Funeral,' indeed."

Lee spoke, "Hey, I'm sorry. This is just the way funerals are out here in the *afueras*. San Lucas must have a hell of a *cuetonero*. Those were incredibly righteous firecrackers. My ears still haven't recovered. Let's go have some *ponche,* the three of you look like you could use it. I should have known there would be a funeral. One of the hitchers mentioned that someone from the village lost a child."

Courtney glared after the band.

"You mean to say that a family has lost a child and the village is celebrating with a band and fireworks?!?"

"It's the way that funerals are 'done.' We'll hear more *cuetones* blasting in a few minutes when the casket is laid into the hole."

Lee nodded towards the store.

"Kevin, come on. This poor woman is waiting with her chickens. It looks like the Cherokee passed on through. Just to be cautious, though, we should spend the night here. I seem to recall that a couple of the stores rent out rooms to travelers. I hate to miss those comfy little *cabañas* but that's field journalism for you.

Again, he motioned towards the store. No one moved.

Lee smiled pleasantly. "Come on. Let's have a drink. We can eat in a while. There will be plenty of funeral food for us to scarf."

For the second time that day and perhaps the second time that year, Courtney began to weep.

Seven

By eight in the morning, the women of Huatepec knew about the Cherokee. With the pump down, the spring branch was the sole source of water. Every morning women came with their plastic buckets and their dirty clothes. They got their water, washed clothes, and gossiped. The gossip chiefly touched the eternal theme of morality. The *mitoteras*, the *chismosas* examined the faults and character flaws of neighbors and villagers not immediately present. The riverbank gossip provided the women of the village with the kind of entertainment that others find in soap operas, literature, and seminars in ethical theory. The gossip also provided factual information. In Elena's experience, this information was never wrong.

Concepción Estrada spoke at length about how Viviana Carrera's daughter, Flor, was going to turn out to be a whore if Viviana allowed her to hang out in front of Maldonado's store. Elena listened attentively but reserved judgment. Later, this same Concepción Estrada also said that the strangers in the Cherokee had given Lieutenant Campos a new holster for his hog-leg. Elena accepted this information as utterly accurate.

With important events, like arrival of the Cherokee, the information accumulated over two or three hours. One woman had seen the S.U.V. stopped at the checkpoint. Others noted that the men had come into the village to buy beer at Mauricio Cosme's store. As they discussed the topic up and down the river, one woman after another would add a fact or detail. Elena didn't bother to get the lowdown in its entirety. It didn't take a genius to see that the basic information added up to trouble. She got her water, washed some of the kids' clothes and then beat it back to the house, hoping to catch Felipe before he set off on his fool's errand to Don Esteban Castellano.

Felipe was still drinking coffee and thinking when she arrived. He was in no hurry. The task of the day was onerous. Besides, since the schoolteacher had decided to become a revolutionary, there was no school for Rodrigo, Golfrido, and María Luisa. They were good kids but it took some time to line them out with chores enough to keep them out of trouble. Besides, he liked to look after little Lilián. She was an energetic four-year-old and a lot of fun. He'd brought her a Barbie doll (Hula-Hoop Barbie) when he returned from Chicago. She'd undressed the doll immediately and lost the little hula-hoop, the pink satin jacket and the striped skirt Felipe had liked so much. Lilián loved that naked doll and spent long hours playing with it. When Elena hustled in with her water, Felipe was watching Lilián bury the Barbie up to her neck in a large sand pile just outside the house.

Elena was breathless. She put a piece of charcoal under the coffee pot, waited a couple of minutes and poured herself a cup. Felipe watched Lilián laughing softly. "It's a hard lot for a doll with this one." He laughed, indicating Lilián with his chin. "Why are you burying her, short stuff?"

Lilián did not think the question needed a response. She got out a tiny pink plastic comb and began combing the long blond hair of the buried doll.

Elena laughed. "That's a good idea. Maybe I will bury María Luisa up to her neck so that I can comb her hair. Have you seen that rat's nest? The little ragamuffin won't let me touch it. Where are her brothers?"

Felipe explained. They had chores.

"Well," Elena said, "I'm glad that you are still idling about here. The soldiers have company down at the checkpoint, five thugs in a big black Cherokee. The leader is a *gringo* and two of the others are black."

Felipe's stomach suddenly felt heavy as though he'd been eating lead. Elena's good coffee tasted bitter in his mouth. He nodded for her to continue.

"They are loaded down with weapons, pistols and shotguns. They're low on shotgun shells, though. They gave Lieutenant Campos, the one who almost killed you, a new tooled leather holster for his pistol. They brought booze and porn for the soldiers. Four of them partied with the soldiers. They played the cassettes of porn on the soldiers' VCR. The other one, a silver-haired *gringo*, met with Campos and a bottle of Brandy. The *gringo* is named Sam. He wears his silver hair long and straight like the women on TV. He has a tattoo of an eagle on the world with some sort of fishhook through it and letters around it."

She put her hands on her hips, bit her bottom lip, and closed her eyes, thinking. Maybe she should have stayed a bit longer. The information was pretty sparse. She recalled another couple of things.

"They bedded down while Venus was rising in the late skies. The carousers were like animals in their drunkenness and depravity. Campos and his *gringo* companion laughed and called them pigs. The Cherokee looks new but it has a fuel pump that is about to go out. It is leaking and they are angry that they neglected to bring a spare."

She cast a sideways glance at her attentive husband. She knew he would not be pleased.

She was right. Felipe listened with growing concern. He pressed his lips together and let out air in a puff.

"These men are not soldiers?"

"No. But they have that same angry, arrogant way about them, the same mineral stupidity."

"Will they stay with the soldiers?" Felipe was wondering exactly what kind of deadly trouble these men represented. It could be anything. Was the Army business something other than the idiotic guerillas? In Felipe's experience, guns led to drugs and visa versa. He'd heard of armed men showing up deep in the mountains and forcing Indians to grow poppies and little trees of some sort.

Elena had exhausted her information and wished she'd stayed at the stream for the complete run-down.

"Who knows? Maybe they will stay with the soldiers until they fix their fuel pump."

Felipe watched Lilián play. He felt weary. The men in the Cherokee would not be happy to see a carload of journalists.

"Listen," he said, "the visit to Don Castellano can wait. Instead, I'll make that trip to San Lucas. They make such good *cuetones* there. I could get them from Donaldo Sabino, but he is so tight that I swear he weighs every little ounce of gunpowder. To hell with misers."

Elena clapped her hands. The San Lucas *cuetoneros* were legendary.

"On the way, I'll stop at las Llagas to visit my *compadre* Don Martín Pino. I will ask him to have one of his boys watch the road to stop Lee White, to hold him at Las Llagas. Maybe I can convince him to come back later when all this blows over and the soldiers have gone."

Elena smiled. "I didn't know that Don Martín was your *compadre*."

Felipe noted the smile with annoyance.

"It was only for the primary school graduation of one of his dozens of kids. There was not much to it, but we are now *compadres*."

"Every toothless old coot on this mountain is your *compadre*.

Elena smiled. Felipe was such a kind man he could not refuse people. He did, however, make plenty of advantageous alliances.

"Well, you'd best get going. Don't let Martín sway you with any sob stories. He's certain to be cadging money, maize, anything. Leave now and you'll be back by dark."

"I'll be home, woman, when I finish my business."

Elena smiled. Even Felipe would naturally answer so. Such talk gave men the feeling that they were in charge.

"Yes, Husband, for the love of the saints take the time you need, just don't expect much of a *jaripeo* on the *petate* if you come in late. Here, take some *tortillas* and be off.

Felipe suppressed a smile. He was convinced that his own attempts to keep Elena in line were pointless. He did it out of a sense that tradition demanded it. At least Elena had a quick wit and a lively, vigorous body that did not have a mean bone in it. He took a small plastic *bolsa* for the *tortillas* and set off. His wife watched with a smile as he ambled down the hill towards the village square.

His *compadre* Martín lived in a village, Las Llagas, that was dusty and reputedly crawling with witches. Witches or no, it was a very poor village in a parched section of the morning side of the Sierra, an hour and a half down the road, half way to San Lucas of the beautiful *cuetones*. Felipe would make the trip piecemeal to save money.

Bus fares were expensive. Luckily the Pan Bimbo bread truck delivered each Thursday morning and the Maldonado store was the last stop before Las Llagas. Felipe would buy a Twinkie out of courtesy and ride for free. At Las Llagas, he could visit Martín while the driver supplied the handful of miserable stores that served the needs of the wiped-out village. Felipe could get back in plenty of time to ride along to San Lucas. He'd probably be able to catch the afternoon bus and get back to Huatepec just at dusk. Elena would be pleased.

Miriam Maldonado was full of the gossip of the arrival of the Cherokee. The porn was the aspect of the story that captured her imagination. Miriam loved scandal and titillation.

"It's a disgrace!" She shouted over the sound track of the television. "The depraved hogs slobbered themselves over those filthy movies. Someone should complain to the government. Just think of those swine casting their eyes on the sweet girls of this village. There will be a rape, mark my words."

Felipe nodded to encourage Miriam to continue, not that much encouragement was necessary.

"Those soldiers will go to the *fiesta* of Santiago all stoked up on those evil movies and are certain to pounce on one of the poor Indian hicks who'll come in from the sticks. Those girls ask for it, of course, and only hogs like the soldiers could tolerate the hillbilly smell." She shook her head.

"They should just take those soldiers on the milk run to Ixtlán and throw them out of the plane," she went on. "What they did to you, Felipe? Think of an unwashed Indian girl, stupid as a sack of charcoal. No good can come of this, mark my words. What if a drunken Indian father goes for the soldiers with his *machete*? Then we'll have murder as well as rape to deal with."

An incredibly lurid movie was playing on the Showtime channel of the television set that had recently belonged to Felipe. Miriam had the television playing at top volume. Felipe found it embarrassing.

The sound track filled the little store with the sounds of orgasm while the screen showed a kaleidoscopic montage of light, color, and writhing buttocks. It was hard to take Miriam's moral outrage seriously in such circumstances.

"Has the Twinkie truck made its delivery?" Felipe shouted, ignoring both the movie and Miriam's diatribe.

"Get the Hell out of this store!" Miriam stepped from behind the counter in the direction of one of the spongers who'd stumbled into the entrance and stood transfixed by the images on the television. Miriam's intimidating shout and aggressive movement broke the man's reverie and he beat a hasty retreat.

"Animal!" Miriam shouted after him. She turned to Felipe. "He should be here any time. I saw the truck heading up the road to the Cosme store and it won't take him long to unload the four Twinkies that Mauricio will need for the week."

This was welcome news. For the time being, however, he was still Miriam's captive.

"The men in the Cherokee are not connected to Don Castellano." She spoke with utter assurance of her facts. Felipe wondered how women could learn so much in so little time, especially since Miriam almost never left the store.

She continued. "Still, they are a bunch of assassins. Hirám Carrera saw the American, the one named Sam, on the Totonac side of the San Martín reservoir a few months ago. He says that 'Sam' was a hired gun working for a big shot who had the stupid Totonacs working almost as slaves. Sam has contacts. He puts together little clots of thugs and they do favors for whoever pays the price for favors. Who knows who's hired them. Certainly not Don Castellano."

Felipe pursed his lips, the situation looked grim. "They would chew Don Castellano up and shit him out."

Miriam agreed.

"Don Castellano got the governor to send the idiots, Campos and his pair of slobbering hogs, but these guys in the jeep have other fish to fry. If Campos has any connection to this bunch, you can bet that they are calling the shots. They pull the strings and Campos jumps. They ply the soldiers with booze and porn. It buys them cheap."

Felipe marveled again at the information Miriam had at her fingertips. There is probably no espionage network in the world more

effective than a village full of Nacotec women. Miriam could probably tell him how many times each of the men had farted, how loud,
how long, and how much they smelled.

On the TV screen, a hooded man was raping a terrified woman
at knifepoint. Miriam scanned the screen without interest. The Pan
Bimbo truck pulled up with a horrible metallic shriek. The brake
shoes were obviously shot. Despite the obnoxious noise that set
Felipe's teeth on edge, he was relieved to see the truck. He was on
his way.

Eight

The sun hit the raw road with a force that verged on violence. Exhalations of steam rose from the road and an extravagant riot of vegetable life loomed on both sides, ready to spill over and reclaim the wounded, mud-bleeding surface of the rutted track. It seemed to Felipe that the earth gave forth a great sigh as the morning heat sent steam skyward to form instant clouds that hovered five feet over the road.

How apt to travel an obscure and occluded road. Anything could emerge from the fog. The Twinkie truck roared down the road with a driver who had no apparent concern for the conditions. Felipe supposed that the driver had such confidence in his powers that he no longer even needed to see the roads he drove. They barreled on, whipping the newborn steam to create an ephemeral wake of clouds that quickly closed behind them. The Army checkpoint loomed out of the fog. They sped past the station without exciting a response. The Army was interested in traffic going into the village.

Las Llagas, twenty-six kilometers away, was an hour and a half's drive, even at the breakneck fifteen to twenty kilometer per hour speeds the driver forced from his ponderous vehicle on the disastrous road. Felipe worried about the brakes. When the driver slowed the vehicle it sounded like a train wreck inside the wheels. It was annoying to worry. Elena always said he was a worrier. As if he enjoyed worrying! No one, she said, could avoid the trouble that fate had in store for them, so why worry. He agreed and worried anyway. Perhaps, like the *gringos,* he should get a tattoo: "born to worry."

A couple of kilometers before Las Llagas, the landscape changes from lush forest to a bare, cactus-ridden plain. The road was choked with dust. Just a few hundred yards before the first house of that pitiful village, a vehicle sat blocking the road and listing a bit East. The driver of the Pan Bimbo truck cursed. "By God! It's *gringos!* And the damned fools have a flat. How in the name of Jesus and Mary am I going to get this truck around them?"

A crowd of people surrounded the sedentary vehicle. It was a white bus or van of some sort. Jesus! Lee White was there with a bunch of other *gringos* and a crowd of Indians, apparently from the village. Everybody was standing around looking at the van with curiosity and concern. Lee was wearing a hat the size of a parasol.

"I know these people," Felipe blurted.

The driver's eyes widened and he looked at Felipe to see if there was a joke.

"I think," Felipe went on, "you can get around them if you go on their left side. I'll get out here. I was looking for them."

The driver veered his truck to the left of the van and stopped. Both men got out. The spectacle of *gringos* confronting a flat tire was evidently too good for the driver to miss.

The driver, a tall, bulky Mestizo from Mictlán, pushed his way through the throng of curious diminutive Indians. He considered the tire.

"Flat," he said gravely, correctly summing up the situation.

One of the Indian men, a small thin fellow with wispy gray hair, stepped forward to take a place beside the driver of the bread truck. He assessed the situation and reached a point of agreement with the big Mestizo.

"Yes," he said with confidence, "flat."

No one in the crowd was prepared to argue the point. Everyone stared at the tire, convinced by the reasoning they'd heard.

Lee was staring at the flattened tire as though stout concentration might cause the limp rubber to buck itself up and get on with it. A skinny Mexican in Levis and an oversized Ché Guevara tee shirt was snapping pictures. A tall, strikingly beautiful *gringa* was pacing angrily up and down the road, trailing another Mexican—maybe a *pocho*—who had a camera hanging from his neck. This man was making soothing noises, attempting to calm the furious *gringa*. The Indians absorbed the spectacle, watching with opened mouths and vacant expressions.

Taking advantage of the wake created by the big driver, Felipe made his way to the collective center of the crowd's attention. Lee looked up, astonished. "Felipe!" He said, "is that you!?!"

Felipe assured Lee that it was.

Lee indicated the tire. "Flat," he said.

Felipe looked at the tire. He was pleased to see that it was a simple flat, not a blowout. There was a man in Las Llagas who fixed flats. Felipe hoped that the man was sober but realistically concluded that this was unlikely.

"There's a man in the village back there who fixes flats . . . If he is sober."

Mixed though this intelligence was, it was enough to break the impasse that had developed in Lee's approach to the situation. "Good, we'll get the wheel off."

He looked around and began shouting in English. "Kevin, give us a hand getting the wheel off. We can get a guy in the village back there to fix it."

Kevin turned and walked towards Lee and the others. The woman continued to stalk the road. The wiry Mexican in the Ché Guevara tee shirt now followed her. He was taking photographs.

"Felipe, this is Kevin García." Lee switched back and forth between Spanish and English. "Kevin, this is my *compadre* Felipe Piñeda. You'll have to use Spanish with Felipe. He's from Santiago Huatepec. He's my main man up there, a very nice guy."

"*Muy gusto,*" said Kevin.

Lee shrugged. "Kevin doesn't speak Spanish very well."

This confidence was not surprising.

"Kevin is from Santa Fe," Lee continued. "He is a *Chicano*, a *pocho*. His family is Mexican but he never learned Spanish."

Kevin did not follow what Lee was saying but he recognized the words *Chicano* and *pocho* and felt hot shame suffuse his being. Anger shortly followed. "I understood that," he said, his voice breaking.

"Oh for the love of God! It's a description, not an insult. You just get over here and take the wheel off the van. If I got down and started wrestling with those lug nuts, you might end up having to bury me here. I'm going to talk to Courtney before she murders Checo."

The driver of the Pan Bimbo truck had watched the exchange closely. "He's a *pocho*, isn't he?"

"Yes, but he thought that I was insulting him."

"He looks ready for war." The big man laughed and extended a hand. "I'm Orlando Roybal, at your service. Here, youngster, let's get this tire off. I know that guy in Las Llagas. He'll fix you up in no time. Drunk or sober, the man is a master. Maybe he's a witch, I don't give a damn. He's fixed more of my tires than I can count. Look at this road!! It's like driving on spikes!!"

Kevin smiled eagerly. He did not understand a word the man had said, but he obviously meant to help and was being quite pleasant.

"That's more like it." Lee walked off with Felipe. He was feeling a bit beleaguered. Courtney was apparently angry that they'd had a flat. What did she expect? The road being what it was, it was a miracle that they'd not had a dozen flats. Maybe she was still upset from the funeral incident at San Lucas. Maybe she was getting sick of Kevin. That was inevitable, he supposed. In Lee's experience, women demanded and merited attention. Kevin was too excited about being in Mexico to have much left for Courtney. Checo was being obnoxious. Imagine hassling the poor girl like that, taking his snaps while she was so upset.

"Courtney, Checo, come here, there's someone I want you to meet."

Checo took one last shot as Courtney turned a withering gaze on the men behind her. Lee approached Checo.

"Cut the crap," he said under his breath.

Lee made his introductions and the men shook hands.

"Felipe, would you be so kind as to tell Checo about any new developments in Huatepec. I have to talk to my daughter. I've told you about her, Courtney."

Lee approached Courtney, who stood twenty yards up the road with her arms crossed, her back to him, apparently considering the mountain wall that defined the far horizon.

"Those peaks," Lee said, drawing up even with her, "create this little patch of desert here. It's called a rain shadow. The people who live here don't know they live in a rain shadow. They probably figure that God is determined to punish them. Here, do you want a lollipop?"

Lee reached into his shirt pocket and produced, as if by magic, a watermelon flavored lollipop. Courtney had bought one of these lollipops in a store in Mictlán. She'd loved it. It was burnished with a thin layer of salt, lime juice, and *chile* powder. It was a startling and touching gift. Courtney thought she might cry and stiffened, fighting the impulse with all she had. She took the lollipop without a word, removed the cellophane and popped it in. The wild dance of tastes in her mouth calmed her. She met her father's gaze.

"Trouble with Kevin?"

"No, trouble with you."

"That's not surprising, but you'll need to elaborate. I've learned to live with the fact that I am not a sensitive person. Let's have it. What's bothering you?"

Lee's face was drawn, his eyes pulled back into small tunnels.

"I'm upset at myself . . . and annoyed with Kevin. But you . . . this is so frustrating! You'll listen. You may even tell me that I'm right. And it won't mean a thing. Nothing will change."

He gave her a smile he meant to be encouraging. "Not much does."

She drew a deep breath. "How can you set out on these roads without a spare? The rental agency was negligent in the first place but you're not helpless. You could have bought one. You bought that idiotic hat!" She lifted her head to indicate the damning presence of the hat Lee had spent over an hour choosing in Tepic. "Nothing's planned, nothing's organized. Checo didn't even have film when we left. Here we are, God knows how many miles up this dirt road without a spare. What were you thinking of?"

Lee was shocked. The idea of buying a spare never even occurred to him. He felt almost faint, like he could fall on his face at any moment.

"My God," he finally said. "I never even considered getting a spare. You don't need one. I wasn't surprised that Hertz rented the van with no spare." He took his hat off and wiped his sweating brow. "The idea of carrying a tire around idle, just in case something goes wrong with the others, has not caught on in rural Mexico. In Mexico, if you get a flat, you get help—instantly. Look how much help we've got. He indicated the crowd with a sweep of the arm.

"That is so irresponsible. You just assume that somebody will be there to bail you out."

"It's the way Mexicans operate. If we had a spare, we could have changed it by ourselves in five minutes, not very sociable."

"That is pure B.S. . . . I suppose Mexicans hope for flats so they can be sociable?"

"That sarcasm, Court, is an ugly habit for a pretty girl."

Lee replaced his hat and tilted it back.

Courtney glared and sucked at the lollipop, mastering the inclination to grab the hat and stomp it into the dust.

"No one hopes for flats, but Mexicans accept the fact that things break down."

Courtney hung her head. Lee felt his gut suffuse with warmth. It was touching to see the sad earnestness of her struggle.

"Look, Court, to do the film and the article we need to be prepped. It's not a matter of just getting where we're going and getting to work. We need information. It might be a poor idea to hustle our butts to get to Huatepec. The flat gives us a chance to learn the lay of the land." Courtney listened, astounded. He was convincing on that point at least. She said nothing. She used every ounce of her willpower to resist the sudden desire to simply capitulate. Twenty-five years of yearning for her daddy lurked in Courtney's strained features.

"Admit it, Daddy, however true all that may be, it's still, for you, an excuse for not having the responsibility and foresight to see that we had a spare."

"Well, yeah. It was an oversight." Lee surprised himself.

"If you really cared that much about being sociable, you would have been around from time to time while I was growing up. Instead, you've always been a crapster, avoiding responsibilities and creating excuses. Thanks for the sucker."

She turned and walked back towards the van, leaving her father to study the volcanoes on the southern horizon as he wondered how he had blundered onto this minefield.

Kevin and Orlando Roybal had gotten the wheel off of the van and were loading it into the back of the bread truck. The crowd of Indians began to break up, with many people walking in the direction of the village. Lee walked stiffly over to the van, locked it and extracted a liter bottle of the toxic *ponche* from the store in San Lucas. He cracked it and took a good belt. He approached the Indian with the wispy moustache, asked him to watch the van, and gave him some *pesos* along with the rest of the bottle.

The *desponchador* was sober enough to repair the flat in very short order. They had the repaired tire mounted in less than a half hour. The cost to fix the flat was three dollars. For forty dollars more, Lee bought a 15" wheel with a bald tire to use as a spare. They were ready to roll.

The Pan Bimbo truck had been a huge help. Lee thanked Orlando and gave him his card. To Lee's mild surprise, Orlando also had a card. He owned a pickup truck and a small *"servicio particular"* business of light hauling. He also noted that he would be making an extra Bimbo delivery trip to Huatepec in a couple of days because of the *fiesta*.

"Please tell Kevin that I'll look for him at the *fiesta*. He is a good man and I want to treat him to a *copita* or two of brandy."

The goodbyes all said, the Pan Bimbo truck roared off towards San Lucas and Mictlán. The Indians who'd "guarded" the van made their reserved goodbyes and disappeared onto footpaths. Finally, to Courtney's alarm, Lee cranked up the van, pulled an immediate U-turn, and headed back towards Las Llagas. Courtney told herself to relax. They entered the village and passed through it, heading, like the bread truck, towards San Lucas. They were barreling down the road in the opposite direction of Huatepec, their supposed goal. She watched the odometer. They went a mile, two, then five. Finally she could stand it no more.

CHAPTER 8

"Daddy," she said, feigning a casual tone, "why are we going in this direction."

"Oh! I keep forgetting you don't speak Spanish. We are going back to San Lucas. Felipe needs to buy *cuetones* for the *fiesta* of Santiago that's coming up on Saturday. You heard the *cuetones* of San Lucas at the funeral last night, they are the best ones around, so we're taking him back there. He's got to go, it's for his *compadre*. He's my *compadre*, so I've got to take him. It's sociable, Court. We'll get to Huatepec later than I'd hoped, but what the hell. I've never seen how or where they make those *cuetones*. It should be interesting."

As they drove towards San Lucas, Felipe mentioned that he was relieved to get shut of Las Llagas. The place, he said, had a terrible reputation as a rat's nest of witches. Felipe didn't believe in witches but it seemed to him that bad things always seemed to happen in Las Llagas. The flat was an example.

Felipe thanked God that he had the good fortune to be born in Huatepec, a hustling community full of liveliness and U.S. dollars. Huatepec attracted the Army and the sinister types in the black Cherokee, but that was the price of dynamics. All Las Llagas attracted was buzzards and dust.

Nine

San Lucas, like Huatepec, was a lively place. It lacked the dollars that Huatepec was able to command but that's because it was more prosperous to begin with. The lands of San Lucas stretched through a wide valley. San Lucas was full of rich peasants who squandered their dangerous, envy provoking wealth in lavish *fiestas* that were known throughout the mountains for their sumptuousness and adherence to tradition.

Felipe had no *compadre* in San Lucas. He would later, when he became a man of reputation and substance. San Lucas forged *compadre* connections with an awareness of its status as a chief Nacotec center. Men from San Lucas did not take "just anybody" as their *compadre.*

The town was strung along the valley it had farmed for two thousand years. There was a church and a plaza on the ruins of a pyramid. The village had a linear feel. Roads branched away from the town following small streams across the valley and into the surrounding hills. Felipe had no idea where to find the cuete craftsman. Lee stopped the van at the same store they'd used the night before. Lee had rented rooms and spent enough money to expect a decent welcome and good directions to the *cuete* craftsmen.

It was midday when the van pulled in. Lee was tired and hungry. He asked the woman who ran the store if she would be willing to feed the entourage. She was.

After the simple, sustaining meal of beans, *tortillas,* a bit of pork in a sauce, and a crushed tamarind *agua,* everyone was perky. Nothing like a good meal to arouse optimism. Kevin went on and on about Mexican hospitality. Lee guided the van up the main road. Following the storeowner's instructions he soon found a side road that followed a small stream.

"How far?" Lee asked.

"Who knows?" Said Felipe. "Pretty close. Not too far. She said to just drive up this road until we started seeing people who were missing fingers."

Courtney asked Lee to translate. He did.

"You mean to say," Courtney said, incredulous, "that these people blow up their hands making fireworks?"

"I guess so," said Lee. "You've got to admit that it's pretty chancy work."

He asked Felipe about it.

"They drink," Felipe replied. "They are very respected for their *cuetones,* so they get to go to all the *fiestas.* At the *fiestas,* well, there is always *ponche,* always brandy and people have to accept the generosity of their hosts. Perhaps they smoke cigarettes for relaxation, to calm their shaky fingers."

Lee translated this for Kevin and Courtney.

"Why don't they quit making the fireworks?" Courtney reasoned. "I'll tell you that the first time a child of mine injured itself, I'd look for a safer way to make a living."

"Yes," said Checo, "but you are an American."

They drove up the road into increasingly dense vegetation that bent over the narrow track. They practically tunneled through the indecent excess of greenery. Houses were spaced along the road in sudden clearings that balanced the riot of vegetation with abrupt, if limited, explosions of light. At every house clearing, children and dogs ran in all directions, excited by the appearance of a white van on their road.

At the sixth or seventh house clearing, Courtney noted, to her horror, that at least one of the children running alongside the van was missing fingers on both his hands.

"Ah," said Lee, "here we are."

The van slowed to a crawl. Eight or nine identical lank yellow dogs descended on the vehicle from all directions, barking at the top of their voices while snapping at the fenders, tires, and door handles. A woman walked out of the thatched house. She was missing two fingers from her right hand. She pelted the dogs with stones, showing practiced efficiency, deadly aim, and an arm that delivered strikes at around ninety miles an hour. The dogs retreated to a respectful distance. The woman was dressed in a black pleated Nacotec skirt and a lumpy sweater that had once been yellow. She waved happily and smiled broadly. The mouth matched the waving hand. The hand missed fingers. The mouth missed teeth. These deficiencies, however, had not spoiled her enthusiasm.

The van's doors opened and began to spill people into her domain. She watched attentively and did not seem particularly surprised. If a van was going to suddenly turn up oozing *gringos* from every aperture, it was all right with her. The dogs were less certain and slunk around at the perimeters of the clearing, uneasy yet intimidated.

"Those dogs are good ones," she said. "They are strong barkers," she continued. "They really raise hell. Are you wanting to buy a good guard dog?" She directed the question to Felipe.

"No thank you, although anyone can see they are excellent animals, we are here for *cuetones* with your permission, *Señora*. Is this the place? Do you make *cuetes?*"

"No," she said laughing and holding up her mutilated hand, "I retired." She went on to explain that her husband and son were *cuetoneros*.

Felipe asked where they were.

"Who knows?" She said. "They come, they go. Perhaps my husband is in his hammock just now recovering from that funeral." She smiled slyly. "I said I was retired from making *cuetes*. That does not prevent me from selling them."

Felipe explained that he wanted *cuetes* for the *fiesta* of Santiago in Huatepec. The woman nodded. She went into the hut and came out with a bundle of firecrackers fixed to long sticks. They worked on the principles of bottle rockets. The business ends, the firecrackers, were cylinders about 3/4 inch in diameter and about four inches long.

Although she was on record as willing to sell the *cuetes*, María Crisóstomo de Peña was not inclined to rush the project. Continuing to chunk the occasional boulder at the snarling dogs, she laboriously hauled straight-backed wooden chairs from the house into the yard compound. She then offered her guests coffee, which she made at leisure in a small kitchen hut that was attached to the house.

While she did all this, she talked to Felipe about relatives, *compadres* and *comadres,* and Santiago Huatepec at large. Lee and Checo listened to all the gossip: who was sick, who had died, who had married, who was pregnant, who was gone to "the other side," who was shameless, and so on. Lee enjoyed the situation, but it made Checo nervous. Checo was too reminded of his mother and aunts. They had the same ceaseless preoccupation with everyone else's business and the same greed for scandal. María Crisóstomo's avid continence, her black eyes widening in anticipation of a juicy morsel—this woman was too familiar for Checo to take much pleasure in the situation.

Kevin and Courtney listened attentively, as though they understood. Watching them nod their heads in apparent comprehension while Felipe and María talked, Lee was reminded of the little football troll dolls with bobbing helmets that many Americans kept on office desks or in the back windows of their cars. It was not a particularly complimentary image, but it made Lee feel fond of the young monolinguals.

María Crisóstomo brought coffee so fortified with sugar that Courtney was reminded of a hot pudding her grandmother had once made. They drank the alarming liquid slowly, as though sensing the wallop the sugar/caffeine load would deliver. When everyone was served, María Crisóstomo sat, drew a deep breath, took a mouthful of coffee, and began to talk about how much she pitied the poor people of Santiago Huatepec. It was a terrible shame, she lamented, that the village lacked the services of a real *cuetonero.* Donaldo Sabino, she explained, put together an entertaining *castillo,* but he ignored the basics with *cuetes.*

"Two years ago, I visited my *comadre* Doña Alicia Cosme for the modest *fiesta* of San Miguelito at Huatepec. Oh, it was a shame to hear those pitiful little toots. I felt bad for poor San Miguelito when they brought him out of the church. A saint likes a robust sound, something that knits the world together in adoration. Those *cuetes* that the waster Donaldo Sabino makes sound like a horse farting.

She pursed her lips. Her eyes flashed with indignation.

"What kind of respect can you show with horse farts? I'll tell you that the saints of Huatepec have shown a lot of forbearance. It's a good thing that the men bring dollars, that's what I think. The saints are always mollified when you pin some dollars on them. Now tell me, who is the *carguero* with the good sense to send you for the *cuetes* of San Lucas?"

"It is Don Mateo Carrera and his wife Carolina."

"Ah, yes, Dona Carolina is a fine curer. Just before his death, my uncle went to her for a pain he had in his chest. He was very pleased with her cure and died with her praises on his lips, God rest him. These *cuetes* you'll be taking, they'll build an enormous respect for Don Mateo and Dona Carolina. Santiago will reward and bless them."

She crossed herself with her mutilated hand.

"I always say to my husband that he is doing holy work, that the *cuetes* themselves are a priceless miracle, worth the labor, the worry, the lost fingers, all of it. Young people these days, like Donaldo Sabino, don't approach the craft with care. To them it's the flashiness of the *castillo* that captures their imaginations. Cuetes are just a business. Of course, this is a world of buying and selling. We sell the *cuetes*, we sell them at a price that is almost a gift."

She named a price for a bundle of twenty-five *cuetes*.

Felipe said that the price, however fair it was, was too high. Huatepec, he said, was not sitting in a golden valley of wealth like San Lucas and he could not afford *cuetes* at such steep prices. They haggled pleasantly while María dealt with the coffee.

María Crisóstomo claimed that her *cuetes* were the loudest, sweetest, most beautiful *cuetes* in the world. Her husband, she said, was a great artist, a *maestro*. To prove her point she insisted on setting off one of the *cuetones* as a demonstration. She bummed a cigarette from Kevin, flirted coyly with him while he lit it, and puffed at it expertly, using the gap of a missing tooth as a holder. She carefully separated one of the long *cuetones* from the bundle, holding it by the stick. She then drew deeply from the cigarette and touched the lit end to the fuse of the *cuete*. She held the stick while the fuse burned. The fuse burned merrily and lit powder that animated the *cuete*.

She let go and it took off with a shrill whistle, sailing high into the afternoon sky. At the top of the arc, the whistling stopped and the *cuete* exploded in a flash of yellow light. The narrow canyon amplified the virile production. The sudden noise was assaultive and physically confusing. Atavistic responses took over, mouths dropped, shoulders hunched, and scalps prickled with erectile animation as the mountains seemed to shake. Courtney could feel the fillings in her teeth vibrate with the power of the blast. For a split second, all thought ceased as attention focused exclusively on the sound. Then came the agonized shrieking of the nine dogs. The poor animals yowled and keened in pain.

The woman smiled. "Isn't that the most beautiful *cuete* you ever heard? It takes my husband's fine *cuetes* to bind the world like that. You won't hear *cuetes* like that everyday, I assure you."

Courtney looked at the company. Lee was smiling, enjoying the interaction. Kevin was trying to act cool, like he enjoyed the *cuetes*. His eyes were watering. Checo was staring in open-mouthed horror into the sky where the *cuete* had exploded. Felipe watched the woman.

"They are unquestionably fine *cuetes*," Felipe commented blandly. He was thinking of how entirely satisfactory the *cuetes* were and how happy his *compadre* would be to have such *cuetes* for the *fiesta* of Santiago. Such *cuetes* would certainly outdo the little poppers that the other *cargueros* would buy from Donaldo Sabina. He named a price that he said was his best.

The woman went back into the house and came out with a bundle of small firecrackers and a papier-mâché soldier doll that likewise bristled with *cuetes*. She held up the bundle. "Here, these are the ones you get at that price. And look, here's a soldier Judas. Maybe the people would like to see him jump for Santiago?"

Felipe and the woman continued to haggle while Courtney, Kevin, and Checo recovered from the blast.

"It was deafening!" Courtney whispered. "How can people want anything that would make a noise like that? It was painful."

"Undeniably," Lee agreed with a broad smile. "But look how proud she is."

The woman seemed taller and was haggling with great confidence, obviously buoyed up and encouraged by the strength of the demonstration. The blast weakened Felipe. When he heard the virile artificial thunder stop time and unite the world, he was consumed with desire. He now lacked the sense of detachment necessary to execute truly superior bargaining. He tried to discipline his expression, but he knew he was doomed. The only recourse was to bring the negotiations to a crescendo before María sensed the shift and figured out a way to exploit it.

"I'll pay that price," he said, "if you throw in the Judas and a skein of tiger poppers."

"Why don't you take a few boards out of my husbands work bench while you are at it?" She answered with a broad, if gapped, smile.

Felipe pulled out his money and counted out forty dollars. María Crisóstomo went into the house and emerged with several packets of *cuetones* and a string of smaller firecrackers (the tiger poppers) that Felipe would keep for himself and the kids to play with. To Courtney's relief and satisfaction, Lee had Felipe get some twine from María Crisóstomo. They tied the *cuetes* to the luggage rack. If it rained, they'd put the *cuetes* inside.

As much as Lee enjoyed the scene at María's, he was pleased to see the negotiations come to a satisfactory end. They had just about enough daylight to make Huatepec before sundown. Everyone made their goodbyes to María Crisóstomo, who repeated her attempt to sell Lee one of her dogs.

"They are the loudest barkers you'll ever find," she said proudly.

Lee made another brief stop in San Lucas.

"The Maryknoll Order has a Mission just up the main road towards Las Llagas. I think we'll stop for a minute or two. We're in good shape to roll into Huatepec before dark—even if we spent an hour with the nuns, and we won't spend that long."

"Nuns? Courtney sounded surprised. "Why on earth? Do you know them?"

"It's been a while. I emailed them that I'd be in Huatepec. It was a courtesy. I used to do business with them. I don't know if any of the ones I knew are still here but I want to stop anyway. It'll take ten minutes. These girls have always been into social justice at some risk to their health. It just occurred to me that they might know something about the guys in the Cherokee. According to Felipe, they're lurking around Huatepec. He thinks they may be some really bad actors. It'd be good to know a bit more. I've always had good dealings with the San Lucas Maryknolls. They'll be glad to see us."

"Spare me, for God's sake." Checo snorted impatiently.

"Ah, yes, unpleasant formative experiences with nuns, right?"

Lee had heard some of Checo's horror stories. They were good ones and he was willing to hear them again if Checo wanted to regale the troops.

Checo grunted. "Please keep it brief. This is beginning to seem like a long day."

The mission was modest. It was a house, a large one, three stories, but not the largest in the community by any means. It was the simple rebar-concrete construction style that characterizes the "modern" approach to house building in rural Mexico. It had the raw, brutal look of poured concrete.

It was siesta time and very quiet in the house. Lee had to knock for some time to arouse even one of the village women who apparently worked in the kitchen. She showed Lee into an office where a big boned blond girl in her twenties was typing on a computer. She wore no make-up and had the Scandinavian look of the Northern Plains, Minnesota or the Dakotas. She turned with a smile and Lee introduced himself and then the entourage.

The woman grasped his hand in both of hers.

"The legendary Lee White! I am very pleased to meet you, sir. I got your email. We've all heard so much about you! There's a rumor that you were here, that you arrived during the funeral last night. We were skeptical, but I'm delighted that we were wrong. I'm Sister Remilda. What brings you? How can we help you?"

Lee instantly liked Sister Remilda. He'd always liked the Maryknolls, dorky as they were. He felt paternal and went out of his way to be gracious and do favors, as though his kindness could make up for the poor job he'd done with his own daughters. He told her about his plan to write an article on the conflict in Huatepec and Courtney's plan to do a film on the *fiesta* of Santiago Apóstol.

"How exciting!" She beamed a big broad-toothed smile at Courtney. "You have a wonderful father, Ms. Gerard, but I don't suppose you need me to tell you that. Our order can literally never repay him. He almost single-handedly created the crafts industry in this corner of the sierra. We got most of the credit."

She giggled merrily, holding her hand to her mouth as though getting credit for Lee's work was "naughty."

Courtney, her head swimming, smiled her assent.

"I know you're bound to be in a hurry. . . . You do want to get to Huatepec before dark, so I'll resist the temptation to gush. I'm afraid that the girls you worked with are gone. As you know, we move around a lot. I can only hope that we won't long be strangers. Several of us will be in Huatepec for the *fiesta,* so let's do chat then."

Lee came to the point, telling her about the Cherokee.

"We can use a 'head's up' on these guys if you know anything."

"You are right to be concerned. We've had our eye on them. They've been working in the *municipios* of the Sierra for a couple of months. They're mercenaries, truly terrible human beings who've been oozing north ever since the Sandinistas lost the elections in Nicaragua. The leader is an American, Sam Cooke."

"Are they working with the Mexican Army?"

"As far as we can tell they aren't, at least not officially. We don't know, yet, who is signing their checks. The army has been around, but the army is predictable, almost benign compared to these guys. They have an agenda, but it is pretty veiled. If you are going to get in and get out in four or five days, I expect you'll be safe. Especially when they learn of my little surprise. Be watchful, though."

"Sam Cooke?"

"A real sweetheart. He's fifty-one, and a Vietnam vet. He was born and grew up in southeastern Oklahoma, Broken Bow. He was in the Marines from 1968 to 1974. He reached the rank of Staff Sargent. He returned to Southeast Asia in 1975. He actually wrote a humorous article for "Soldier of Fortune" magazine in 1976. The article implies that he was in Laos. From that point, he's not very visible in the data bases. He lived near Fort Benning, Georgia during the early eighties. He must have worked at the School of the Americas. Most of the real foul balls have run through that snake pit, but I haven't been able to find out what he did. That's it, the visible works."

"I can fill in the blanks. Any idea what he's like?"

"He speaks Spanish with an accent, talks a lot, reads. One thing, he likes to give people rides. Three weeks ago he picked up two nuns from Puebla at the bus station at Mictlán. They were coming here for a visit and were naive enough to accept a ride."

She rolled her eyes and rocked back in her chair with an exaggerated shrug of disbelief that anyone could be so foolish.

"They rode all the way up here with those five thugs. It was awful. Sam stopped in the middle of nowhere to give his 'boyos' a round of target practice. While this was going on, he got into the back seat with the girls from Puebla and read them a story from William Faulkner about tied mules being hit by a train. He told them that he liked to have someone religious perform oral sex on him while he read Faulkner."

Her lips tightened and her nostrils flared as though she were withholding unseemly laughter. "He said that he sure hoped he never lived to see a 'string of nuns' hit by a train."

Sister Remilda gave her attentive audience a big grin. She obviously found aspects of the story amusing. She continued. "With the peasants the rides have often included beatings disguised as fights. You know, one of the 'boyos' pretends to take offence at a remark and then pounds the poor peasant. They've also done a lot of malicious property destruction. The behavior seems sociopathic, and it looks like Mr. Cooke's got an agenda. He isn't riding up and down the Huatepec road for no reason."

Lee watched sister Remilda until her eyes met his. He held her gaze and took a deep breath. "You aren't involved in the pump incident and the mini-insurrection up there, are you?"

She smiled as though pleased that Lee considered it possible. "No. As you know, Huatepec is pretty anti-clerical. We know our place. My surprise for Mr. Cook is that I'm 'outing' him on the web. I have typed up reports of the criminal acts and intimidation along with a little bio. I also managed to take a bunch of photographs I'm going to post. I was just working on codes for the web page."

"Seems like a lot of work."

"The web page will expose Sam and make his employers nervous. It may get him fired. His owners are probably concerned about visibility. If I can out Sam on the web, they could be next. Imagine the embarrassment. Anyway, If you are interested, give me your email address again and I'll send you what I've got, even stuff I won't be able to post on the web page."

Lee took out a note pad and wrote cultwkr@aol.com. He handed it to her. "I had no idea the order was into surveillance and intelligence to this extent. I guess you have to be."

"Amen." She giggled with delight, enjoying the small, trite joke. "We are not exactly INTO it, but it does pay to know something of one's enemy."

She stood. Lee was astounded. She was huge, maybe six feet tall and seemed to loom over everyone. "Now don't think me rude, but I've told you more than you need to know already. I'm going to throw you out. You really do not want to be on that road after dark. I'll pray for you and will look forward to seeing you on Saturday or Sunday. We're invited to feast with Don Mateo Carrera and his wife Carolina."

"Ah! Felipe here is Don Mateo's *compadre*."

Sister Remilda shook her finger. "No, no, no. If we get into *compadre* gossip, you'll never get to Huatepec!"

A couple of minutes later they were back in the van heading east into the highlands. Checo spoke, voicing a conviction that no one would dispute. "Sam Cooke has quite an adversary."

"Busy girl," Lee agreed, "and just a whiz at intelligence."

For Felipe's benefit, Lee and Checo did a re-cap in Spanish of the conversation. Felipe said little but drooped and looked so unhappy that they cut it short. Lee and the others were short-term visitors. Felipe would have to deal with the threat Sam Cooke posed as long as he chose to stay, and that was on top of the army.

Felipe heaved a sigh and talked at length about the situation in Huatepec. He tried to include every detail of the conflict between the villagers and Don Castellano, the group of disgruntled villagers Dzul had assembled, the way the *fiesta* had eroded Dzul's support, and the menacing presence of Campos and the soldiers. Hoping to balance his account of the village, he also talked about the excitement in the village because of the *fiesta* of Santiago Apóstol.

The trip up the mountain was uneventful and the weather was mild. For Lee, driving the happily dry road during the daylight hours was pleasant. They climbed steadily and moved from zone to zone. They'd started the trip into the sierras in the *"tierras calientes"* where they drove through Cotton, cacao, and cane plantations. As they climbed into the *"tierras templadas"* they went through intentional forests of banana trees, plum, guanábana, and passion fruit. In the broad valleys, they passed the rich *milpas* of corn, beans, and squash that sustained the lavish *fiestas* of San Lucas. The road went relentlessly up towards the *"tierras frías,"* through the ubiquitous *milpas* of corn and beans that grew at all elevations. Beehives, promoted by the government in a hugely successful program, were everywhere.

Despite the uniformity of cornfields, beehives, and farm animals, however, the entire face of the land changed every fifteen minutes or so as they drove along the road to Huatepec and the Nacotec highlands. The variety of the landscape was endless and surprising. Places like Las Llagas, deserts in the midst of monsoon-soaked highlands, provided the region with the *pulque* that Lee loved. Beyond Las Llagas they entered a zone of pine forests broken by corn, bean, and amaranth fields as well as dispersed villages made up of log cabins. There were startling fields of cultivated flowers; irises, daisies, carnations, and mums for the flower trade. Extravagant golden carpets of marigolds were raised as an additive for chicken feed to create yellow yolks that seemed rich and nourishing.

The many villages all had a tenuous feel despite the fields, orchards, and gardens. To Lee, the mountain villages seemed tentative, like fleas on a great dog. If the dog ever shook hard enough, the fleas would all fall off. The area, along with all of central Mexico, was vulnerable to cataclysmic earthquakes.

Thinking of natural catastrophes, Lee thought of the people, the peasants, the villagers and their vulnerability. It seemed ironic that in a land of unstable tectonics, the greatest catastrophes were invariably the products of greed, cruelty, and prejudice.

Ten

"Lee, we need to think about what we are transporting in the van."

Felipe was feeling uneasy, tight in the neck. Lee and the others did not seem to fully appreciate the gravity of the situation. The optimism of the wealthy and powerful was irrepressible and far from surprising. It was the Felipes of the world who invariably paid the price.

The sun was beginning to set. The high tropical air was filled with vapor and went golden, burnishing the entire world as though El Dorado really existed. They were about ten kilometers from Huatepec and Felipe had urgent concerns.

"The soldiers will want to take a look. Maybe we should prepare ourselves. I am thinking about the pump. It is not imported, is it?"

"No, I bought it at one of the Basque hardware stores in Mexico City. I've even got a receipt."

"You should not tell Campos that the pump is a gift. Instead, say you bought the pump on my behalf for the village and that you'll be reimbursed. He knows that I am a village policeman. The boy there, Kevin, he has equipment and so does Checo. It might be good to stop for a minute and make a list of all the equipment. You might save yourself some bother that way."

Lee hadn't been thinking about the checkpoint. He supposed he was slipping, losing his attention to detail. Felipe was absolutely right. Taking a few minutes to prepare themselves could save hours of heartache. They were traveling pretty light. They could probably generate an equipment list in ten minutes. Checo, who'd been listening, agreed. Lee pulled off the road into a little clearing at the edge of a marigold field. Courtney woke. Kevin quickly got out, went behind a tree and peed.

Lee told Courtney she should take a walk to enjoy the sunset and the marigolds. What a beautiful, bright, contentious girl she was. He needed to do something to make peace with her.

Checo got out paper and began listing his cameras and lenses. Lee asked him to add a cassette tape recorder, a mini-cassette voice recorder, and the rented three eighty-six laptop Zenith. Kevin returned. Lee suggested said that he get all his camera bags out so that Checo could add the film equipment to the inventory list. Kevin felt his neck get hot. He set the camera bags on the ground.

Checo pointed at one and dutifully listed the video camera, lenses, and cassettes Kevin pulled out. He pointed at another which had a tripod, a thirty-five millimeter camera, a Polaroid camera, zillions of rolls of film, a light meter, a couple of battery powered high-tech lights, umbrellas, and foils. Checo pointed at the new camera bag Kevin had hoped against all reason that no one would notice.

Kevin wet his lips. "That one has three new lenses for the thirty-five millimeter camera. One is a wide angle, one is a distance lens, and the other is coated for use in special light situations."

"Yes, go on."

"Then there is a nine millimeter machine pistol, a sound suppressor, two thirty-two shell ammunition clips, some allen wrenches, some miscellaneous accessories and spare parts that I don't understand, and seven hundred rounds of boxed ammunition. There are also some film magazines for the Polaroid."

Checo quit writing. He blinked. He looked at Lee, but Lee was watching Courtney in the marigolds. Checo watched Courtney along with Lee. It was a good pastime. He pursed his lips. He guessed that Kevin was getting sick of the way Checo had been busting his balls and had decided to return the favor.

"You're joking," he finally offered.

Kevin drew a deep breath. "No, I'm not. I bought the pistol. It was going to be a good will gift for the guerrilla leader."

This time, Lee heard. His mouth fell open.

"Jesus! I hope you are shitting us! How the hell? . . . Do you know? . . . Do you have any idea how illegal that is, how many years we could all be in prison for transporting weapons?"

Kevin's hands were shaking, but he pressed on. The only way out of the situation was through it. He opened the bag, pulled out the orphan-maker and showed them with an empty clip how it fit together.

Felipe watched Kevin assemble the gun and wondered what Elena was going to do without a husband, what his children were going to do without a father. The sight of Kevin's gun was one of the two or three worst moments in Felipe's life. Even the situation with Campos had not been so bad. With Campos, Felipe had sensed that there was a pathway through the difficulty. Watching the young *pocho* handle the gun, Felipe knew that he was a pawn for forces beyond his control.

Lee had a very different feeling. His pulse raced, his heart pounded, and his chest seemed to open with a rush of a sudden heat at the back of his neck that washed upwards into his skull. This combined to give him a quick intensity of pleasure he recognized at once. Lee had found no thrill that could match it. Sex paled.

When Checo saw the gun, a pulse of anger passed through him, anger so strong that his field of vision narrowed and he almost fainted. While Kevin gave his demonstration, Checo slowly recovered his composure. How he yearned for Mexico City. Why had he come? He pictured his studio, the coffee shop where he hung out, even his lousy, trashed-out apartment. He was homesick. He missed his city. The further they went into the lovely mountains, the more nervous and on edge he became. The vast sky felt brutal, savage, uncontained. The air seemed to lack substance. Breathing it made him feel light, airy, insubstantial—like he might float into the ionosphere as a greenhouse gas.

He felt a lump in his throat that'd been there all day, even before this. It was probably dangerous to be so angry. Checo could feel his pulse in his head and imagined the elevating pressure in his circulatory system. Was this it? Would the sudden surge of anger reveal a compromised blood vessel ready to balloon out into a fatal aneurism? Would he die of rage out in the sticks and never see his beautiful city again?

He took a deep breath. Let it go, he thought, let the anger wash away like water. He's only an ignorant boy and no harm has yet been done. Lee would have to deal with it. It was Lee's fault. Lee would never again be able to chide him for small things, like having to stop and pick up film on the way out of town. Amazingly, Checo's anger began to ebb, to dissipate as he focused his thoughts on the pleasant possibility of being, for once, one up in the relationship with Lee.

The men were standing in the clearing. The last oblique golden rays of the setting sun illuminated the scene that Courtney interrupted. Kevin, having assembled the gun, was in the process of breaking it down. Lee, Felipe, and Checo watched in a paralytic funk. Courtney could not see exactly what Kevin was doing. Somehow recalling the nearly throttled chicken, Courtney thought that Kevin had another chicken.

"Let it go!" she said.

Kevin obeyed. He dropped the gun. The stress was getting to him. It'd been a stupid idea to get the gun and even stupider not to have told Lee and Checo about it. Now it was time for him to take his medicine.

Lee walked over and picked the gun up. It was light, had good balance, and felt professional, competent. It'd been stupid of Kevin, but at least he'd gotten a nice piece. Lee had not touched a gun for more than fifteen years. It made an oddly reassuring heft in his hand. The gun was a man-killer. It had no other possible utility. It was a practical tool for strained situations, a beautiful example of form married to function.

Lee remembered the peaceful sensation of having killed people, threatening, dangerous enemies in Vietnam during the Ia Drang Valley fighting. In fifty years of life, Lee had found few sensations more blissful than the sudden feeling of safety, security, gratitude, and accomplishment that preceded the inevitable self-loathing that went with homicide. The little machine pistol made Lee nostalgic. It was so much nicer than the graceless M-16 that'd served him so well in Vietnam.

He had a powerful desire to keep the gun. Kevin obviously had no business with such a weapon. "Look, this is foolish in so many ways that I hardly know where to start."

Courtney stepped forward.

"Daddy," she said, "what in God's name are you doing with that gun? Are you going to shoot the chicken?"

Lee looked at Courtney. "What chicken?"

Courtney peered at him.

"Where's the chicken?" she pleaded. "Kevin was holding a chicken when I walked up."

Kevin spoke. "No Court, it was the gun, the gun I told you about, that gun."

He pointed.

Lee held up a hand.

"Quiet. Both of you. I do not want to hear one more word of this drivel. This is partly, maybe mostly, my fault. You couldn't have known just how restrictive the gun laws are down here, but Jesus, Kevin, we're working together here. I'm confiscating the damned gun. If any authorities find this gun or any of the ammunition, then our ass is really grass."

"Checo, for God's sake translate what's going on for poor Felipe. He looks about ready to bury. Courtney!" He snapped angrily. "You knew about this gun? It came out of your budget? You didn't see it fit to tell me?"

"No!" Courtney snapped back, "I did not know about the gun until yesterday. It's on Kevin. You'd better quit waving it in my face, I'll tell you that!"

Lee turned, glaring.

"Don't you dare get snippy with me. I am apparently unable to take anything for granted. I should have seen this coming. You should go back to your expensive fucking school and complete a double major in Humility and Spanish. I'm sick of you and your half-assed, superior little *gringuita* judgments. Your beetle-browed, half-wit boyfriend there has put us at risk with his tinhorn romanticism. I've had it. I'm tempted, Courtney, to take you and your squeeze on into Huatepec, and put your adolescent asses straight on the Mictlán bus. It's a red-eye, leaving about 11:00 tonight."

Courtney stiffened.

"Try that, and I'll . . ."

"You'll what? Hassle me a bit more about the spare tire? Rag on me about my hat? Cut us out of the credits for your masterpiece?

I'm listening, Court, what'll you do? What do you think, Checo? Are we quits with these dipshits?"

Checo had been quietly reporting to the dejected Felipe. He didn't hear all that Lee had said. Lee repeated the question.

Checo smiled. It was petty mean, but he enjoyed the fact that Kevin was in trouble with Lee. Now Checo could be magnanimous. It was rich.

"Too much trouble. It's a romantic thing to give a gun for the revolution. He probably thinks it's some kind of *Chicano* solidarity. Anyway, he needs to work off the money he spent for the gun. And look at Courtney. She's choking with rage. If we fire her, she will have a stroke before she's even able to murder Kevin. So let's be big-hearted." He gave Courtney a big lascivious wink.

Courtney blushed. She did not know how to take Checo's behavior. He was being pretty offensive, but she felt tickled and thrilled. Especially since her dad was being such a complete jerk. Kevin had got her into this. What a humiliation! She turned on her father.

"This is nothing more than a bunch of macho crap. The three of you can draw lots and the winner can take that gun and shove it straight up his ass. I'm disgusted with all of you . . . except Felipe."

Lee pressed his lips together. His nostrils flared and twitched. "Okay Towanda. I'm to think about this over night. I want to discuss it privately with Checo in a situation where he doesn't feel obliged to be a comedian. I want to discuss it with Felipe. He's sick with worry."

He closed his eyes, took a breath, and skewered Kevin with an icy glare.

Kevin hung his head dejectedly. He looked almost as unhappy as Felipe.

"Now what I want you to do, Kevin, is to wrap the boxes of ammo in plastic bags and bury them at least a foot deep right over there in front of the corner post. Put this gun back in the camera bag and bury it separately over here by the van. It's like a toxic substance. We have to make sure it does no harm up here." He handed the pistol to Kevin.

Kevin did as he was told. Lee watched, utterly conflicted and shocked at his own reaction. He wanted to keep the gun yet knew he couldn't. He could barely stand to leave it. At least it would be close at hand.

Checo and Courtney helped Felipe finish the inventory.

"Courtney," Lee interrupted her attempts to re-pack a camera bag. "I was out of line, the way I spoke to you just now. I'm sorry. You are a smart, good-hearted girl. I was upset. It would have been better if you'd told me about the gun when Kevin told you. I understand your hesitation, though. I don't blame you for getting mad."

Surprised by the apology, Courtney nodded nervously. She didn't want him to see how pleased she was, but that burst of warmth in her chest was so familiar and pathetic. She'd still crawl over broken glass for a word of praise or simple kindness from her dad.

When they got back into the van, the sky was almost completely dark. Insects, locusts or crickets, were making a racket that nearly precluded conversation.

The incident left Lee rattled. He drove thinking that he was too old for this shit.

As they drove through the gloaming twilight, Felipe worried about the menace of Campos—armed, arrogant, and dangerous. Finally, he spoke—almost shouting against the tumultuous tropical uproar of insects.

"*Compadre,*" he addressed Lee, "I think you should stop at the little stream, and allow me to hike up the path to my house. I'll take the *cuetones*. I've told you about Campos and the things he said. If you drive up with me, then he will know instantly who you are. Perhaps he'll get nasty, cause you problems and delay. Without me, he might just wave you through."

Lee nodded. He was half amused at Felipe's anxiety. He had certainly passed through more checkpoints than Felipe. Checkpoints are pretty much the price of third world travel outside the typical tourist routes.

They crossed the little stream and Lee stopped the van. Felipe took the *cuetones* and disappeared into the darkness and the staccato buzz of insects.

Shouting to make himself heard, Lee had everyone inspect their papers, the tourist cards, passports, drivers licenses, receipts proving ownership of the expensive film equipment, the recently drafted inventory lists, the van rental agreement, and even prescriptions for medicine. This took a while. Lee did not usually take such precautions. He thought that officials at checkpoints should wait as long as it took him to find whatever it was they needed to see. Why make their jobs cushy? Kevin's little surprise, however, and Felipe's anxiety had worked to raise Lee's anxiety. Similarly, Courtney's criticisms had stung. He could be as well prepared as any of her jumped-up Syracuse film instructors! If shouting at the top of his voice in the maddening darkness of an early evening was what it took, he was certainly up to it.

Lee found his paperwork in just a minute or two. He got out of the van while Kevin, Courtney, and Checo searched in the barely adequate light from the van's interior dome. Outside, it was alarmingly dark. Hundreds of fireflies darted around, but the randomness of both their illumination and movement somehow made the night seem even darker. The moon would rise in an hour or so.

Eleven

A few minutes later, Lee pulled the van into the turnout that marked the Army checkpoint. The tents were pitched in a clearing away from the trees that harbored the raucous insects. Appreciating the relative quiet of the place, Lee scanned the area. There were two vehicles beyond the tents, an Army jeep and a black Cherokee.

Three men approached the van. Soldiers with guns, the familiar but antiquated M-16s, flanked a thin, diminutive officer with a side arm. His hair looked as though he had just left the barbershop. This officer was obviously Campos. Felipe's description was perfect.

"Well, well, a very pleasant and good evening to you, Meester. I am Lieutenant Ezequiel Campos at your service. It is my duty to inform you that you are proceeding into a zone that may be dangerous, close to insurrection. This is not a place for tourists, Meester. . . . "

"White," Lee said, "Lee White, at your service, Lieutenant. The village just up the road here is our destination. We'll be going no deeper into the mountains. We appreciate your concern for our safety. If the area is 'close to insurrection,' I can safely conclude that no hostilities are now in progress. Understanding the risks, we prefer to go on ahead as planned, taking all due caution." Lee loved the formality that Spanish offered him in such circumstances.

Campos allowed the beam of his flashlight to play around the interior of the van.

"The road is open," Campos responded pleasantly. "We do not wish to restrict movement. We must, however, inspect all persons and vehicles that pass this checkpoint heading south. I need to see papers for everyone in your party and the vehicle."

He took the offered papers.

"Now, kindly step out of the vehicle and the soldiers here will take a peek inside while I review these. Just step into the tent."

Checo asked if he could stay with the vehicle to "help out," (meaning that he'd keep an eye on the soldiers). Campos had no problem with that arrangement. Lee threw the keys to Checo, who began opening doors. Lee, Courtney, and Kevin followed Campos into the spacious tent.

A Coleman lantern blazed like a double sun lighting the interior to midday intensity. This was the "office" tent. There was a card table with pop bottles, ashtrays, a deck of cards, a miniature radio/television/VCR, and a partly folded road map of the state. There were five or six folding chairs. The furniture and tent were color-coordinated in the predictable olive drab.

Campos graciously asked his guests to sit and began to inspect the papers. "Ah! So you are the famous Lee White, the 'cultural worker?'"

Lee indicated that he was Lee White.

"Then I suppose you are here to do some 'cultural work?' It's none of my business, of course, but I am a curious man and the conditions here do not give me much latitude to indulge my curiosity." Campos smiled as though self-disclosing an amusing but intimate fact about himself.

Lee believed him. Even if he was a sadistic fascist, as Felipe had indicated, he was probably a curious man, out of his skull with boredom. "I call myself a cultural worker when I am working with artisan products, which, from time to time, I buy and sell. Just now, however, I am here as a journalist. We will be making a film of the folk festival of Santiago which the village of Huatepec will shortly celebrate . . . "

"How interesting!" Campos said with fervor. "How exciting! I am hoping, of course, to enjoy the *fiesta*, I believe in expanding myself with investigations of peasant customs. In my own way, I too am a 'cultural worker.' Unfortunately, we soldiers must enjoy such events from a discreet distance. We are outsiders here and must be ready in case our assistance is required, yet in the background, lest our uniforms and firearms frighten the celebrants or stir resentment."

He gave his head a sad, sideways shake along with a forced, bemused chuckle. "The village is under some strain due to the presence of troublemakers looking for an excuse to mount an insurrection. Very unfortunate." He turned his attention back to the papers. "Ah, your associate outside is a Mexican, Sergio Rivera."

Lee indicated with a nod that this was true.

"And your daughter there, with her . . . husband."

He shuffled papers. Lee did not correct him. Mexicans understand kin relations much better than they understand the apparently arbitrary ways that Americans connect on the basis of profession, interest, class, and coincidence. Kevin made sense to Campos as Courtney's husband: fine.

"Hum, Kevin García" Campos mispronounced "Kevin" so atrociously that Lee sensed it was purposeful. The Lieutenant then cast his gaze towards the young man. "How do you do, Kevin García from Santa Fe, New Mexico? Your tourist card indicates that you are in movies. What's your role? Are you a movie star like Jimmy Smits or Charles Bronson?"

Lee interrupted. "Excuse me Lieutenant, but he does not speak Spanish."

"Oh, what a shame! Then I cannot have a heart to heart with my New Mexican brother. I am mortified to say that I speak no English. I missed the advantages of a decent education. I've never spoken to a . . . what do they call them? . . . 'Chicano.' And I thought this was my big chance."

At this point Checo strode into the tent followed by the armed, shuffling soldiers, Ignacio and Jesús. Ignacio was carrying the Judas *cuete* doll. Felipe had taken the bundle of *cuetones* but had evidently forgotten the Judas. He shuffled forward, pushing past Kevin and Courtney, and placed the doll on the table next to Lee. He handled the doll with great, exaggerated caution.

"I discovered this bomb."

Campos noted Checo's Ché Guevara tee shirt. He stared, shook his head paternally and gave another small, forced chuckle. He then considered the Judas doll. The doll actually looked like Campos. It was a soldier Judas, paper mache festooned with firecrackers. It was shaped into a crude human form with a painted Army uniform, side arm, and baseball style Army hat. The details of Campos' uniform matched perfectly. The face of the doll had been painted with a moustache and a sneering, brutal expression. Lee thanked God that Campos had no moustache.

"What do you say about this?" Campos shifted his gaze from the doll to Lee.

"Nothing. What's there to say? It's a Judas doll. They are for Easter, Good Friday. You know. You must have played with them when you were a kid on Good Friday. It's a toy."

Lee was suddenly conscious of the universe of smells. In the tropics there is always something on the breeze. The fecund odors of the lowlands, gardenia, frangipani, and human shit had given way to the brisk, no nonsense scent of the pine forest. Talking to Campos about the Judas doll, Lee realized that the odor of his own sweat, a pungent, aggressive, metallic smell, had overwhelmed and replaced other smells in the world.

Campos gave no indication that he smelled the rank B.O. that Lee felt that he was exuding into the suddenly close and crowded tent. He examined the Judas doll without touching it or approaching it more closely. Instead, he shot glances at the exits as though apprehensive, uneasy.

"Ah, so this is a toy, *Señor* White, a child's toy? Caporál Ignacio called it a bomb and I must say that it is more a bomb than a toy. I certainly would not be happy to have it explode in this tent. I pray to God that this is not the type of 'toy' you would give to your children, *Señor* White."

Lee took a look and tried to make an impartial assessment. Campos was right. The Judas doll was not the kind of toy he'd allow any child of his to even touch. Ignacio likewise had a point. The little doll bristled with serially fused firecrackers that were the size and shape of shotgun shells. Eight were visible and the doll could well carry an internal load as well. Lee shuddered to think how many ounces of gunpowder the little doll might pack and what kind of a wallop it could deliver if the various charges detonated simultaneously.

"It's sold as an amusement, like a *castillo*," he finally said. "It's not meant to harm or destroy anything. People set them off to celebrate. It's a custom."

Campos smiled largely, benevolently and took in the room with his warm gaze. "Isn't this amusing. How you will chuckle over your Brandies recalling this conundrum. The 'cultural worker' sees 'customs, amusements, toys for use in celebration.' The poor soldier sees a bomb, with his image, if not his name, affixed. Take a look at your amusement there with the eyes of a soldier charged with the task of keeping the peace in a zone of discord and insurrection. Judas in the form of a soldier of the Republic. I am trying to imagine your delight, Meester White, when you touch a match to this effigy."

Checo, noting the rank smell and ashen countenance of his old friend, decided that it was time to intervene. He cursed himself for the tee shirt, sourly thinking that he'd give it to Kevin. The tee shirt put him into the underdog role. It could not, however, be helped. He spoke. "We're going to use it to open the film. It's nothing compared to the firepower that they use for special effects in commercial movies—it's nothing—and we certainly did not have any insults in mind. Please don't take offense; confiscate it if you must. We can do the opening scene with *cuetes* in the studio if we must."

He dropped his voice as though sharing a confidence.

"By the way, Lieutenant, we need to have an authoritative individual for the film—someone who can talk about security issues and breaches of the peace that occur during *fiestas*. We want to dramatize the positive role that the Army plays in the Mexican countryside."

Campos said nothing, but looked up at the ceiling and took a deep breath. Checo winked at Lee. He was certain that Campos was losing an internal struggle. Instead of moving to the next point in his harassment, he was imagining himself on film.

"Well, I am a busy man, and as I was telling Meester White here, the Army must work very discreetly, on the distant edges of the *fiesta*, given the level of tension in the village. We can discuss the film later." He drew a deep breath, as though anticipating an unpleasant task. "I am sorry to say that I am going to have to confiscate the explosive device regardless of its supposed utility in this film. I also regret having to say that I am forced to hold on to the papers of Meester White and the other foreigners. My superiors may require further explanations. I may need to detain Meester White and the others. They will not want to wander without their papers."

At this point, the flap of the tent moved slightly and another man moved into the crowded tent. He was maybe 6'2", gaunt, and wiry. His hair was silver and shoulder length. He wore a tank top, Levis, and Frye boots. He smoked a cigar and had a tattoo on his right arm that Lee recognized as the logo of the U.S. Marine Corps.

"I've heard about all of this I care to hear." His Spanish was competent but peculiar. "Give them their papers, Ezequiel. A bird in the hand is more likely to shit on your wristwatch than a bird in the bush. Let them go and hope to hell that they are the biggest threat in the mountains. And let them take their firecracker."

He then turned to Lee and spoke in English.

"Saigon, Class of '68 . . . jarhead, you, pardner?"

Lee felt a terrible constriction in his body. It ran the entire length of his spine, from his coccyx to the foreman magnum, where his neck met his skull. He wondered. Did he have Vietnam stamped right into the middle of his forehead or what? Was it evident to everyone, or just the rest of the mutants, sociopaths, and just plain Joes who'd "done" Vietnam?.

"'67," he said. "Ia Drang Valley, Army."

"No shit? No wonder you can't drive."

Lee said nothing.

"Sam Cooke."

He offered Lee his hand. Lee shook it.

"Sam Cooke?"

"Yeah. I used to get ragged about it all the time, 'Chain Gang' an' shit, but what doesn't fuck you dead fucks you tough as the Good Book say. You all go on. I'm purely clueless about y'all mean motor scooters n' bad go-getters, but I got sick of lying there listening to old Ezequiel giving you a yard of shit."

He smiled and rubbed his eye.

"We passed you on the road? I thought then that you were probably hooked up with the nuns, the 'Little sisters of Granola,' and were in on their project of convincing the Indians that they ought to murder all the *Ladino* bastards from here to the Tierra del Fuego as the sure route to Christian fellowship. The Lord works in fucking mysterious ways and I figured you tooling up the road singing

'Dominique' in three-part harmony. 'Spose I was wrong. You know what, though, those little gals are sure fun to toss out of helicopters. It relieves a lot of stress."

He gave Lee a wink.

"Y'all oughta try it one of these days after you roger their little butts. Puts a whole new slant on the idea of 'The Flying Nun.'"

He laughed raucously.

"You are the worst driver I've ever seen. Having to put up with your driving is hassle enough for you-all's entourage there, so I yanked this old boy's chain for you. You'd better just get your asses in and out of this area as quick as possible. The bad dog here is a sorry motherfucker, but he is smart and he is almost a third as mean as me. He will figure out a way to fuck you up. 'Cultural worker,' my ass. And remember, 'forewarned is fore-fucked.'"

Campos handed Lee the papers and motioned with his chin to take the Judas doll. "We can talk about the film at a later date," he said mildly.

As they got into the van, it was Checo's turn to be puzzled. The *gringo*, Sam, had spoken so rapidly that Checo thought he might have lost the thread of his comments. "What did he say?" Checo demanded of Lee as they lurched away from the checkpoint.

"You don't want to know," Lee replied. He left Checo, Courtney, and Kevin to piece out the discussions at the checkpoint. Checo reported on the Spanish side of the conversations, Kevin and Courtney argued about what Lee and Sam Cooke had said about throwing nuns out of helicopters. Courtney was faint with horror and disgust.

Kevin was gibbering. "I admit it sounded like that. I mean, that's what I thought I heard, but . . . I don't know. Maybe it was metaphorical. I mean, could you get away with . . . "

"ENOUGH!" Lee interrupted as he piloted the van along the chancy streets of Huatepec.

"It's what he said alright. Who knows if he is lying. He probably is, but the story is around, it doesn't much matter if he's lying. What matters is that he used the story as his calling card, his way of announcing himself. It's a way to get one up and stay that way. We can't let it bother us."

Courtney was feeling genuinely sick.

"How can you say it doesn't matter? Just hearing it makes me feel violated."

"That's the intent. Fact is, if you build helicopters, guys like him will throw people out of them."

"What a horrible person."

"Yup, a real sweetheart. Sister Remilda has him pegged. The U.S. exports the type to conflicted areas all over the world. It shouldn't surprise us that he and the fine lieutenant are the gatekeepers. Somebody's got to keep the downtrodden trodden down, and these good boys make a career out of it. They gave us their leave to get in, do our stuff, and get out, as long as we are right snappy about it, which dovetails with our plans."

Thank God it was not more than a couple of kilometers to Felipe's house. Lee looked forward to nothing more out of life than a couple of slugs of *ponche* and a good night's sleep. Elena, voluble as she was, would surely forgive him if he just crashed. The day had gotten fatiguing as it wore on. It'd be nice to just kick back for a while, even half a day. The scene at the checkpoint was nothing out of the ordinary, really—just travel in the hinterlands of the empire, sometimes tricky. Checo, Kevin, and especially Courtney, would give the situation an ample complement of anxiety, so that was covered. Lee had the advantage of knowing the ground. Huatepec was a lovely, dynamic village. Felipe and Elena, in Lee's opinion, were two of the finest human beings on the planet. His love for Elena, Felipe, and their children was something unique in his existence. Lee loved deeply, but seldom found simplicity in his connections. His love for *la familia Piñeda* was a treasure, unalloyed, straightforward, and easy. With these *compadres* Lee was able to relax. As he bumped up the gouged, precipitous street and Felipe's house came in view, Lee felt the tension in his chest begin to release. He could not recall ever having been so glad to get anywhere.

Twelve

By eight in the morning on the day of the Vísperas de Santiago the women of Huatepec knew that Lee White and his entourage of *gringos* and *chilangos* had arrived. They also knew that Campos had harassed them and that Sam had intervened.

Hours passed, the information became increasingly refined and accurate. The English interchange between Lee and Sam was a source of frustration and resentment. Just like *gringos* to have a crucial conversation in English!

"The ones in the hills" got only the crudest, most basic facts about Lee and the others. At ten in the morning, nine-year-old Bonifacio Feliciano, Indalecio's son, showed up at the camp with a kilo of *tortillas*, a dozen eggs, a ceramic bucket of cooked beans, and what he'd heard of the morning's streamside gossip.

Jorje Dzul had been brooding since Felipe's visit. The news of unarmed *gringos* bearing pumps did little to improve his mood. Once the pump was running, the material rationale for protest would be gone. *Fiesta* obligations had already thinned Dzul's ranks of supporters. It took constant badgering to keep even Oswaldo and Indalecio, men who idolized Dzul as a soccer star. Others, like Efraím Estrada, who theoretically attended meetings, were increasingly unreliable as the *fiesta* approached. Furthermore, the village ran on dollars and was vulnerable to *pochismos* of all sorts. Jorje Dzul smelled the diabolical scent of the CIA on Lee White's gambit with the pump.

Once young Bonifacio had gone, Dzul spoke to Indalecio while Oswaldo dealt with the food.

"It's fiendishly clever of the *gringos* to show up with that pump."

Indalecio shrugged. "At least they're not armed. The ones in the black Cherokee . . . "

Dzul bit at his lip. "What arrogance, though! What an insult to come unarmed into this zone! With movie cameras! They'll be filming their benevolence. The effect on our work will be devastating unless we act at once."

Oswaldo was scrambling eggs and heating *tortillas*, Indalecio began gobbling beans. Dzul got a bowl as well. The cadre was not as well provisioned as it might be, he noted, but that was the way of guerrilla struggle: you had to depend on the people you sought to liberate.

"We'll force them to taste the fruits of their arrogance. I say we take the pump before they have the opportunity to present it to the village, before White's cabal of *gringos* starts spreading dollars and fraudulent good will. The moment belongs to us, all we have to do is seize it."

The men ate. Dzul nourished himself and felt grim satisfaction. He'd always known it would come to this, a confrontation. *Subcommandante* Dzul and his lean cadre would face the bloated immensity of the CIA.

At the exact moment that Jorje Dzul and his two man Army were gorging on beans, eggs, and *tortillas* in the insurgent camp, Checo Rivera got devastating news. The airplane that came in from the state capital and did the milk run to Ixtlán had brought in a passenger, a *chilanga* in a mini-skirt and platform shoes who'd given his name to startled villagers when the plane landed.

It was Rocío. Checo was sure of it. The list of people who would show up in a peasant village dressed like a whore and asking for Checo Rivera was, thankfully, short. His momentary attempt at denial, "perhaps it's a mistake," was too pathetic to provide even five minutes of grace. As bad as it was, however, Checo saw immediately that it could have been worse.

The household had gotten up early. Elena fixed an impressive breakfast on her charcoal hearth and two-burner stove. The kids ate and ran, evidently preoccupied with chores and excited about the next day's *fiesta*. Lee had gone off with Felipe to see his *milpas*. Elena went to the stream to wash clothes. Checo took his camera and went with her. Courtney tagged along with a new toy, a digital camcorder, leaving Kevin to ready the rest of the equipment.

The streamside coterie of peasant washerwomen was pulsing with excitement. They'd been gossiping for hours and now they had something truly juicy. Elena called Checo over to hear the news from a toothless old woman. Checo listened with growing apprehension as the old woman described the arrival of Rocío, an event unparalleled in Huatepec history.

Witlessly pleased that Courtney did not understand Spanish well enough to know what was up, Checo rallied his energies quickly. Lee's affection for Minerva was so biased that Checo had neglected to tell him of the affair with Rocío. If he could get to Rocío quickly, he could get her to maintain the deception. Sure, it'd involve a little lying, but Lee was a good enough friend to make the effort worthwhile. The affair with Rocío was, of course, going nowhere and did not compromise Checo's resolve in regards to Minerva. Minerva didn't even know about Rocío. Lee, however, was irrationally judgmental with Checo's small indiscretions. It was Lee's fault that Checo had to lie to him.

Checo's wiry body was awash with contradictory sensations. Dread, expressing itself as shortness of breath, competed with lust, expressing itself in the customary way.

Elena watched Checo's reaction to the news about the scandalous woman who was asking for him. She was able to correctly identify male duplicity, its attendant agonies, and the adulterous root of Checo's discomfort.

"*Hijo de la Chingada*" she whispered under her breath. What if Checo brought the strumpet into her home?

Courtney was videotaping the scene, dozens of colorfully dressed Indian women washing clothes in the little stream. She paid little attention to Checo and did not notice Elena's moment of scorn and anxiety.

Elena was pleased to inform Checo that he didn't need to worry about the airport. If he wanted to find the woman who'd flown in, all he had to do was go to Miriam Maldonado's store. She gave him directions and volunteered to keep an eye on Courtney.

There was continual streamside speculation about the woman. (Was she a whore? Was she a *fotonovela* star? Was she Lee White's Mexican fiancée? Was she Linda Ronstadt?) As soon as Checo headed off to Maldonado's store, Elena let everyone in on the certain knowledge that the woman was Checo's illicit lover.

Checo made his way out of the riverbed and onto the road that paralleled the stream below the village. He found the Maldonado Store almost at once. Inside, as in Mictlán, he was overwhelmed. What was it about canned sardines? Red cans were stacked to the ceiling on all sides and Checo wondered momentarily if a sardine cannery had established a factory store in Huatepec. The noise in the store was likewise astonishing. A television perched in the midst of the sardine paradise. Rocío, dressed in a red leather miniskirt, a buff suede bomber jacket, white pantyhose, and red platform pumps was sitting on a stool with her arms on the counter watching TV. She wore a black wig with a single braid that must have been a meter in length.

So completely did Rocío's red skirt and pumps match the sardine cans, that for one insane moment, Checo thought the tableau had to be a shoot for an ad campaign to sell canned sardines. It was the kind of gig Rocío often worked. The TV was turned to top volume. Next to Rocío, on the other side of the counter, a woman in a Nacotec pleated skirt and embroidered *huipil* likewise watched the TV. This woman sported two black braids, even longer than Rocío's. The women had similar faces; dark, even darker than Checo's, with high prominent cheekbones, full lips, and tapering chins. It was odd how the heart-shaped face of the young woman matched the heart-shaped face of the older woman. They could have been mother and daughter. The fact that the women were apparently quite chummy enhanced the impression. Against reason, Checo wondered whether by some appalling coincidence, Huatepec could be Rocío's hometown.

The women watched the *telenovela* with a running nonverbal commentary of arched eyebrows, pursed lips, and shaken heads. The program was one that Graciela watched, "Cuna de Lobos." It featured an evil, controlling matriarch with a patch on one eye. Checo

had long felt that this was a genuinely sinister character and half suspected that Graciela watched the show to pick up tips on effective
means of controlling the lives of family members.

The woman in the Nacotec skirt and *huipil* was, of course,
Miriam Maldonado. In addition to the women, Checo slowly became
aware of the fact that there were three men in the store. The men
stood beside the door, rubbing their hands and arms, and conversing by speaking directly into one another's ears. Each of the men had
a clear plastic cup of *ponche* that he was nursing. These men, Checo
later learned, were Rocío's bearers. She engaged them to carry her
bags at the moment she alighted from the plane. Rocío did not travel
light. Her presence in this small village *abarrotes* store was utterly
incongruous, yet she seemed completely at ease. It occurred to Checo
that Rocío, who'd come to Mexico City from someplace in the state
of Veracruz, might well have grown up in a village like Huatepec.

The scene in the store so overwhelmed Checo that he lapsed into
a dazed, fugue-like state, standing three paces inside the door. He
stood there, his eyes glazed and his mouth open. A commercial came
on and Miriam hit the mute button, inundating the store in an aggressive and disheartening silence. Rocío rolled her head on her neck as
though she had a crick. She saw Checo. Caught off guard, she gave
a little shriek, jumped to her feet, and put her hand to her chest.

"Ay, Checo, you scared the life out of me. Here, close your mouth,
little sweetie." She scampered over, tousled Checo's hair, and gave
him an affectionate embrace, kissing both his cheeks. "They let me
fly the plane, Checo, the pilot let me take the controls. I dived that
plane and pulled it up. I want to take lessons when we get back to
Mexico. Will you take flying lessons with me, Checo? Do you know
how they take off from these villages? They just push the plane by
hand along the ledge of a cliff and just drop it right off the edge. It
falls, the engine catches, and off we go! You've got to go back with
me in the plane. I want you to see me fly the plane. You can help the
pilots push the plane off the cliff. You just jump in at the last minute.
It's exciting. It'll make you young!!"

Checo thought of pushing a plane off a cliff, jumping in at the
last minute and then waiting for the engine to catch. The image came
easily and he felt great weariness, as though his feet were made of
lead. He felt like he was eighty and that this woman was sure to kill

him. This was Lee's fault. Checo ought to be in Mexico City taking Marisol and some of his nieces for a nice outing in Chapultepec Park. It was the kind of thing Minerva would appreciate, the kind of thing that would provide him with a pathway back to his family. Instead, Lee White had lured him away from the sanity of Mexico City and now a wild woman had followed him to this remote mountain fastness. He did not have the energy or will to resist and would probably be jumping off of cliffs into airplanes within a day or so.

Rocío introduced Checo to Miriam Maldonado, who asked Checo if he was Rocío's father.

"He's my uncle, my Dutch uncle," said Rocío. "And he spanks me when I am naughty. Hey! Are you going to spank me, Uncle? I think I have a good spanking coming. Here, help these poor men. They carried my things all the way from the airfield and you can help them take my things up to my room. I have the cutest room and it has the most fantastic view."

Rocío instantly mobilized the men to carry her many packages and suitcases upstairs to her room. Miriam led the way, chattering and boasting about what wonderful rooms she had for travelers to rent. The concrete house had been built by degrees. The upper stories were newly built. The house surrounded a yard with a well. The family used rooms above the store and below the guest wing. Electrical sockets and plugs hung from the walls and ceilings. Bare bars of reinforcing steel graced the exterior corners. Rocío's room was about three meters square with gray, unpainted concrete walls. The furniture consisted of a twin sized bed and a night stand with one drawer. It was a completely generic space, a space of unparalleled and secure impersonality. "Cute" was not a term that jumped to Checo's mind as he inspected the bunker-like quadrangle. Still, Checo could not help but admire the spare uniformity of the place. It was a place with no character, nothing to intrude on one's privacy and sense of who one was.

Miriam stood outside the door looking down on the courtyard. She beamed and indicated her house with a sweep of the arm.

"Better than any hotel in Mictlán, that is some bed isn't it? You can sleep all day on such a bed!" She laughed. "What luck you have! The rains have come, by the grace of God, and you are here for the *fiesta* of Santiago. What luck you have!"

CHAPTER 12

The heat of the day hit Checo. The village was high in the mountains and the morning had been very cool. It was smart of Rocío to have worn the bomber jacket. The high sun, however, had heated the concrete surfaces of the house and those surfaces radiated heat. Checo wavered and tried to focus on the small, energetic presence of Miriam Maldonado. Rocío's porters-men stood at the door of the room. Miriam and Rocío stood in the door and admired the room. Checo felt that Rocío had to be sweltering at this point. The bomber jacket was bound to be hot, suffocating.

"Rocío," he said, "let us get your things into the room. Then, before you get involved in anything else, we need to talk."

"See," Rocío feigned fear to Miriam. "He is going to get me in that room and spank my poor fanny!"

Miriam laughed and laughed. "Well, I won't allow it," she finally said. "This is my house and I make the rules. It is a decent place with no spanking and no scandalous behavior. You, boys, get those bags in there and on the double. I hope that you didn't pay these slacking loafers yet. You've bought them *ponche*. Here now, give them a *peso* each. That is enough. My boy could have carried these few packages all by himself for a *peso*."

The men, trembling and out of breath from hefting the back-breaking cargo, deposited the packages, got their *pesos*, and left. They looked to Checo like they should take their money and head straight for the nearest chiropractor. Miriam hustled downstairs after them, obviously worried that they'd lift something from the store if they could.

Rocío sat on the bed and astonished Checo by bursting into tears. "That Miriam is just like my mother. The day I walked away from my village was the day my life ended." Rocío wept, missing her mother.

Checo felt that the circumstances of his existence were utterly beyond his control. He watched his mistress weep without a clue as to what to do or say. The apparent fact that Rocío had grown up as a peasant was somehow horrifying. He wanted to get out of the room, out of Miriam Maldonado's domain. God, he missed Mexico City and the light, avaricious Rocío he had wooed and bedded so casually under the benevolent gaze of La Diana.

"Look," he said, "I've got to get back with Lee and the others. You can come. I'll tell Lee that you're here to model for another project I'm doing, that I had a brainstorm and sent for you. He is my wife's best friend . . . "

"And you don't want him to know that I am your *puta*," she said. "All right . . . Do what ever you want to me. I'm nothing, it doesn't matter."

She began to sob loudly.

"No, that's not it. I want my friend to like you. But he needs to get to know you before he finds out that I'm sweet on you. If you weren't important to me, it wouldn't matter if he liked you or not."

This was all true and it was all a lie. Rocío and Minerva, each in her own way, would make Checo pay for trifling with Rocío. That was certain and Checo felt that he deserved it, primarily for the poor job he was doing as a father to Marisol and Rudolfo. He walked over to the bed, gave the sobbing Rocío a kiss on the head and made his exit feeling like an utter heel.

Kevin was glad when everyone left. He had not been alone with the cameras and equipment for days and he had missed them. Getting equipment set up was a way to make sense of things. Before Lee left with Felipe, Kevin got him to open the van so that he could get all the cameras, lenses, lights, meters, tripods, everything. Lee took off, locking the van and Kevin took the equipment into the compound outside the house where there was a long table. There, lens by lens, camera by camera, he began a methodical inspection, cleaning, testing, setting, and preparing for the work that awaited. Elena, Courtney, and Checo left and that was just as well. Kevin needed some space after the claustrophobic sojourn in the van. He also had a slight bellyache. He'd eaten lots of beans since his arrival in D.F. and supposed it was catching up with him.

He chewed a Rolaid and looked up and down the valley. It was early yet and mist lingered here and there. Light picked its way among the high peaks to fall across the village in long, sultry bands of muted color. Close at hand, the muting effect broke down and the shortening shadows emphasized the separateness of each leaf, each mud-puddle, each furrow, each pebble.

There was no hurry. He planned to spend at least four hours prepping the equipment. He approached the task with the sensual pleasure that craftsmen take in their tools. He loved the metal and glass, the precise and exquisite tooling. He could feel the tension draining from his system. About a half hour into his prepping project, a great uproar suddenly erupted in the compound of the house next door. A woman exploded from the house cursing at a dog. The dog had an eggshell in its mouth and beat a nimble and prudent retreat. The furious woman gathered the remaining eggs and went back into the house. The dog slunk into the compound. Stopping to see if the woman was giving chase, the dog scanned the compound. When it saw Kevin, it gave a start, drew itself up, and cowered, blinking and cringing. Kevin watched. The dog met his gaze, hung its head, and dropped the eggshell. Watching, Kevin felt a great pain in his chest. He spoke to the dog.

"Hey, don't be ashamed. You have to eat. Poor bastard."

The dog looked wary and alert.

"So let it go, bro."

The dog left.

"Bye, bye, bro," Kevin said. "It's the flapping fucks, isn't it?"

He cleaned lenses with a vengeance, feeling the pain in his chest move up his spine, with the evident ambition to become a headache. Letting go was easier to say than do. Around nine-thirty the morning mist cleared and the sky was vivid blue. Kevin didn't notice. His expansive phase was on hold. He brooded and did his work, preoccupied with his headache, tummy troubles, and his habitual resentment of his parents. He was a sitting duck when the guerillas grabbed him, his nose buried in the innards of a camera.

Jorje Dzul actually had to speak to get his attention. "Meester!" he said, "in the name of the oppressed people of the western hemisphere, I arrest you for crimes against humanity."

Kevin pulled himself from his distracted state and looked up to see a short muscular man about his age. The man wore Levis and a tee shirt that read "Rage Against the Machine" in English. He also wore a plain blue ski mask and carried what looked like a starter pistol. He'd made his announcement in Spanish. Kevin had no idea what he'd said. Two other men in ski masks stepped out of the plot of banana trees across the path from the compound. One of them carried a shotgun that looked like a museum piece.

Jorje Dzul had no idea that Lee White was so young. It figured that he was a *pocho*, a Mexican from the other side who'd turned his coat and anglicized his name. He motioned for White to put his hands on his head. He did so. Dzul ordered Oswaldo and Indalecio to grab the prisoner and pat him down for weapons. They did.

Dzul, Oswaldo, and Indalecio were some of the few Huatepeceños who did not recognize Lee White on sight. It was poor luck for Kevin (and, ultimately Dzul) that Dzul's path had never crossed Lee's. As for Oswaldo and Indalecio, they were both married to women who for years had sold their embroidery to Lee through the crafts cooperative. The wives knew Lee on sight and would have known instantly that the young *pocho* was not Lee White, who'd pumped so many dollars into their pockets. Oswaldo and Indalecio did no crafts and ignored "women's commerce" as beneath them.

Dzul wanted the pump. He asked Kevin about the pump. Kevin repeated his original claim, "No hable Español." And Dzul believed him. He looked over the equipment Kevin had been prepping. It was obviously photography equipment, no luck there. He walked over to where the van was parked and *mira,* there it was, the infamous pump. He cursed. The damned pump was a good one, a large hunk of metal with a switch box and wires. It looked heavy, far too heavy for Oswaldo and Indalecio to lug up to the camp in the hills. Dzul did not want to leave the pump in the van. It was a valuable commodity in the war for the support of the village. Still, it was not going anywhere. They'd have to confront Felipe Piñeda to commandeer the pump. That would not pose an insurmountable difficulty. Still, Dzul was frustrated. He'd expected one of the cheap, light, flimsy pumps. It was just like the *gringos* to bring an ostentatious gift.

He returned to the compound where Oswaldo and Indalecio had Kevin looking down the barrel of the ancient cannon. He grabbed a camera case, roughly filled it with the lenses and equipment, and handed it to Kevin to carry. With that they moved out, hustling Kevin across the rutted road to a footpath that skirted a banana orchard. Kevin moved quickly. He felt nothing. It was as though he was suddenly incorporeal. He carried the camera case and followed Dzul. The other two followed at his heels. Dzul was elated. They'd pulled off the "arrest" without having been seen by anyone.

Dzul's self-congratulation was entirely unwarranted. The spectacle of a *gringo* sitting outside working with exotic implements was too interesting to pass unnoticed. Pregnant Rosaura Cayetano, who'd been so disappointed in her egg-sucking dog, had kept vigil with her slacker husband Nazario. Similarly, Rodrigo and Golfrido Piñeda had neglected their goats. They had climbed a tree to watch the *gringo* at his work. In addition, José Gabriel Ponce had used the *peso* that the movie star had given him for helping with her bags to buy a second snout-full of *ponche* in anticipation of the *fiesta* of Santiago. He'd stopped beside Felipe Piñeda's house to take a mid-morning nap in the shade. The "rebels" had almost stepped on him when they stopped to put on their ski masks. He'd roused himself and watched the little drama of the arrest unfold. He'd seen everything and knew that the "rebels" had made a mistake. The chubby *pocho* was not the legendary Lee White.

José came "within a hair," as he later said, of attacking Dzul in his indignation. So, contrary to Dzul's view of the hermetic arrest, no fewer than five eyewitnesses had seen the entire incident. Naturally, the accounts of the incident were very different. Nazario Cayetano and José Gabriel Ponce so differed in their stories of the event that an enmity developed between them that poisoned their relations for some time.

Thirteen

The feast day of Santiago fell on a Saturday. The *vísperas*, the vespers of Santiago, would be at sunset Friday. At that time, the community would unbend and allow the German missionary priest from the mission at Mictlán to actually enter the church at Huatepec to celebrate the vespers mass. He'd show up "looking like a wrestler," as Elena said, with a little bevy of the Maryknoll nuns from San Lucas. They'd do the mass and stay respectfully in the background while the *cargueros* managed the remaining festivities. There would be a procession to take Santiago out of the church and give him a little air. Eight brass bands would show up to serenade the saint. *Cuetones* would shatter the stillness of the night sky. But the big thing would be the *castillo,* a complex of fireworks that Donaldo Sabino had built for the *vísperas.* The *castillo* would go off in a tightly scripted series of spectacular effects such as spinning wheels of exploding *cuetes,* strobe-like pulsations of light and sound, and concentric rings of sequentially exploding fireworks dioramas that led the delighted eye and ear into a mythic labyrinth of fire, light, and mind-numbing sonic blasts. The *castillo* would cost the eight *cargueros* more than two hundred dollars each. It took Donaldo about six weeks to prepare a *castillo* and a full day to put it up.

By midday Thursday, the rhythm of life in Huatepec began to shift. The streets were full of women and children carrying bundles of flowers to the church. *Fiesta* bread was baking in dozens of ovens all over the village. A convoy of trucks rolled into the village bearing the logo of the Martínez Shows, a carnival that featured several generator powered rides and an equal number of hand-powered rides that worked when the roustabouts physically turned the wheels that ran them. Barkers with loudspeakers who came to sell new and used clothing and plastic utensils of various kinds arrived with the carnival and began setting up to sell their goods. The village began to fill with visitors from nearby pueblos, as well as a whole contingent of Huatepec natives who'd moved to the *barrio* of Nezhualcóyotl in Mexico City and worked in a linoleum factory there. Other villagers had come in threes and fours from Chicago and Des Plains, Illinois; Vidalia, Georgia; Bakersfield, California; and elsewhere by car, bus, and plane.

For Courtney, the spectacle was so extravagant and so unexpected that it nearly eclipsed the anxiety that had gripped her heart and constricted her breathing since Dzul and his followers had grabbed Kevin. Felipe convinced everyone that the best course of action would be to go about their business until Dzul made a contact. Felipe, Elena, and Lee agreed that the "ones in the hills" were unlikely to harm Kevin. They would want something.

Courtney walked through the village with her new digital camcorder, determined to get the footage even though Kevin was missing. Checo was helping her out, mainly just walking around with her and providing moral support. He'd been very sympathetic and his technical assistance was superb.

The mounting fever of activity in the small town was as startling to Checo as it was for Courtney. All over the village, pigs were dying. Courtney had never heard the astonished shriek and rhythmic cries that mortally wounded pigs send into the world when their throats are cut. She was horrified. Off the plaza, just across the street from the village pool hall, she filmed the slaughter of one of the unfortunate animals.

The pig was tethered by one back leg to the axle of a decrepit and probably defunct taxi. A man on a bicycle had a sharpening stone that he ran by setting the bike on a block and attaching a rubber belt to the back tire. The belt turned a gear wheel which transferred the motion to the sharpening stone. The apparent owner of the pig, a barefoot man with lank gray hair, an aged cowboy hat and ragged green pants watched closely. A huge copper cauldron was propped up against a tree and a fire of wood and charcoal was burning merrily in the street a few yards from the pig. When the first knife was ready, the man in the green pants pulled a cord out of his pocket, played out a loop and flipped it in front of the pig. The pig soon stepped into the loop. With practiced ease, the man in the green pants snapped the cord, secured the foot and stretched the pig out on the ground. He tied the cord to a light post, mounted the prone hog and began shaving the rough hair from the pig's neck. A woman in a pleated Nacotec skirt and *huipil* came out of a house carrying a large pottery bowl.

When the pig was shaved, she slid the bowl under the oddly compliant animal's neck. The man in the green pants took another newly sharpened knife and approached the pig. The new knife was long, very thin, and came to a sharp, narrow point. He grabbed the hog by the snout and plunged the knife into the animal's neck. The animal gave the astonished and horrified shriek that Courtney had been hearing every few minutes for what seemed like an eternity. Bright red blood blossomed as the man extracted the knife. He re-positioned the bowl beneath the pig's throat. The pig cried, seemingly in rhythm to its own traitor heart, which pumped its lifeblood into the waiting bowl.

Rigid with disgust, Courtney filmed as though the act somehow shielded her from the reality of the situation. Then it was over. The pig was dead. The cauldron was set on the fire and the man in the green pants went to work, first shaving then skinning the animal. He cut the skin into small pieces, which he threw into the hot copper cauldron.

The crisp smell of wood smoke on the breeze gave Courtney a small, pleasant moment in the midst of the grim slaughter. She looked at Checo. "God, I can't help but think of Kevin. They've got him up there somewhere. Confined, probably tied like that poor animal."

"Just keep filming," Checo said. "Lee will think of something. He was a soldier, after all. He got lots of medals in Vietnam."

Courtney did not reply.

At this point, Rocío walked up. She was dressed more practically than Checo would have anticipated. She wore ultra-tight designer jeans, cowboy boots, a black silk blouse, and a baseball hat. She sported her black wig with the long braided ponytail.

The sudden crisis of Kevin's disappearance had provided Checo with cover. He'd told the distracted Lee that Rocío was a model. He claimed that on impulse he'd called her because of idea he had to make some pilot prints in the village setting for an ad agency. Lee had ignored the patent absurdity of the story. Now Checo introduced Rocío to Courtney.

Courtney was polite and extended her hand.

"Tell her that these are my people," Rocío said to Checo.

"But . . . they're not," he said. "They couldn't be. You are a *Veracruzana*."

"Yeah," she said, "But I never spoke Spanish until I was six and hiked down the hill to the primary school. My mom and dad were Huastec."

"But these people are Nacotec."

"So what? It's the way I lived. This girl is making the movie. I can tell her what's going on. You can't. See the pigs? I swear that my mouth begins to water when I hear them cry out. Oh, I can't wait for them to cook the *chicharrones*. God, Checo those pig skins are heaven."

"What's she saying, Checo? Tell me." Courtney's forehead bunched in annoyance. "I can tell that you don't want to go into it, but I am sick of never knowing what's up. Don't get evasive with me, I know what a bullshitter you are."

She glared at Checo as though he were personally responsible for the fact that she knew no Spanish while everyone else did.

Checo rolled his eyes. What a mess. The presumption of American women had amazed him since he first encountered it in California. Mexican women, of course, dominated their territory and threw their weight around plenty, but they didn't do so until they'd amassed immense power. Rocío, for example, would walk up and issue orders. But there was sense to it. Rocío had him by the short and curlies—she'd worked at it. American women, however, even little girls, presumed to order men about with no rationale whatsoever. Courtney was supposed to be an intern, a gofer, someone to "cut wood and carry water" for the privilege of working with him. Instead, she called for translation on demand. The fact that he was bilingual, he supposed, qualified him for the privilege of serving the princess. He drew a deep breath and complied.

"She says that these are her people and that she salivates when she hears the pigs squeal. She says she can't wait to eat the fried pig skins."

Rocío took the Camcorder from Courtney and began messing around with it. Checo raised an eyebrow.

Courtney noted Checo's concern and smiled.

"Don't worry, she can't hurt anything. I cut off the battery pack when I handed it to her. Tell me what else you were talking about, don't try to get out of it!"

"Look, I was arguing with her. Do these look like 'her people' to you? She is a model and a movie star. She maybe was born in the sticks but she is as far away from peasant life as you can get in this country."

Now Rocío interrupted, addressing him in English. "Checo, you do not comprehend nothing. Ha! Yes I speaking English. Like Vicki Carr. Like Sonia Braga. I go make Hollywood film. This are my people, Checo. Cortee comprehend, I think maybe."

Courtney shook her head. She did comprehend. Her eyes met Rocío's and conveyed affection, woman-to-woman affection, which apparently did not extend to Checo.

Checo drew a deep breath. These women were pulling together across the linguistic divide to break his balls.

Rocío spoke to him again, returning to Spanish.

"Tell her that she has to seize the world at the time of *fiesta*. That's the will of God. The saint needs it. Do you think they like it in those dark churches all year, hearing nothing but whining and ass-kissing? No. The saint wants to hear the band. The saint wants to enjoy the drunken people. The saint wants the flowers, the bread, the pig meat! You know, Checo, that before the Spanish, my people had no pigs? They ate the Aztecs for their *fiestas*. That's what I think when I eat that pig meat. It's my enemies I feed on. Tell her!"

The man in the green pants evidently specialized in killing and skinning. When this was done, he signaled three younger men to take over the butchery. He called the woman to take the bowl of blood, lit a cigarette, and watched the skins fry in the huge cauldron. Checo did not want to be doing this. He wanted to lose Courtney so that he could spend some time with Rocío, some bedtime, before Lee resolved the Kevin situation and they had to get to work. The sight of Rocío's behind working inside her Levis was devastating.

He spoke first to Courtney. "She is saying things that prove that she is losing her mind."

He turned to Rocío. "It's you that I'll soon feed on. Let's get her to begin filming again so we can sneak off to your room. I have to work, you know. We won't have much time. So you just quit talking nonsense. It'll upset this girl and we'll be stuck with her from now on."

Rocío was not particularly responsive to Checo's ardor but at least she answered him in Spanish. "Is she a director? You said she was a director. Maybe she will give me a job in her movie. Maybe I need to have her talk to my agent. Look, you wait. I'll give you my key and you can come to my room, slyly, with stealth, like a proper lover. Miriam does not want scandals but she knows what's what. We can't waltz through that store and up to my room in the middle of the day. You just come sneaking up the stairs under the cover of night. I tell you these are my people. We can't carry on without shame, not here. I will go around with this *güerita* and show her where to point her camera. NO! NOT THERE!"

Sure enough, to Checo's horror, Courtney had the camera again, had the battery pack reactivated and was filming the slow progress of an Army jeep that was bumping up the road towards them. Checo pushed Rocío in front of the camera.

"Strike some poses," he ordered. Rocío responded. Mexican women, thanks be to God, are quick to dissemble in tricky situations. Now as the jeep approached, Courtney appeared to be filming a model doing . . . maybe a commercial or something. The jeep rattled past.

"Courtney," Checo said patiently, "Don't EVER film or photograph the authorities, especially the Army, unless you are doing their portraits or something. Lieutenant Campos is a shark."

He wiped his brow, regaining his composure. "This is bad for my blood pressure. I could do with a midday rest. Rocío wants to go around with you and show you what to film. Her English is not great, but do what she says. She'll keep you out of trouble."

"Rocío," he changed to Spanish, "you understood some of that. Keep an eye on her. I'll do like you said . . . later. I'll tap. Wear something . . . you know . . . silky."

The women bid him goodbye and set off exploring the village. Checo turned and walked towards Felipe's, the direction the jeep had taken.

Lieutenant Campos had a patch of eczema flaming out across his forehead. He applied light friction to the patch as Ignacio drove up the hill to Felipe Piñeda's house. This delicate rubbing gave him pleasure so deep and gratifying that he wondered about the utility of wealth. If a man could find so much pleasure in the simple act of scratching an itch, what good was wealth and what justified the trouble it took to amass it?

The answer was, of course, "plenty." Campos was devoted to money and understood the advantages of wealth. Still, he liked to spin things out. Such gymnastics kept him mentally alert. It was interesting. In one sense, every free and simple pleasure was like a fart in the face of the wealthy. In another way, though, he supposed it was a challenge. Leave it to the rich to eventually figure out how to levy tolls on the act of scratching an itch.

Campos was lost in philosophical reflections on itching when they passed the middle-aged *chilango* idiot who'd been wearing the Ché Guevara tee shirt. He was with Lee White's beautiful *gringa* daughter and they were making a film—porn, from the look of the model they had. He wondered where they'd found her. She seemed vaguely familiar. He smiled. Maybe she was a porn star and he'd recognize her if he saw her boogaloo.

As they drove along, it chanced that Jesús, one of the soldiers, began to scratch his testicles. Ordinarily Campos didn't notice the animal urges and rituals of his underlings. In this case, however, he'd been giving the issue a bit of thought. The crude behavior was almost mocking. Campos watched with irritation. His eczema seemed to heat up just watching the moron scratch.

"GET YOUR HAND OUT OF YOUR FUCKING PANTS!" he finally shouted. "I ORDER you to stop scratching at once!"

Jesús was not a defiant man. He hesitated a moment but kept scratching. The truth of the matter was that he had a hell of an itch, an itch that moved and expanded as he scratched at it. He'd leave off when he got to a good stopping point.

"DO YOU HAVE WAX IN YOUR EARS, YOU SON-OF-A-BITCH! I ORDERED YOU TO STOP SCRATCHING!" Campos had been enjoying himself. They were out on a very pleasant task. Soon he'd interrogate the good Señor Worm and his *gringo* friend about the alleged kidnaping. Now this scratching incident had ruined his anticipation of the interrogation.

Jesús continued to scratch.

"Christ, boss, give me a break. My nuts ITCH!"

Campos unbuttoned his holster button and touched his pistol.

"Don't make me use it," he said with ominous blandness. "I'll see you hauled up before a court-marshal at this rate."

Campos was actually trembling with fury. Jesús finally left off scratching and glowered at his superior officer.

Lee's brow wrinkled in worry. It is always, he thought, a strain to have an associate kidnaped by guerrillas. It is one of those unfortunate developments that universally hinders projects and casts a certain pall over otherwise happy situations. If these preoccupations are seldom the building blocks of pleasant conversation, they give those involved a lot of latitude for dire speculation.

Lee and Felipe sat on straight-backed chairs in the compound of Felipe's house, looking dour as they quietly explored the many prospects for catastrophe. Of the three people at the compound, only Elena had managed to stay cheerful.

"Look at the two of you, what a couple of sourpusses. It's no surprise to me that the morons of the monte up there have done nothing. What can they do? The main risk is that the boy will die of boredom if he has to listen to Dzul! It's a blessing that he does not know Spanish, I'll tell you that."

Elena was pacing, using the wooden spoon to emphasize her points. "Esmerelda Feliciano has about had it. She has been doing all of Indalecio's work for the *fiesta* and having to send that little wiseacre Bonifacio up there with food. Poor Kevin is probably choking on the food. The woman is no cook. Still, she is ready to pull the plug, I'll tell you. She's about ready to send her brothers after that ninny Indalecio."

Lee spoke up. "Elena, I have no doubt whatsoever that you are right but I don't know Dzul. It's hard to wait. I brought the boy here. I am sitting here fighting the urge to arm myself and take care of business."

Biting his lip, Lee felt as though he had a weight on his chest.

Felipe looked up at the mountain and grimaced. "I know. I am a policeman and here I sit. It's best to wait yet I cannot wait without concern. Jorje Dzul has come unglued . . . he spoke of a 'people's tribunal.'"

Elena gave a snort. "What people? All he's got are those louts Indalecio and Oswaldo. Stop worrying, they will soon show up at the door with a list of idiotic demands. You'll talk and the boy will come back. At least we know where the *pochito* is and we know that he is OK. Esmerelda got that much out of Indalecio. Mark my words, he will be back for the *fiesta*."

At this point, Felipe heard the roar of an automobile that was about to burn a clutch. He looked down the disastrous street and saw a sight that filled him with dread. An Army jeep bearing Campos and one of his brutes was lurching up the hill towards the house.

"Look," he pointed with his chin.

The jeep parked at the gate. Campos swung out of the jeep and walked briskly into the compound. Jesús followed, taking a clandestine swipe or two at his itchy testicles.

"Ah, it's the cultural worker and the village police force. A very fine good day to you Meester Lee and *Señor* Officer Worm. Mrs. Worm, I presume. He bowed at the waist to Elena. "There was talk of giving the Army a role in the movie. The question must be clarified."

Lee spoke up. "An equally fine good day to you Lieutenant. I'm not sure I can help you. Courtney, Kevin, and Checo are concerned with the film. I am not. They are not here."

Campos looked about the compound as though he might find Courtney or Kevin under the stove or behind the door to the house.

"I have heard an astonishing rumor. Now, you may not credit it, but someone told me that a contingent of armed men took the boy away at gun point. Isn't that absurd?"

Felipe glanced at Lee. Neither man replied.

Campos walked up and down as though taking the measure of the compound. He whistled '*Cielito Lindo*' between his teeth.

"He is gone," Lee finally replied. "Apparently he left with some villagers. We've heard the rumor but doubt the part about the arms. What would villagers be doing with arms?"

"That very question is one I have been asking myself. I wondered, what investigations have the police launched to explore this allegation? As I told you the other evening, I am a curious man and I also have a great deal of experience in such matters. I am going to offer you my assistance, *Señor* Officer Policeman Worm."

Felipe shuddered visibly and spoke. "We are waiting. If Mr. White's associate is free to come and go, then he will shortly return to begin his work in filming the *fiesta*. If there has been foul play, then the culprits will shortly contact us with demands."

"Well," Campos smiled, "I must advise you that the law of the republic forbids you to molest citizens until such demands are, indeed, made. I would hate to have to take you into custody for violating the civil rights of teachers, soccer players, and peasants. I have heard the word 'kidnaping' tossed about very freely in the village below. There are penalties for false accusations. We live in a free state, *Señor* Worm. Our companions are free to come and go as it pleases them. Did you or Meester White attempt to hold the young filmmaker against his will?"

Lee spoke up. "Certainly not. He has gone off and we are simply waiting for him to return. We have no control over rumors."

"Unless you are the source of the rumors." Campos turned on his heel and met Lee's gaze. "I have evidence that outsiders have worked to destabilize this village and turn it against constituted authority. I certainly hope that this is not the 'cultural work' you have undertaken to do here."

Campos paced up and down. With each point he looked at Lee and stabbed his index finger into his palm. "Tomorrow the *fiesta* of Santiago begins. It is a pretext for revolutionists disguising themselves as priests and nuns to descend on the village. I find it curious that you have chosen this moment to make your own visit here. The young *Chicano;* was he determined to make a film that would point out the role and merits of the Army in maintaining order? Is that why you've gotten rid of him?"

Campos turned dramatically on his heel, looking Lee straight in the eye. "And what about the debauched Chilango, the degenerate with the Ché Guevara tee shirt?. It appears that he is a pimp. He is parading his tarts up and down the village, drumming up *fiesta* business. I just saw him!"

Lee glared at Campos and took a deep breath as he fought to master the hot flash of anger that'd surged up his back and colored his cheeks when Campos referred to his daughter.

Jesús, standing in back of his superior officer, allowed himself an indulgence. The soldier let his right hand wander into his right pants pocket where he resumed the furtive scratching of his itchy testicles.

Campos drew himself up and took a deep breath of his own, obviously preparing to make his summation. "You," he pointed at Lee, "are here thanks to the intervention of one of your countryman. His sentiment will sour quickly if he learns that your presence constitutes a threat to the moral stability of the *municipio*."

At this point Checo walked into the compound. His appearance momentarily distracted both Lee and Campos. They craned their necks to see who'd walked in.

Elena had heard enough and had enough. There were limits. She advanced on Jesús, brandishing the wooden spoon. "You get the hell out of my house, you slobbering goat. I will not have you whacking off in the presence of my *compadre*. This man," she indicated Lee with a nod of the head, "is my *compadre* and I will not tolerate the disrespect!" She raised the spoon over her head. "Now get the hell out! GET!"

She swung at him as hard as she could with the spoon. He danced away, his face stricken with astonishment. She advanced. He backed up straight into Campos who was turning towards the sudden outbreak of pandemonium. Campos lost his balance and fell to his knees. Taking advantage of the collision, Elena swung again and hit Jesús with the spoon, right in the middle of the forehead. Jesús reeled and retreated, stepping on Campos' hand. Campos, who'd been pulling himself to his feet, howled in pain. Elena aimed another blow at Jesús and missed. The momentum caused her to lose her balance. She fell. Jesús turned his back and fled abjectly from the compound.

Elena admonished the stunned, stricken Campos from the floor. "We are decent people here, Sir Lieutenant."

Campos had gotten to his feet. He was holding his hand and giving his painful fingers a gingerly inspection. He stood for a moment breathing heavily, his being awash in contradictory impulses. Internally, rage warred with the need to save face. The latter proved stronger.

"*Señora*, I did not see Private Moya's behavior. He will be dealt with severely. My business here is finished. With your permission, I have duties to attend to."

He pulled himself to his full height and walked out of the compound with all the dignity he could muster. Lee and Checo followed. Felipe helped Elena to her feet and came after.

Jesús turned the jeep around with difficulty in the narrow street. He killed the engine twice. Finally, as they began to drive away, Campos spoke. "You'd better learn to control that mad woman, *Señor* Officer Worm . . . and be careful during the *fiesta*. Lots of bad things can happen in the disorder of that *fiesta*."

Lee, Felipe, Checo, Elena, and the kids who'd suddenly materialized, watched the jeep flee down the hill towards the checkpoint.

Checo spoke. "So, did I miss something?"

Fourteen

Jorje Dzul was fit to be tied. Both Indalecio and Oswaldo had disappeared. It was the damned *fiesta* of Santiago! Now here HE was, with a prisoner of war—a war criminal, in fact—and he could not convene a Peoples' Tribunal to try him. A tribunal required three judges. Dzul, a stickler for revolutionary protocol, would have to hold his prisoner until after the blighted *fiesta* when he could reassemble his cadre.

Kevin was trussed up in Dzul's hammock. He was wishing, as he'd wished almost every minute since he arrived in Mexico, that he spoke some Spanish. He was, in reality, an ally of the guerillas who'd captured him. How could he tell them?

Not that it was so bad. From his hammock he could actually see Felipe's house in the distance down the hill. He'd know where to go if he was able to escape. Not that he felt much like going anywhere. The arduous uphill hike had sapped his strength. It was getting hot and he felt a lingering something in his guts. Two of the three guerillas had disappeared and the camp was pretty lonely. The hammock was comfortable but . . . Oh no! Something was definitely wrong with his stomach. He felt a sharp, intense wave of pain. God! He was going to have the runs! The sudden imperious summons left poor Kevin with limited options. He struggled against the nylon parachute rope that they'd used to tie him to the hammock. He shouted, *"Por fávor, Señor, tiene dolor."*

Dzul was leaning against the wall of the thatched shack and was cleaning the little twenty-two pistol. He considered the suddenly animated prisoner.

Kevin was able to relieve himself a bit with a titanic fart. It was not very dignified, but it sure felt good to let it go. *"Por favor, caca,"* he said, humiliated.

The noise of the prisoner's fart was followed by a stink so foul and dense that Dzul was immediately convinced that the protestations of the prisoner were genuine. He did not relish the prospect of cleaning up a mess. Besides, unlike the CIA, his cadre of insurgents would respect the Geneva Conventions. Let the Red Cross inspect!

He began untying the prisoner. It was tedious work. The imbecile Oswaldo had tied the prisoner, making a complex of tight knots that were difficult to undo.

The relief Kevin had felt at the release of the gas was unfortunately temporary. As Dzul fumbled at the knots, Kevin felt his intestines twist and distend. The pain was astonishing and sudden! Like nameless legions of his countrymen, Kevin tried to remember if he had drunk suspicious water or eaten suspicious food. He recalled his precautions, the bottled water, the lettuce removed from *tacos,* the mayonnaise scrapped off of *tortas.* The fruit agua he'd had in San Lucas, that had to be it! How can you ask such a nice woman if she uses bottled water to make her tamarind drink!? SHIT! Kevin was in agony. The universe had collapsed into one dread concern: could he hold it in until the guerrilla leader got him free and he could get to the bushes?

Finally, the last crucial knot gave way and Dzul had his sweating prisoner free. Kevin jumped, hit the ground and ran two, three steps out the door of the shack. That was all he could do. He dropped his drawers and quickly squatted. To his surprise he vomited! Then in a massive convulsion, he relaxed his sphincter, blistering the ground with a hot liquid spray. The cramps possessed him for a seeming eternity. He took a deep breath and wished he had not. He did not realize that the human body could produce such a smell. He vomited again.

Dzul was horrified. Would the poor man die? Would he, Dzul, end up himself in front of a war crimes tribunal for allowing a prisoner to explode from diarrhea? And the smell!! Surely the plants beside the path would wither and die. Shaken, he found a bit of newspaper and handed it to the prisoner.

Kevin wiped the searing liquid from his behind, pulled up his pants and took a few steps away from his production. He had the astounding insight that giving birth had to be something like the experience he'd just had. He breathed deeply, being certain to partake of the cool air of the afternoon breeze that blew the intolerable stink into the mute hills. His collapsed intestines felt as though they were lying flat and spent against his spine. An intense, electric surge of well being animated his body from the tips of his toes to a point about a foot above his head. He felt that he could almost cry from pure joy. He stood for a moment and looked out over the valley. How wonderful it was to be alive! What a magnificent world we humans are allowed to inhabit!

Oblivious to visionary states, the practical Dzul approached. He held the pistol and carried a shovel. He handed the shovel to Kevin and indicated the obvious use he had in mind for the implement . . . He was ashen and his hands shook.

Kevin realized that he could grab the shovel and brain his captor. The balance of power had shifted. He took the shovel and cleaned up the mess. Dzul waited in the hammock. Kevin finished, returned to the shack, and sat on the floor propped up against a pole. He tried to talk to Dzul.

He pointed to himself and to Dzul.

"Amigos,"

Dzul smiled weakly.

"No hable Español" Kevin continued, *"Habló Inglés?"*

Dzul did, in fact, speak some English. It was one of the subjects he taught the children of Huatepec. He drew a deep breath, feeling overwhelmed with the thousand ironies of the situation.

"You sick," he said.

"Yes," said Kevin. "Why did you bring me here?"

"Your country makes war on poor peoples. You are CIA, *Señor* White?"

Dzul had lost his purchase on the values that animated his existence. Damned peasants, he thought, and their damned *fiestas!* He was near tears.

Kevin smiled, thinking of Lee and his oversized hat, the target of the revolution.

"I am not Lee White. I am not CIA, I am a photographer. I am here to help make a film with *Señor* White. He is a journalist and a good man, not your enemy."

Dzul looked blank. He did not understand most of the words and he didn't care. He did understand that he'd grabbed the wrong man. It was all over. He ought to just go back to Huatepec and the school . . . Except the students wouldn't show up anyway on the day of the Vísperas de Santiago. Damned peasants! How *Subcommandante* Marcos managed in Chiapas was beyond him.

Kevin began to notice unmistakable signs that his feeling of well being would be fleeting at best. His muscles felt weak. His head pounded. His stomach began to churn.

"Can I rest on the hammock?"

Dzul looked up. He could see that Kevin was looking poorly again. He slid off the hammock.

Kevin collapsed into the hammock, suddenly very cold. He was sweating. He began to shiver. Dzul watched, appalled. It was obvious that Kevin could not simply walk away out of his life and back to Felipe Piñeda's house.

Kevin threw another fart and recalled the intense shame he'd felt at six when his mother diapered him for messing his trousers. He was shaking from the peculiar cold and tears ran down his face.

Dzul watched with growing concern.

Kevin spoke.

"Do you love your mother?"

Jorje Dzul stared and blanched. He bit his lip and put the gun back into the oversized holster that hung from one of the posts. He was reeling with confusion and rage. Ten minutes ago, the American was his prisoner. Now sick, farting, and released for humanitarian reasons, the guy was actually lying there in his hammock insulting his mother. Dzul walked over to the prone, hallucinating filmmaker and punched him in the nose.

"You love you mother?" he said, turning the insult around.

Kevin was too feverish to give much attention to the blow, which he barely felt. He was bleeding a bit.

"Yes, of course I love her but I hate her too. She really lays in the guilt for all she's worth, I'll tell you that, bro."

Dzul missed most of what Kevin said. The rush of his anger

had passed. He decided to ignore Kevin's insults as the ravings of a sick man.

"I will going for you friends. You wait. You sick. They come, help you."

When Courtney and Rocío walked into the courtyard at Felipe's, Lee White was sitting with Felipe and Checo in straight-backed wooden chairs, watching vultures ride the mountain updrafts. In his revery, Lee recalled the lovely feel of the nine millimeter machine pistol. He yearned for it, nostalgic for the weight and balance of the beautiful little weapon. He considered his beloved Courtney, appalled that he'd spawned such a creature. She was keyed up, every muscle tight, every movement sudden, clipped. Even in the strains of the circumstance, kidnapped boyfriend and all, she seemed to radiate mastery and condescension. Amazing.

Elena hustled here and there serving pulque, and a hurry-up *comida* of beans, *tortillas,* and *guisado.* Along the way she took time to admonish children and cast baleful glances at the men, none of whom moved to help her.

Rocío spoke to Checo in Spanish.

"I like this girl. She told me about her boyfriend. We can do something, Checo, I know it."

Checo gave Rocío a pained glance and motioned to her to be quiet.

"Kevin was right." (Lee was speaking Spanish.) "We ought to have done everything possible to get arms to the guerillas. I wish I had that lovely gun."

Felipe spoke. "Lee, we have no guerillas here. Just a school teacher and a few men who admire his soccer playing."

Checo chimed in. "Lee, forget about arms. Forget about that gun! You are making your *compadre* nervous. What kind of a guest are you?"

"I'd love to just hold it, No wonder the U.S. keeps making atom bombs. The damned scientists and generals probably just like to look at them, touch them, and feel all that precision, all that beauty . . . by the way, are you going to introduce us to your . . . friend?"

Checo introduced Rocío. He told his lies.

Rocío walked over to Lee and shook his hand. "So," she said in Spanish, "the legendary Lee White."

He considered Rocío. There was no question whatsoever that Checo was fucking her. Checo lied about almost everything, that was a given, but when he was actually ashamed of his behavior, he got a shifty quality to his demeanor that spoke volumes. Lee trusted Checo much more than he trusted more strictly honest people because he was certain that Checo was honest with himself. Rocío was surprising. She had a buxom, peasant quality that Lee wouldn't have guessed appealed to Checo, however much it appealed to Lee. She was astoundingly familiar. Why?

"You, you are a film star . . . I've seen you in . . . "

"*Nalgadas*—that's what Checo calls them. He is so superior. It's pure snobbery. But I want to tell you, we can find Courtney's boyfriend. I know these villages. Hell, I was born in one. You can bet that everybody knows where the boy is. Some of us should stroll over and talk to them. They probably are so poor that they would have to borrow bullets to shoot anyone."

Felipe spoke up. "You are right, we already know where he is. But I am convinced we should wait. They are not bad men, just foolish. The situation is dangerous because of the Army. If we don't hear something soon, I will walk up to their camp by myself to speak with the leader."

Courtney spoke to Lee. "Daddy, what is going on!? I am trying to be patient but I haven't been able to follow the conversation."

"Well," Lee said, "where to start?"

The tone in Courtney's voice, that timbre of self-righteousness and demand, resonated in Lee's skull. The voice was Hannah's. Lee felt something like a dog's urge to bite and shake. Attempting to master the impulse, he spoke blandly. "No news on Kevin, but we had a nasty visit from Lieutenant Campos. Elena chased him away with a spoon. I just met Rocío. She is having an affair with Checo that he has not been forthcoming enough to tell me about. I'm sitting here getting a little sick of everybody's agendas. Kevin had his." He looked at Checo. "Checo had his," he indicated Rocío with his chin. "And you? You've had an agenda from the get-go, haven't you Daughter?"

He smiled broadly. He didn't know exactly why he'd thrown down on Courtney but it felt right, warm, relaxing. Something about her "trying to be patient" had set him off. Having that gun on his mind did funny things. "You think, your film will be good for Indians. You really believe it, too. Yeah, right . . . pure delusion, self-congratulatory bullshit. You don't even like Indians. They make you kinda . . . uneasy. Your agenda is career advancement, pure and simple. You and your Syracuse mentor! Fucking spare me. I wish I'd left the lot of you at the foot of the mountain and brought a load of guns instead."

Courtney's voice trembled when she spoke. "Has anyone ever told you that you are an arrogant person?" She fought to hold down the confusion and searing hurt that flared in her chest.

"Yes, often. And, I might add, correctly. Has anyone ever told you that you dissipate your powers in needless vigilance? You use up all your wariness in idiotic concerns and have nothing left for real threats." This was, Lee realized, kind of irrelevant in the present situation, but it was nonetheless true. He congratulated himself. She needed to hear what he'd said.

"I'm worried about Kevin." She raised her voice over the sudden din of barking dogs.

At that moment, Jorje Dzul was braving the false ferocity of the dogs as he walked into the compound. He smiled. Earlier in the day, when they'd kidnaped Kevin, the dogs had not even bothered to raise their heads.

Courtney, still reeling from her father's blindside attack, scrutinized this man, obviously the "rebel leader" who held Kevin captive. She felt that despite his slight form, Jorje Dzul was an imposing figure. He had a broad, sloping, somehow regal face of the sort that the stone craftsmen of Palenque had immortalized.

Felipe jumped to his feet and opened his mouth to speak. Dzul lifted his hand with the schoolmaster's imperious gesture of silence. To Courtney's amazement, Dzul had a slightly preppie look. He wore khaki colored Chino pants, a Rage Against the Machine tee shirt, yellow socks, and deck shoes.

He spoke.

"Good afternoon, Felipe, Elena. I apologize for having to interrupt your get-together."

"This is your house, Jorje. Let me get you a chair. Could you use a cup of coffee, *pulque?*"

"Many thanks, but no. I am here regarding a rather urgent situation. I want to speak to Lee White."

Lee moved towards the entry way and extended his hand.

"I am Lee White, sir, completely at your disposal and attentive to your every word."

"Sit down! Please, Mr. White. This concerns your young associate, Mr. García."

Lee sat.

"We have provided your friend some revolutionary education. I have come to tell you that Mr. García has fallen ill. It's not serious, but he is certainly in some discomfort. He has the affliction that so often affects tourists who visit the republic. I am inviting you to the camp. You can take Mr. García to proper medical care."

Lee waited a moment, allowing a brief smile to flit across his face. "You are . . . *Comandante?*"

"Jorje Dzul, simple Jorje Dzul, pleased to be at your service . . . sir . . . "

"Well *Señor* Dzul, Felipe told me of the problem with the well and I know something of the basis for disgruntled feelings among the peasants. I am a journalist and hoped to report on the . . . circumstances. We can speak of that later. I am concerned about my friend . . . "

"He has fever. He has cramps in his guts. He is weak, too weak to walk this distance unaided."

"Should we take medicine?"

"Certainly, if you have it. The sooner he gets a good dose of antibiotics, the sooner he will be well. I only wish that poor Indian children had the good fortune to have such medicine available. Diarrhea is a big killer of children in these mountains."

Elena, apparently unable to bite her tongue, had a comment. "Yes, and it'd be killing more were it not for my *compadre* and the business he brings with his crafts enterprise. Women sell their things and are able to buy medicine."

Jorje Dzul said nothing. He had enough experience with Elena to allow her the last word. He'd acquitted himself well in the encounter with Lee White, but it'd been effortful. Now was not the time to confront Felipe Piñeda's presumptuous wife.

Within a few minutes Felipe Piñeda's busy courtyard was empty except for the dog, the chickens, and Yoli. Lee, Dzul, Checo, Courtney, and Rocío were in the van headed up the treacherous road to the spot where Kevin languished in his fever dreams. Felipe, Elena, and the kids were hot-footing it over to Don Mateo's to help with *fiesta* preparations.

Jorje Dzul was pleased that Felipe Piñeda had fish to fry. The absence of Piñeda meant that Dzul did not have to watch his tongue. Elena Güerra was a notorious gossip, an uppity woman, a real shrew and ball-buster. Felipe was an ass-kisser, a *lámbe*, a man corrupted by his visits to *el otro lado*. It was hard to speak expansively in the company of such people. Now, however, Dzul sensed opportunity. Lee White had shown him respect. A clever revolutionary always uses the resources at his disposal, and Dzul was once again feeling the clever revolutionary.

"The conditions here are appalling." He directed his conversation to Lee as the van bumped its way up the disastrous road. "The Indians live like serfs. When a white person, one of the *gente de razón* walks down the street, the Nacotecs have to remove their hats and move out of the pathway. I seized on the outrage about the pump to foster awareness."

Lee knew that this was the sad truth. He was, however, tickled. What a choice revolutionary and with a genius like Checo, what photographs they'd have! Lee made no attempt to control the conversation which he translated for Courtney and recorded on his little voice-activated cassette recorder.

Courtney spoke. "I don't get it. Isn't everyone in the village an Indian? Isn't this guy himself an Indian? He has a classic Indian face, like the statues at Palenque."

Lee translated this and waited to enjoy the response. Rocío burst into laughter. "Cortee thinks I am Indian too," She laughed. "Just because I've got *huarache* bunions on my feet and didn't speak anything but Huastec until I went to *primaria*. I did play a little *indita* in one of my movies, oh that was a scream. I worked my *nalgas* to the bone to raise myself, to not be a beast of burden hustling along the highway with my bare feet and my *ayate* full of onions . . . and then I get that part as an Indian—what a comedy!"

"I'd like to have seen those *nalgas* of yours before you worked them to the bone," laughed Checo. "The full moon in its splendor must have had an equal."

Lee's translation of Rocío's comments did little to relieve Courtney's confusion.

Checo tried to help.

"What she means," he said, "is that being an Indian in Mexico is to be poor and a bumpkin. Rocío was born an Indian, but now she's only an Indian when she gets a movie role as an Indian. That's what she thinks is so funny."

"But . . . if a person is born Indian, how can they . . . Aren't there reservations?"

Rocío had more to say. "At *fiestas* everyone is an Indian. Just give me a bowl of *posole* with a big hunk of pig meat and a few *copas* of *aguardiente* and I'll be ready to kill all of the *gachupines*, cook them up for the next batch of *posole*, send their souls to hell, and ship their bones back to Europe."

Lee smiled and translated. Checo pulled at his shirt and looked uncomfortable. Jorje Dzul tried to force a chuckle, but it came out sounding like a cough. "*fiestas* sap revolutionary energy and keep the poor Indians in chains. The *cargueros* spend thousands of dollars, millions of *pesos* on the *fiesta*. They just piss it away on illusions! Stop here!"

Lee was amused. For a man committed to a communal, egalitarian society, Dzul certainly had an imperious way about him. Lee stopped the Dodge. Everyone got out. The "road" was bounded on both sides with a dense undergrowth of banana trees.

A quarter hour later, the entourage arrived on foot at the guerrilla "headquarters" Kevin was sitting, huddled and shivering, on the ground beside the hammock. He'd had several episodes of diarrhea and vomiting. He'd cleaned up the mess on each occasion, but a sickroom smell hovered in the air. His nose had bled all down the front of his shirt. He looked terrible.

Courtney ran to him. "Oh God, what happened? He's bleeding, he's bleeding!"

Dzul looked down, ashamed. "He said something about my mother and I punched him in the nose. He was having fever delusions. I'm sorry."

Now Checo laughed. As an aside he spoke to Lee. "So he insulted the guy's mom. That's some class. Here he was kidnapped and sick. That's some spunk. I didn't know he had it in him."

Lee was not paying attention. He walked up to Kevin and handed him two five hundred milligram Ampicillin capsules and a soft drink. Kevin took the pills and gave the entourage a big goofy smile.

"You'll be OK. The antibiotics work great. You'll feel a little rocky through the evening, but you'll be fine by morning."

Kevin drank the soft drink thirstily.

"God, what a painful condition. The cramps were amazing. I think I just set myself a new standard for humiliation."

"Well," said Checo, "don't feel too bad. In the U.S., whenever anybody mentions Mexico, people start talking about diarrhea. Just imagine what it's like for us."

Checo and Courtney helped Kevin walk. The path to the car was a fairly steep downhill grade through lush second growth jungle brush.

Checo held forth. "This *gringo* association of Mexico and diarrhea is a national curse. It is not an exaggeration to say that many Mexicans would be willing to go to war over shit."

Kevin began to laugh. His face twisted with pain but he could not seem to stop. "But it's not just an association. I think I just proved that."

"Of course it's not just a *gringo* stereotype. Mexico is a third world country. Mexico City is literally awash in shit. The vacant lots and alleys of the city are full of shit. In April it dries, flakes, and blows up and down the street in clouds. We breathe it and form little composite shits in our lungs. Diarrhea lurks everywhere. So when Americans start in on Mexico and diarrhea . . . well, we can't deny it. We just clam up."

Lee was leading the way down the path. He was listening with obvious delight to Checo's comments and had something to add. "What Americans do in Mexico is beyond belief. It's eternal. It's going on right now, this minute, any minute. Americans, mixed company, are sitting in their sixes and sevens around tables in Puerto Vallarta, Guanajuato, D.F., you name it. They're having their dinner and cocktails. They're talking about how cheap everything is and what great bargains they get. They're sharing truly hair-raising details about their bowel movements. I saw a guy at a fancy restaurant in

Uruápan order a double shot of brandy, mix in an equal portion of Pepto Bismol, and then propose a toast to Mexico."

Checo laughed. "Just imagine the waiters. They probably pissed in his soup."

Fifteen

With Kevin safe, Courtney went into production mode. For the first time since the first jarring wolf whistle at the airport in D.F., she felt competent, in charge. She'd make her film, by God. She was the only one who knew how, the only one with the breadth of skills to direct. And direct Courtney would, right in the face of her father and his judgments.

First, asking no man's leave, she hired Jorje Dzul. It made good practical sense. Having him around would help her dad get material for his article and he could help Kevin out with the equipment. Besides, Courtney was impressed with Jorje Dzul. He'd shown concern for Kevin's suffering and had even made a nice, formal apology for the error he'd made in arresting Kevin. He did not back away from his position, his outrage at the bosses and landowners. She liked that and wanted him to be involved in the film. Dzul agreed instantly, noting that, for all practical purposes, the Huatepec cadre had disbanded for two days in honor of Santiago Apóstol. He went with Kevin to check over the equipment they'd grabbed up during the failed kidnapping.

Courtney moved on. She had about twenty-four hours to get everything ready. It was barely enough time. She wrote notes. She prepped Checo on her conception of the stills sequencing she'd need him to provide. She lined Kevin and Dzul out on the set-up and testing of the equipment. She reviewed the footage that she and Rocío had shot, wishing she could see the stills from Checo's Pentax. Putting aside her resentment in the interests of the film, she huddled with her dad to pick his brain and get a better grasp of the *fiesta* process. She briefed everyone on the support that she expected during the filming project.

Kevin spent the waning hours of the day recovering and showing Jorje Dzul how to load the cameras, how to hold the light reflecting umbrella, and how to manage the lights. Dzul, to everyone's delight, learned very quickly and had a good eye for detail.

Courtney was increasingly confident. Maybe her dad was right. Maybe the film was nothing more than resumé-building. Was she that crass? Maybe, but at the moment, she was professional. She sensed the momentum of skilled people on the move, ready to do what they needed to do. Things had shifted with Kevin. The kidnaping and the illness had moved Courtney. After the incident with the gun, she'd been ready to dump him, eject him from her bed and fire him in the bargain. Now, though, as she watched him work, she felt closer to him than ever before.

The antibiotics worked their magic and Kevin rebounded with liveliness, zest. It excited Courtney to see his confidence with his craft, his willingness to issue orders to his supposed mentors, as well as his new helper, with such good humored authority. Courtney felt intensely alive, vibrating in every cell as though she were privy to a wonderful secret.

For his part, Kevin was awash with adrenalin. He'd see that Courtney got the footage she needed!! He rushed about, showing that heady sense of mastery that is the inevitable issue of an effective dose of antibiotics. He'd been weak, trembly, and very, very thirsty. As the afternoon wore on he drank eight *cocas dietéticas* and ate several packages of lime-flavored corn chips from the Maldonado store, just the right therapy, evidently, for an annoyed digestive system.

Kevin felt like he was the luckiest human being on the planet. He lacked nothing. Being alive and being just "simple Kevin García" was plenty. His quest for his Mexican roots had paid off in an unanticipated way. It was wonderful, too, to just forget about his bowels. There is something about intense pain. The world of attention shrinks as the pain expands. When the pain stops, it's as if intelligence and attention are keener, more effective, oddly rested. He knew it would not last, but was determined to make the most out of the situation . . . AND he wanted to make love to Courtney. Her competence, her slightly imperious air, her swift graceful movements, the way her features softened when she was actually working . . . this was, for Kevin, powerful stuff. Every time Courtney hustled by, Kevin's pulse quickened and he felt lightheaded.

By sundown Courtney was able to relax. She had everyone organized and the pressing tasks were mainly completed. Across the valley, bands were playing and *cuetones* deafening all sentient life as the day wore on into evening. Rocío was at Maldonado's getting dressed and gossiping with Miriam Maldonado. Felipe and Elena were at Don Mateo Carrera's house helping with the endless *fiesta* preparations. Lee and Checo were relaxing outside and bantering with Dzul.

As Courtney and Kevin sauntered into the house to have yet another look at the camcorder footage, Kevin took charge. Interrupting Courtney's warnings about the limitations of the digital camcorder, he quieted her with a finger to her lips. Pulling her against his chest, he opened his shirt and pushed her into a dark recess between a chest of drawers and a hanging *ristra* of *chiles*. They made fast sweet love on the fly, with their trousers around their ankles and their knees trembling uncontrollably. In the tender moments after their lovemaking, Courtney wept gently, sweetly, happily.

"We're starting over. You know that?"

Kevin nodded. He did not, in fact, know what she meant. "Sure."

"Everything had to do with my Dad. He loves Mexico. He was always in Mexico while I was growing up. That's what drew me to you. If I could be close to a Mexican, it'd somehow connect me to him . . . my dad."

"So now you see your mistake. I'm no Mexican. You've hitched up with another *gringo*."

Courtney laughed. "You were as close as I could find. Anyway, I am trying to be serious."

"That's pretty hard, Court. I mean, here we are with our jeans around our knees and our bare butts sticking out. I'm still a bit queasy. I dunno, maybe we could get our soundings on 'the relationship' later."

Courtney laughed some more. She was facing outward. It was Kevin's big butt and ludicrous plaid boxer shorts people would see if anyone walked in.

"I just need to let you know, that's all. Being with you was a sick way to connect with my dad. It was not fair. It was probably even racist. What you said, though, that I'm hitched up with a *gringo.* What's that about? I mean . . . it was funny, but . . . ?"

Kevin smiled a sheepish smile. "Up there with Dzul I realized that I really needed to lighten up. I mean, we get press credentials that let people know that we're who we say we are. But there aren't any '*Chicano'* credentials and I have to get used to it. Otherwise, my only option is to run around screaming 'I'm not a *gringo!'* at the top of my voice and pull stunts like the one with the gun. Jorge and I are going to get to know one another as we work together, not because of some '*raza'* mystical bullshit. I'll worry about what kind of *Chicano* I am later . . . *ése."*

Courtney had nothing to say but plenty to share. Grazing his cheek with her tongue, she dropped to her knees, nuzzled, licked, nibbled and stroked as he hardened and the backs of his thighs quivered. Kevin held Courtney's head and breathed, at first deeply and then in quick shallow gasps. The mounting tension peaked at last as a fusillade of *cuetones* shattered the peace of the high valley.

The sumptuous encounter was brief. Lee, Checo, and Dzul didn't even suspect. Courtney took pleasure in the one load of semen dampening her panties and the other slowly digesting in her tummy.

Lee and Checo stood behind the van. Dzul was inside admiring the pump.

"Checo, unless something changes we'll need to learn a new language. If we speak Spanish, Dzul will eavesdrop. If we speak English, the 'children' will hear. It's hard on us, *amigo,* accustomed as we are to discreet and delicate conversation."

"Eek-spay ig-pay atten-lay. I doubt that Kevin and Courtney ever learned it and Dzul could never figure it out even if he knew English—which he doesn't, not very well."

"Shit, let's just speak English. Kevin and Courtney are bustling and oblivious, and no wonder. How often do either of us say anything consequential? You, for example, have nothing consequential that you could even possibly say in this setting."

Checo smiled. Lee was accurate there, if insulting.

Lee shook his head and shrugged. "And I'm worse. Did you see how I went off on poor Courtney? Did you see that stunned look? She could not believe I was being such a jerk," he laughed.

"I believed it," Checo laughed. "I've watched you, you're jealous of her! In your mind, she gets all the breaks you never had . . . "

" . . . And she's talented, Checo! God, she annoys me. I can't even take any credit at all for how great she is, how contained and professional she is. So shoot me, I threw down on her. Yes I'm jealous of her, jealous of her Pillsbury Dough-boy stepfather, and jealous of her tight-ass, prissy professors. I had no idea I was so petty and small minded, but what the hell, I have an excuse. I'm under stress and all I can think of is Kevin's damned gun. You know, it's just a swell little piece, Checo. No wonder the nuts in the National Rifle Association want the damned things. No wonder all of the teenaged gangsters have them. I hate that it's buried out there."

Lee pulled his pants into "sagging" position. He was, of course, wearing the huge *sombrero* he'd bought in Tepic and the combined effect was unimaginably ludicrous. Then, to Jorje Dzul's astonishment and Checo's mixed distress and amusement, Lee did a clumsy version of a moonwalk, spraying Felipe's compound with bursts of imaginary ordnance.

"Woo wacka woo wacka woo wacka wow wow
Woo wacka woo wacka woo wacka wow wow
Come wit it now! Come wit it now!
Gonna touch steel, yo, all you mother-fuckers,
'copter shakedown, your asshole puckers
Wit da sure shot, sure ta make tha bodies drop
Terror rains drenchin', quenchin'
thirst of da power dons'
five sided fist-a-gon
Rally round da family! Wit a pocket fulla shells
Rally round da family! Wit a pocket fulla shells

Rally round da family! Wit a pocket fulla shells
Rally round da family! Wit a pocket fulla shells
Woo wacka woo wacka woo wacka wow wow
Woo wacka woo wacka woo wacka wow wow."

Checo just rolled his eyes. "I have known for years that you are a serious lunatic. Where you come up with this shit is beyond me. First it's that *bolero* tape, now this. You 'relate' to this?"

Lee continued his enfeebled hip-hop moves.

"Just chillin,' watchin' my flanks, yo . . . Righteous band, Checo, Dzul has one of their tee shirts. 'Dey da shit' as the children say."

He heaved a theatrical sigh.

"I just wish I had a 'pocket fulla shells' right now along with that little machine pistol we buried."

Checo made no reply but grimaced, hoping to convey the depth of his annoyance with the topic of the machine pistol.

"You were right about Courtney, though," he said, hoping to move the subject. "She's got more professional ambition than social conscience."

"Yeah, but we're all here at the expense of the Indians. Don't fucking single out my daughter! White people, people like you and me have taken everything physically possible from the Indians, enslaved them, exploited them, the whole *enchilada*. Now we show up to pick at what's left, the dances, the songs, the rituals, and the pathetic struggles of people like Dzul. We're buzzards, *compadre*, lets just have that straight from the get-go. Courtney is just more likely to really achieve something. I'm jealous and I'm ashamed. I had absolutely nothing to do with Courtney's upbring-ing. I totally abdicated."

Lee heaved a great sigh and pulled his pants up. He closed his eyes tightly and opened them quickly, forcing himself to change the subject.

"I've been meaning to ask you, Checo, how'd you ever come up with Rocío? She's not your type. She will ruin your sense of order, method. Anyway, she's fatter than decency demands. You're a bohemian. Just let me have a shot with her. You need a skinny black-haired, white skinned, pot-smoking artist with a beret. Rocío is brown, Rocío dyes her hair and wears wigs. Rocío is a demon, Checo. She'll fucking kill you. Anyway, I can tell you are looking for a way out. Give me a break, Sergio, you've got Minerva and you know she's the best."

Checo continued to grimace. Lee'd managed to come up with a topic even more annoying and threatening than the orphan-making machine pistol.

"Yes," he said, "but Minerva is a perpetual *Señorita,* a *fresa, muy, muy, muy especial.* Even a *gringo* can see that! It wears on you, Lee, don't you get it? And Rocío is her opposite, 'hot to trot!' You're worse than my mother. At least my mother doesn't want to horn in on my outside poon."

Lee glanced at the door. "Here come Courtney and Kevin. Let's switch to Spanish. Dzul's the only one who'll understand what we're saying and this shit will mystify Dzul."

It was around eight. Courtney pointed out that they'd done about all they could do. Unless Lee and Checo could think of things that still needed doing, it was time to call it a day. Courtney felt that she was ready to get her footage.

Neither Lee nor Checo made any arguments. Things wouldn't start cooking until probably the next afternoon. That gave them the morning to pull anything together they'd overlooked.

Since the Piñeda family would be staying at the Carrera compound in anticipation of the *fiesta,* there was no protocol. Kevin began rolling out his sleeping bag. Courtney followed suit. Lee went to sleep in the van. Checo, sensing an opportunity to sneak a visit to Rocío, said that he wanted to take a walk. He left with Jorje Dzul who was looking forward to sleeping in his bed in the little house next to the school. The trip down the hill convinced Checo that he didn't have the energy for the rigors of love making with Rocío. He walked up the hill regretting that he'd walked down. Since leaving D.F., the days had an eternal, endless quality to them. Unfortunately, Checo's energy was finite. It was depressing to have an eager lover just a few steps away and lack the strength to do what it'd take for the pleasure and solace Rocío would give so readily. He struggled up the hill wishing he'd not left the house. Like Lee and the others, Checo was asleep by nine.

The filming began in the churchyard, between two and three in the afternoon, a couple of hours prior to the *vísperas* Mass. The scene for Kevin, Courtney, and Checo was unbelievable. They'd picked up Rocío at the Maldonado store. Rocío and Lee seemed very much at home. They spelled one another, fielding the endless questions. Dzul helped Kevin with his equipment, but held himself aloof from the unseemly chaos in the churchyard.

The entire village had converged on the Church. Eight brass bands crowded into the church yard. They more or less took turns playing, but at any particular moment at least three bands would be playing. Representatives of the various *cargueros* set off volleys of mind-numbing, ear-shattering *cuetones*. Three troops of dancers that Lee identified as *"Negritos," "Santiagos,"* and *"Segadores"* danced intermittently to the band music. Hordes of women wandered from one group of spectators to another with liter bottles and plastic buckets of the powerful, toxic *aguardiente ponche.* They pressed plastic cups of *ponche* on everyone. Other women hustled by in a constant multicolored stream, carrying arm loads of flowers into the church. Yet others, in small groups of three or four, carried baskets of pink cornbread, white *tortillas,* fruit, and candy into the Church. The priest and nuns were nowhere in sight. Lee speculated that they'd hustled right into the church preferring to ignore the pagan chaos of the churchyard.

Felipe managed to find Lee and the "film crew." He reported that Elena was at Don Mateo's house cooking. She'd be along or not, depending on how long Carolina needed her help. Everyone was invited to eat at Don Mateo's after the *castillo.*

Felipe had seen Campos and his two-soldier Army. They were watching the festivities from a discreet distance up a side street where they sat on a wall.

Kevin, under Courtney's direction, was filming with grim determination. Checo and Courtney were overwhelmed. Courtney surveyed the crowd and estimated that around eighty percent of the adults were drunk, drunker than she'd ever been in her young life. It was going to be difficult for everyone to maintain composure and professionalism.

Checo snapped photos and Courtney monitored Kevin. Rocío shouted explanations and pointed out shots. They had arrived at just the right time. Four young men in costumes with flashy be-mirrored *sombreros* rode horses to the doors of the church. The doors swung open and into the church went mounts and riders, followed by one of the brass bands. Inside, these mounted dancers, the *"Santiagos,"* forced their mounts to dance on the hard stone floor in an incredible display of horsemanship. The horses danced forward, stopped, and backed up clicking and wheeling, responsive to the band's martial air.

At the front of the church, the mounted figure of the saint, Santiago Apóstol, was displayed on a litter surrounded by flowers and baskets of bread, fruit, and candy. The horses approached the altar and danced before the saint. Confined in the limited space of the church the band was deafening. At length, the mounted dancers turned their horses, retraced their steps down the aisle to the doors of the church and out into the churchyard. The band followed and the followers of at least one of the *cargueros* hoisted the litter bearing the saint. Amid the riotous noise of their band and another that'd just arrived, they carried the saint down the aisle and out the door. Others grabbed the baskets of bread, fruit, candy, and flowers. They followed the saint down the aisle.

As the worshipers bore the litter into the churchyard at least ten *cuetones* were launched in a tightly choreographed series, along with a string of a hundred or so smaller firecrackers, obviously the inferior work of Donaldo Sabino. The pealing bells of the church made a deafening counterpoint.

Outside the church, the crowd set the litter in the center of the churchyard. The supporters of another *carguero* quickly arranged a spectacular altar of flowers and bread at the feet of the saint. The *Santiago* horsemen backed their horses away from the center of activity, parting to make way for the *"Negritos"* troop, thirteen boys and one *"Maringuilla,"* a boy dressed as a girl complete with a skirt, apron, and *huipil*. The *Maringuilla* carried a basket on "her" head and danced in short mincing steps. The *"Negritos"* looked like colonial era soldiers with black pantaloons, white leggings, black jackets, and mirrored headdresses that covered their faces. They danced a spirited, clattering dance reminiscent of the horses.

Rocío gave a running commentary.

"The saint likes to see the setting sun, he likes to hear the beautiful music and enjoy the *cuetones*. He's cramped up in the church all year. All year, he, in there is listening to people, their prayers, their greed, their fear. The *fiesta* gives the poor saint a way to enjoy himself, to see the people dancing, to see the people drunk. The little saint, he likes to look at them."

She made a sweeping gesture that encompassed the crowd.

"They are drunk," she continued, "not worrying about nothing. It's how they pay respects to the saint. Look how the bands drive the dancers, how the *cuetones* blast. People lose their greed and hate and jealousy for a day.

Rocío, like the village women, was drinking heavily. The "crew" was surrounded by women with buckets of *ponche*. Courtney and Checo had to accept drinks but were pouring them out every chance they got.

Lee led Courtney and Checo around showing them what they should shoot. He was also looking for the nuns and the priest. At Lee's suggestion, Courtney had Kevin filming the *Segadores* dancers who, with their own band blaring an unearthly waltz, danced in a corner of the churchyard a few yards away from the *Negritos*. The Segadores enacted a situation where a dancer in a white-face mask and extravagant *sombrero* handed out money to dancers in the white costumes of peons. The *Peón* dancers danced indolently, shuffling slowly and waving their money. Another *Maringuilla*, in women's clothes, danced coquettishly around the masked dancer making supplications for his money. Kevin was running out of film. He looked around for Dzul, who he'd asked to carry another loaded camera. Dzul was nowhere to be seen. Kevin shouted to Lee.

"Have you seen Jorje? I need another cassette. I've only got about ten minutes of film left."

Lee hustled off to look for Dzul but first he needed to see that Courtney got film to Kevin. Across the chaotic churchyard, he spied Courtney and Rocío drifting along. He didn't see Checo. Lee made his way across the disorderly tumult, stepping over drunks who lay scattered here and there. Courtney was looking a little bleary. Two

Indian women were pushing one another in a loud argument over which of them would get to dance with Courtney. Rocío was dancing with another Nacotec woman.

"Courtney," Lee yelled above the din. "Get a cassette to Kevin. He is over there filming the other dancers. Where's Dzul?"

Courtney broke free of her admirers and lurched toward Lee. "He said he needed to leave for a minute. I think he just needed to pee."

She headed towards Kevin.

Lee closed his eyes and cursed. Felipe walked up. "Hello, *compadre*," he said.

"Ah Felipe, good, you can help me. Dzul has disappeared. We'd better go look for him. I have a bad feeling about him going into the *afueras* on his own. Where would he have gone to piss? I mean close by."

Felipe pointed up the street. A hundred yards from the church there were the ruins of a walled house compound. The walls would offer a reserved man like Dzul the modicum of privacy he would require. The two men hustled up the street, passing Campos's parked jeep. The soldiers were nowhere to be seen. Lee and Felipe glanced at the jeep and then at one another.

"Shit," cursed Lee.

As they approached the wall of the compound they could hear the beating that was in progress. Lee stopped and motioned for Felipe to do likewise.

"The two soldiers, will be kicking the shit out of Jorje while Campos watches," Lee said. You walk around there and approach them. In your capacity as policeman, ask them to explain themselves. Stall. I want you to figure out who has guns in reach. Probably only Campos. The others will have laid their guns aside to do the beating. I want you to give one cough for each one that has a gun within reach. If I hear one cough, only Campos is armed. Got it?"

Felipe hesitated.

"Look Felipe, we have to stop it. I have to make a gesture and work out an understanding. You are going to have to trust me on it. The only way we can make the situation safe enough for me to parley from strength is to take out the guns the soldiers will have laid aside. Point out the guns the instant you see me."

Felipe nodded. "Don't take any chances."

Lee nodded. Felipe rounded the corner and saw the predicted tableau. Jorje Dzul was lying on the ground between Ignacio and Jesús, who were kicking the prone figure in a desultory fashion while their boss looked on in apparent delight. The soldiers went about their work with the heavy deliberation of routine. They beat poor Jorje Dzul with the same enthusiasm they would have brought to the task of ditch digging.

"You two," Felipe shouted. "Quit kicking that man at once."

They quit with the air of disgruntled workers who were more than happy to have their labors interrupted. They did not, however, move away from their moaning victim.

"Ah," said Campos. "It is the good *Señor* Worm, the policeman saint who does not beat his harridan wife. Hello Officer Worm. In our recent conversation, I told you that Ignacio and Jesús were musicians. They were just now providing some free music for the vespers of Santiago. They've been accompanying this songster here. He is ready to sing for his supper. He is going to sing us a little song about the famous water pump rebellion. Maybe we should make it a duet."

Felipe had scanned the scene for guns. Sure enough, Ignacio and Jesús had propped their guns against the wall he had just rounded, several yards from the inert and moaning Dzul. Campos, as expected, was wearing his pistol in its snapped holster. Felipe coughed once, a rattley, phlegmy sounding cough.

Things then happened very quickly, though they seemed to Felipe to be in slow motion. Lee, giving a terrifying shout, rounded the corner and launched himself into the midst of the situation.

Felipe pointed. "By the wall!"

Lee turned, saw the M-1s, and moved nimbly. He snatched up the guns and flipped them end over end into an adjacent pig pen. He then gave the astonished Jesús a push. Jesús stumbled backwards and knocked into the hulking Ignacio who fell heavily onto Dzul. Lee then took a step back, folded his arms over his chest, and watched Campos fumble with the snap on his new holster. The process was almost painfully slow. By the time Campos had his sidearm in hand, he was surely cognizant of the fact that Lee, with the element of surprise and a good hundred pound advantage, could have easily disarmed him. Instead, Lee simply waited.

Fixing the startled Campos with a stare, he spoke. "Begging your pardon, Lieutenant. I urge you to please stay away from my people. I am here at the invitation of the people of this village. This man is on our film crew. I will not tolerate having my employees molested. I am a man of peace and mean no harm to anyone, but I will defend my people. You understand. He is under my protection."

Campos shook his head in the affirmative and spoke. "I make no apologies. I also must warn you about the weapons. The rifles that you have taken from these morons and given to the hog . . . those weapons are the property of the republic."

He fixed Lee with a cold, yet composed stare and holstered his pistol. "I don't think you want to complicate your offenses against the peace with the charge of theft of government property. I am going to take Private Moya and Corporal Buendía. We are going to take a turn about the plaza, *Señor* Cultural Worker, and then we are going to drive back to the checkpoint to file reports. I expect you to see that the guns are collected and placed in the back seat of the jeep." As he spoke, he emphasized his points, stabbing his index finger into the palm of his hand.

Lee was impressed. The man had dignity. He was a worthy adversary.

The Lieutenant continued. "I also suggest that you consider yourself and your entire party to be under house arrest. Do your cultural work, Meester Lee White, take the time you need. You will have to pass the Army checkpoint and then you and I will make a trip to certain authorities in Mexico City. There you can explain your practice of giving support to subversives as well as your assault on Mexican Army personnel. Perhaps you will be deported. Perhaps you will face charges."

"The guns will be in the jeep."

Campos raised his voice. He apparently did not like to be interrupted whether with backtalk or agreements. "I'm not finished! *Maestro* Jorje Dzul there, the Mayan Marxist, should know better than to stir up strife and animosity in a peaceful village. I was doing my own cultural work, educating the educator. Your countryman, Sam Cooke's methods are less refined."

Lee glared at Campos. He needed to do something to maintain parity. "Sam Cooke is a pimp. Don't tell me that you disagree. I have no fight with you beyond the fight that you bring needlessly to me. As far as Sam Cooke goes, I know him, I know his type. He is very bad news for you, this *municipio,* and this country. Don't let assassins like him compromise the integrity of the Mexican Army."

Campos smiled rather largely when Lee mentioned the integrity of the Mexican Army. He took a breath and allowed the calamitous din of a barrage of *cuetones* to die down.

"As a representative of the Mexican Army you are so keen to safeguard, I remind you that the unsoiled integrity of the Mexican Army is scarcely your concern. I am, however, inclined to overlook what some of my fellow officers would characterize as presumption."

He stared at Lee with no hint of the smile he'd allowed himself for a moment. "I have a suggestion or two myself. My advice is for you and Sam Cooke to not use Mexico as your battleground. You *gringos* fight one another in every corner of the world save your own. I cannot tell you how insupportable it is to have to endure your ilk. Sam Cooke, as you so elegantly put it, is a pimp."

Campos looked at the ground and shrugged wearily. "I wish with all my heart that the two of you would just go straight to Hell along with the communist nuns, the insulated drug lords, and the helpless bovine tourists. I would have my men kick the dog shit out of vain little maggots like *Maestro* Dzul everyday lest they continue to attract hyenas like Sam Cooke. Take your grandeurs and your *gringo* squabbles elsewhere, *Señor.* Don't destroy my country with your fraternal battles."

He raised his head and met Lee's gaze. In the odd quiet the deafening *cuetones* created, the men examined one another's souls. Campos had one last comment. "Now as I said, gather up the weapons and leave them in the Jeep. Do your scabrous culture work at your leisure and get out . . . or at least try to."

With that, Lieutenant Campos, hurling curses and threats at his retreating subalterns, strode towards the plaza.

Felipe and Lee eyed one another.

"Well," said Lee, "that went about as well as could be expected."

Felipe beamed, looking Lee up and down.

"*Ay compadre,* You are fortunate you are not an Indian. Campos would have fainted dead away from shock . . . and then instantly killed you. . . . Yes, I'd say it went about as well as could be expected."

Dzul was bloodied and groaning in the mud, apparently unable to rise. It'd be awhile before he got back into his midseason form as a soccer player or revolutionary.

Lee pointed at Dzul with his chin. "Would you mind tending to Jorje for a minute. I suppose I am going to have to fight that hog for the guns."

The hog, who'd watched the confrontation with weary detachment, was huge and looked dangerous.

Lee went around the wall and gingerly hopped into the pigpen. "Nice piggy-wiggy,"

The impressive porker grunted with interest and annoyance.

"Easy now, papa's just going to ease on over and grab those indigestible rifles. Yes, yes, that's a good hoggy-woggy, don't want to eat papa now do we?"

Luckily, the pig's interest in Lee, though avid, was fleeting. The animal was evidently still digesting the last person who'd come into his pen. Lee was able to grab the gun and get out of the piggery in record time.

"If there was a gold medal for the process of soothing furious pigs, I'd definitely be in the hunt." Lee commented in English to his perplexed *compadre*. Continuing in Spanish he pointed towards the plaza with his chin. "Let's walk these guns down to the jeep. Jorje can take his leisure there in the mud. Five minutes one way or another is not going to make much difference to him at this point."

As instructed, they left the guns in the back seat of the Jeep.

Lee spoke. "Your Lieutenant Campos is a more interesting character than he seemed at first. He sounded almost like Dzul."

"I was thinking the same thing," said Felipe. "But Mexico is full of comedians."

"Yeah, I'm laughing my ass off. Let's gather up Dzul, get him to the clinic, and get back to the *fiesta*. The priest is probably celebrating the mass. There's a moral here. 'If you style yourself a revolutionary, take care where you piss.'"

Sixteen

It was getting dark and the German priest was concluding the mass. Lee wanted to speak, however briefly, with Sister Remilda, who was listening to the mass with a couple of the other Maryknoll nuns. He knew the priest from an earlier visit. The guy was as impermeable and inscrutable as Lee could imagine. The nuns needed to know about Campos and Sam Cooke. The various cracks about the "communist nuns," "the little sisters of granola," and the horrendous reference to pitching nuns out of helicopters added up to a perspective that the Maryknolls needed to bear in mind. Given his run-in with Campos and the obvious interest of Sam Cooke in Lee's affairs, he wanted to make the contact with the nuns swift and discreet.

"You might as well stay out here, Checo, and be sure you get some stills of the *castillo* before they light it. I want to have a word with those nuns. Those girls need to know what's up."

"Go ahead. I don't suppose it's their fault that nuns ruined my life for years. I even had to put off my marriage for three months. Minerva has never recovered."

"What? I'm not following this. What do nuns have to do with putting off your marriage?"

"Minerva, you know, the woman you worship, my wife? You recall her, she's about this tall."

He held his hand level with his chin and Lee rolled his eyes.

"Do you really want to hear this now? Someone is probably going to throw up on us any second now . . . "

"No, go on. It'll be reassuring to hear one of your Godless tirades in the midst of this drunken insanity. Let's go into the church. It might be quieter in there and that's probably where I'll find Sister Remilda."

Checo followed Lee inside. Mass was going on, but the crowd standing just inside the door was in a conversational mood. Most of the talk centered on the *castillo* and whether it would rain. *Ponche* circulated. Lee declined. "Now, about the delay in your marriage?"

Checo snagged a *copita* of *ponche,* drained it and launched into the story, his eyes bright with enthusiasm.

"Minerva's anorexic mother insisted that her dipso-priest brother celebrate the marriage. So we made the banns. Well the blighted church record showed that as a kid, I'd never completed my catechism. I missed two classes and went through my confirmation on provisional status. We had to put off the marriage for three months while I re-did my catechism."

"I can't see that would have made much difference. You were already *schtuping* Minerva weren't you?"

"Well, it cost Minerva's father hundreds of thousands of *pesos.* The fact that I was already banging his daughter didn't make him feel much better. Minerva, you see, was already a couple of months pregnant. She got so upset that she got acute gastritis and was in the hospital for a week. The Church wouldn't bend."

"I don't see how you can blame nuns."

"You will. At twenty-nine I had to go through a complete catechism class with a raft of snotty little Catholic rich kids. *Fresas!* The nuns that ran that show were the most horrible human beings ever born. They actually managed to turn all of the kids against me. I came within a millimeter of failing my second catechism. The nuns treated me like a sex fiend."

Lee smiled. The image of the twenty-nine year old Checo in catechism with a bunch of pre-adolescent *"fresas"* was one to savor.

"Great story. Sister Remilda would probably enjoy it. I just wish I got along with my own daughter as well as I get along with the nuns."

"Jesus, Lee, figure it out. You have something in common with the nuns. How many *gringos* give a rat's ass about the Nacotec Indians? You and those nuns, by my count. Courtney has ambition you resent and you can't look at her without drowning in guilt. You're a hero to the nuns and a disappointment to your daughter. What do you expect?"

Lee opened his mouth to speak but Checo raised his hand.

"Silence! I have listened to you dissecting my marriage and you'll, by God, listen to me. Anyway, I'm getting claustrophobic in here. The fucking church is lucky I don't have access to the neutron bomb . . . In fact, I'm going to leave. The sight of that German eunuch is making me sick."

Checo sauntered outside the church.

The mass was winding down. Though the church was packed with people, almost no one was paying even the slightest attention to the priest. Santiago's litter was set up to the side of the main altar. People were paying their respects and seeing to the floral arrangement for the saint. The front rows were packed with the inevitable "crows," the black-festooned women who haunted the church and attended every conceivable mass, especially the funerals.

In the very front row, Sister Remilda and two other white women in their mid-twenties sat looking crisp, clean, and wholesome in that energetic, left-wing, people-helping way which, for Lee, was so touching and so familiar. They were dressed in cotton dresses and running shoes, and wore their hair up and invisible under their bandanas.

When the mass was over, Lee made his way to the front of the church. Along with the priest, the women would be going to a *carguero's* house to eat a *fiesta* meal and giggle with the women of the household. They'd have no interest in the *castillo* and might well slip out a side door to make their sojourn to the *carguero's*.

The nuns were on their way to have a look at the decorations the Indians had put up for Santiago when Lee intercepted them.

Sister Remilda grasped his hand in both of hers. "So glad to see you arrived safely."

"Well things have been pretty tricky." He told her about the kidnaping and the recent confrontation with Campos.

Sister Remilda introduced her wide-eyed companions, Sister Judith and Sister Mary Agnes. Father Josef would be along.

Lee did not like Father Josef very much, but he did have to admire his persistence. He'd been the only priest in the mountains for as long as Lee'd known Felipe.

"I know Father Josef, but it's you I need to talk to."

He filled them in detail on the situation he'd encountered with Campos and Sam Cooke. He warned them to be aware and watch their flanks. Sister Remilda bit her lower lip, half closed her eyes and slowly nodded.

Sisters Judith and Mary Agnes seemed nervous and kept glancing towards the exit that was apparently behind the altar. Lee hurried his remarks. In his view, the pump incident and Dzul's short-lived organization of his "guerrilla group" made the Maryknoll presence at the *fiesta* extremely dangerous. He was fairly certain that Campos would stay away for a while, but he was less certain about Sam Cooke. Cooke had doubtless learned that the rumors of an insurrectionist group were exaggerated. Chances were that he would turn his murderous attention elsewhere. Lee took a deep breath and told them what Sam had said about raping nuns and throwing them out of helicopters.

Sister Remilda smiled as though Lee'd cracked a joke.

"We appreciate your information and your concern. I think we're OK though. Our tactic is to force them and their kind to either leave us alone or murder us in public, in front of the world. We won't be on the roads by night and we even buddy up to pee. Anyway, they've probably spied enough to know that we are not a real source for the revolutionary groups."

Lee really liked this girl. Every successful humanitarian enterprise in human history depended on the intelligence, humor, and stalwart competence of people like Sister Remilda to create the "growing good" of the world. She'd make her benevolent contributions almost anonymously on her way to the "unvisited tomb" that George Eliot described as the destiny of the Sister Remildas of the world. Lee found her charming and part of her charm was that she made no effort to be charming.

Lee began to edge away. He'd delivered his intelligence. It was shocking how young the nuns were, the same age as Courtney and Kevin. The vulnerability of all the young people made him feel nervous, sad, confused. His throat tightened.

Sister Remilda was quick to notice Lee's move to retreat. "Listen, thanks again. You are always welcome to visit, pass some time and brainstorm with the girls. You are an inspiration to the order. I'm not sure you understand how important your work has been in ending the exploitation of Nacotec crafts people. You cast a long shadow, Mr. White." She took his hand again and looked directly into his eyes.

"Stay safe and don't feel you have to do anything about this Sam Cooke," she said. "The struggle is long term. One torturer more or less is not going to matter in the long run. He'll leave Huatepec, as will Campos, when they figure out that there's no real insurgent group. So don't take any risks!"

Lee grinned. That was almost precisely what he'd wanted to tell her.

Father Josef was leaving through a door in back of the altar. Sisters Judith and Mary Agnes turned to follow.

Sister Remilda spoke. "Last night we stayed at Don Mateo Carrera's. Tonight we stay at Don Jerónimo Pombo's. We have to hit all of the *cargueros* or they get jealous and have drunken *machete* fights. Please stop for a chat on your way down the mountain."

She gave Lee a big hug and a kiss on the cheek. She then turned and hustled to catch Father Josef and the others.

Lee watched her go and felt his eyes tear up. He wondered again at how easy it was to care for this plain, earnest girl and how difficult and gnarly it was with the beautiful, accomplished Courtney.

He turned to go out front for the *castillo*. It was too crowded to move and he felt the unmistakable weight of two soft full breasts as they were lovingly laid across his forearm. He looked down to see those self-same breasts straining against the silken constraints of beige satin to flatten against his arm in a most pleasing way.

"Rocío," he said, "You have a pleasant way of announcing yourself."

Rocío smiled lasciviously as she watched Sister Remilda make her way to the door behind the altar.

"*Monjas,*" she said. "*Putas, cabronas, hijas de la chingada, ¿qué quieren estas pendejas religiosas?*"

"More to the point," Lee said rubbing his forearm against Rocío's breasts. "What does the famous star of the *nalgadas* want with the legendary Lee White?"

"Who knows?"

She brushed back and forth lightly allowing Lee to feel her stiffened nipples. "Except that Checo is preparing to dump this poor girl to crawl back to the Ice Princess. Ay Checo; he is a loveable man, he taught me about art, the bastard, and now I am ashamed of my stupid movies. Poor Checo, he is afraid of Indians."

"Let's go out. Call me old-fashioned, but I feel uncomfortable feeling you up in church."

"Well, you have scruples that most priests lack but we don't want to miss the *castillo*, do we?"

They walked slowly out of the church. In the churchyard they quickly found the rest of the entourage surrounding Kevin. The sun was setting and he was using a portable light and the umbrella to illuminate a drunken band which played accompaniment to the dancing *Negritos*.

Courtney and Kevin were very lovey-dovey. They were staying in constant physical contact even as they worked. This gave Lee a warm feeling in his midsection. Felipe and Elena stood with Checo, shouting explanations, something about the situation—the *Negritos*, the band, the *castillo*, the imminent dinner at Don Mateo's house, or the carpet of drunken Indians that writhed like wounded soldiers on the battlefield of the village churchyard. Lee was unable to hear.

He looked around and took stock. He and Kevin were the only people among the hundreds that he could see who were not drunk. Even Courtney had apparently absorbed some of the *ponche* that'd been pressed upon her from every side.

Having noticed Lee's disgraceful sobriety, Indian women mobbed him with bottles of malodorous *ponche*. Rocío gave a tipsy giggle and continued to rub her breasts against him. He took a bottle and drank as though determined to correct the oversight that had kept him sober so deep into the *fiesta*. A bandaged and drunken Jorje Dzul was at Kevin's side, manning the umbrella that cast light on the anarchic brass band that was offending the coming night with a wild cacophony of ornamental noise. Never breaking breast contact with Rocío, Lee crossed in front of the band to join Felipe, Elena, and Checo. He looked around. All eight bands were playing at once. All three dance troupes were dancing, including the mounted *Santiagos* who pranced their horses among the drunks that were passed out here and there. As if the din from the bands and the carnival were not doing enough to deafen the celebrants, *cuetones* were going off at regular intervals.

Lee had seen and participated in dozens of similar *fiestas,* but he was always appalled and a little frightened at the collapse of social order. People were grabbing one another to dance. Fights were going here and there, those witlessly brutal if ineffectual mutual batterings of drunks. People were staggering, falling, crawling, laughing, crying, and shouting. The din was terrible. Rocío spoke directly into Lee's ear. "They are impatient for the *castillo.*"

Sure enough, a small knot of men, one of whom had a flashlight, approached the imposing *castillo* that dominated the front of the church. The litter bearing Santiago emerged from the church door to be greeted with a great shout from the crowd. Santiago was placed just a few meters from the *castillo.* The bands quit playing and a dramatic hush settled over the anarchy. The man with the flashlight lit a cigarette and held the glowing end of it to the mother fuse that unified the *castillo.*

The *castillo* erupted with light and sound. There were bells, there were whistles, there were wheels, rockets, fountains, explosions inside of explosions, as the spark made its way level by level through the engineered labyrinth of light and noise. As usual, Lee felt that he was beginning to hallucinate as he saw a sequence of tableaus and dioramas in light; armies on the march; a great figure of Zapata on his horse rallying the revolutionary forces; a silhouette of Sor Juana de La Cruz writing poetry in her sanctuary; eagles and jaguars locked in a grim struggle with skeletal figures and a butterfly Army; Benito Juárez driving his distinctive carriage; mountains shaking and volcanic devastation falling on decayed recumbent cities; Cantinflas tricking a top-hatted *rico;* and finally, Tonantzín, the Virgin of Guadalupe, rising slowly to utterly dominate the summer sky. The *castillo* went on and on, creating a new time, an ephemeral eternity that could never collapse into the soulless drudgery of entrenched, unvarying poverty.

And then it was over. The churchyard was utterly still for a second or two that had the feel of a yawning abyss. The first thing that Lee heard was Felipe speaking to Checo.

"The *castillo,* you see, is the entire *fiesta* in miniature . . . "

Lee could see that he continued, his lips were moving. Lee could not hear what he was saying. As though animated by a single force, the eight bands had, at that moment, begun to play. A moment later, the carnival rides started up to provide a calliope OOM PA cadence to the cacophony. An acrid cloud of smoke from the *castillo* enshrouded the village like fog.

Rocío pulled up Lee's shirt and rubbed her satin covered breasts against his bare back. "That was a very good *castillo*." She reached a greedy little hand around to gently and secretly caress the inner margin of his thigh.

Lee's attention returned unbidden to the secure, sensuous feel, the balanced perfection of the little semi-automatic Kevin had brought for Dzul. The *ponche* sat like a dollop of molten lead in his stomach. Warmth radiated from his lower belly and suffused his extremities as he allowed Rocío to stroke away, naughtily teasing at his upper thighs and brushing her nipples against his back. While this was going on Lee allowed himself to enjoy the fantasy of confronting Sam Cooke with the little pistol and watching the hail of bullets reduce the cold sadist to a mound of bloody rags.

Seventeen

A half dozen women had been sitting on the ground in the court-yard of Don Mateo's since midday. They'd made literally hundreds of *tortillas*. As *cargueros*, Mateo and Carolina were obliged to feed all comers. Pigs had been dying for days and were cooking over charcoal in huge vats of *posole*. Cases of soft drinks and beer were stacked everywhere and there was a fifty gallon oil drum full of *ponche* made of *aguardiente*, pineapples, oranges, lemons, and red *chile*. Bunches of ripe bananas, baskets of pink *fiesta* cornbread, and sacks of sugar balls with pistachio-nut centers arrived with people who'd been at the church. The bread and candy had been crucial to the altar decorations for Santiago and now that they were blessed, they'd be eaten along with everything else.

Elena's *comadre*, Carolina, was worried about Jorje Dzul.

"How does he look? Did those men beat him badly? Say what you will, Elena, but he's no more foolish than most men."

"The man is a moron. Thanks to Lee White, he'll live in spite of his suicidal stupidity. Campos could have walked up there at any moment and wiped out the entire weak-minded bunch of them."

"I never said different," Carolina said, stacking *tortillas*. "What I said was that he's no more foolish than most men. Most men do not have the solitude to fully express that foolishness. Mateo, for example, has hated Don Esteban Castellano since before he was born. Several times a year Mateo wakes up and says to me:

165

'Carolina, he has finally pushed me beyond endurance. I am going to kill him.' And he means it! He just never gets around to it. For Mateo, murdering Don Esteban is a chore and a dream. He has goats to look after."

She took a generous swig of *ponche* and continued.

"And what does Jorje Dzul have? He has the school and the soccer team, not enough. He has no family, no *compadre,* no animals. As a supposed atheist, he shirks his duties to the saints. Worst of all, at twenty-nine he lacks a wife and kids to anchor his imagination. And it's our fault. We won't allow our girls to marry him."

"The government brought him here to teach, not marry."

Elena provided the conventional response with interest. Carolina had always argued against matching Dzul with any of the marriageable damsels infesting the village.

"Is he a *capón,* a gelding? No *comadre,* he is not. He is a man like other men with urges and drives that seek an outlet. If Mateo had no anchor to his life, he'd be in prison for the murder of Don Esteban. And by the way, there is nothing weak-minded about the impulse to create a revolution to bring the rich to their knees."

The women making *tortillas* murmured agreement. Elena smiled, recalling her wild spoon attack on the soldier.

Carolina continued. "For our men to act on these impulses, however, would be suicidal. Men lack the craft, strategy, and patience to preserve themselves. I tell you, young lady, we should have seen this coming. There might have been a massacre. There's nothing the oppressors like better than a massacre to remind everyone who is in charge and whose butts are black."

Elena laughed, having thought the same thoughts herself. Still, she disputed. "So it's our fault that Jorje Dzul tried to create a revolution from the hatred and despair of our men?"

Carolina drew her lips together. "No, our fault is that we did not provide him with a wife and a heavy burden of obligation. I tell you, *comadre,* a married man cannot afford to go down in a hail of bullets. It's the solitary souls who bring death into these mountains . . . men like Campos, Dzul, Sam Cooke, and your *compadre* Lee White."

Elena frowned, her temples pounding with sudden anger. Her *comadre* was about to step over the line. Just let her! Just let anyone start in on Lee! They'd get some of what she'd given that animal Campos had brought into her house. "What? Don't forget what Lee White has done for this village."

If Carolina noticed the flash of anger in Elena's eyes, she did not show it. "All I am saying is that we should do what we can. I plan, for example, to find a wife for our normal school revolutionary, and I expect you, *comadre*, to help me. Your little cousin Susana Güerra would do just fine."

Elena straightened a stack of *tortillas*, took another ball of masa, and began to pat it into a *tortilla*. Felipe had just walked into the compound. That meant that the *castillo* was finished and the ravening hordes would soon arrive to devour everything in sight. It was nice to see him. She was one lucky woman!

"Susana would be a good choice. . . . But perhaps she has her own ideas." Elena was as bland and noncommittal as she could be.

Carolina smiled and shook her head. "What could be a poorer guide for a young person than her own ideas, *comadre*? Answer me that. Just look at what has happened to Jorje Dzul through having his own ideas. You will help me, won't you?"

Elena said that she would. She'd warm to the project whenever Carolina chose to be less high-handed. Elena owed her elder, her most important *comadre*, immense respect, but there were moments when expressing that respect had an onerous quality. Elena was ready to enjoy the *fiesta*, damn it! Just the sight of her husband opening a beer to drink with Don Mateo got her hot. Surely Carolina did not expect her to trail Susana across Jorje Dzul's nose immediately?

While their wives discussed matchmaking, Felipe and his *compadre*, Mateo Carrera, discussed the pump. Felipe explained.

"So my *compadre*, *Señor* Lee White, has brought this powerful pump from Mexico City. In my view, however, only someone of your stature can be entrusted to see that the pump is properly installed."

Don Mateo, a diminutive man with lively eyes and white hair, laughed. "What you mean is that you do not want to bear the expense of providing a *fiesta* when the pump is installed." He laughed and regarded his young *compadre* with tilt to his head and a softness to his eyes.

Felipe smiled.

Don Mateo continued. "Perhaps in early October we can give formal cognizance of the pump with a *fiesta.*"

Felipe and the other men smiled and passed around a pack of cigarettes. People were starting to arrive from the church, mainly the spongers from Maldonado's store and the hicks from the *afueras* who did not seem to eat between *fiestas*. For the next few days, the skinny, shit-eating pigs of twenty mountain villages would live in bliss upon the indirect munificence of Don Mateo. Regarding the rag-tag Army of dinner guests beginning to arrive, Felipe and the other *compadre* of Don Mateo Carrera had to laugh.

"Who could have imagined," Don Mateo commented, "that people so drunk could move so fast?"

Felipe, like the others, was amused. The first wave of dinner guests was really something to behold. If there was a square centimeter of shirt, pants, dress, or *huipil* that did not have a rip or tear, Felipe would have been surprised. It was obvious, too, that few of the locust horde were willing to expose their clothing to the injurious practice of occasional laundering. Later, when the past midnight hanky-panky became general, the rips and tears would provide convenient access to the various portals of pleasure.

Felipe laughed, feeling an odd mix of pride and disgust with the *arrimados* that were swarming the tables and expertly snagging beer, bowls of *posole,* and big fists full of *tortillas*. He opened his mouth, laughed out loud, and spoke to Don Mateo. "Just imagine how your guests would terrify the *gringos.*"

Considering the rag-tag army of *arrimados* bent on feasting and booze, Felipe could understand why *gringos* were so nervous about the Mexicans that roofed their houses, babysat their kids, and cleaned their homes. No wonder the *gringos* were shitting themselves with fear and dispatching killers like Sam Cooke to central Mexico.

Felipe had been swilling *ponche* and beer since the encounter with Campos. He went to open another beer and saw Lee and his entourage trooping up the road followed by the band, the dancers, and the rest of the guests. Felipe found it amusing that the *gringos* had arrived nearly as fast as the Army of spongers.

Events had been crowding poor Checo. He did not feel up to another *fiesta* event. The drunkenness and chaos were getting old, and the *castillo* had been emotionally draining. He told Lee to go ahead to Don Mateo Carrera's house; perhaps he'd join them later.

So, as the entourage began the westward trek to the *carguero's* evening feast, Checo walked north. He was shaken, having seen an image of Minerva's face in the *castillo's* labyrinth of light. He wandered for a quarter hour and ended up in front of Maldonado's store.

"Did you come to spank your friend?"

Miriam smiled. To his discomfort, Checo blushed. The situation with Rocío was more embarrassing now that it had run its course.

Miriam was sensitive to Checo's discomfort. She opened two soft drinks, handing him one.

"I hear that your associate, the *gringo,* and Felipe Piñeda gave the Army some lessons in polite respect."

Did the woman have a catalog? Was she psychic? Did she just sense the topics Checo would find disturbing?

Standing in the Maldonado store watching Miriam Maldonado swill the *sidral* she'd opened for herself, Checo felt a wave of self-loathing surge through him to center in his forehead. The trip had been just brimming with insights into unpleasant truths. Lee White was, of course, to blame. Lee had talked him into this endeavor, forced him into this little crucible of unsolicited self-examination. He took a long drink of the apple-flavored *sidral.* Miriam Maldonado was eyeing him, obviously expecting conversation. What was it about these women who ran these *abarrotes* stores? Give such women some elbow room and they'd rule the hemisphere.

"The soldiers were beating the teacher. Lee White and Felipe intervened. They are *compadres. Señor* White feels responsible for the safety of the teacher because his daughter hired him to help with the film."

"You'll find no tears shed in this village over the discomfort to the soldiers. I am a business woman, *Señor,* and I'll tell you that types like that will soon ruin my investment. I only wish I could have seen the looks on their faces!"

Checo was immeasurably glad that he had not seen the looks on anyone's face. He drew a breath and wondered how to extricate himself from the situation. He had not come into the store with the notion of discussing one upsetting topic after another. Like Rocío, Miriam Maldonado took some resisting. She did occupy her space. Noting that among her other enterprises, Miriam operated a *'larga distancia'* service, Checo decided instantly to give Minerva another call. He told Miriam that he wanted to call his wife in Cd. Juárez to try to convince her to come back to him. He figured that he might as well tell her straight out. Like the woman in Mictlán, she was almost certain to listen.

"Ándale pues," Miriam smiled and took the piece of paper with the number Checo scrawled. Checo looked at his watch. It was almost nine. With any luck she'd be home. Miriam put on an ancient headset and dialed the number on a decrepit old unit that made Checo feel like he was in a movie, one of those classics from the golden age, a Tin Tan flick or a Bogart. Miriam got that look of vacant expectancy, that paralysis of the face that afflicts people who are aware of the fact that a phone a world away is ringing. She leaned forward and signaled to Checo to pick up the phone she'd placed on the counter.

"¡Bueno!"

Checo's heart literally fluttered. He had always been impressed with the way Minerva could convey her congenital optimism with that lovely upward inflection of her *"bueno"* on the phone. It suggested that life was, indeed, *bueno*. It was also *bonito*. With Minerva, it was seldom *barato* but then, as the *gringo* pop song says, two out of three is not bad.

"Minerva, are you aware of the fact that marrying you was one of the best decisions of my existence? I'm calling you from Huatepec. It's in the middle of the Sierra Nacoteca. Lee has gone off the tracks and is probably going to get us all killed."

"Checo, for God's sake, I just walked in the door. I need to pee. I need to get Rudolfo ready for bed . . . no, Rudolfo, you can't watch 'Free Willy' again. OK, OK *'Calle Sésamo'* is OK, but just one . . . Now Checo can you call back in five minutes? I've . . . "

"Just take the phone with you. I'm your husband. I promise I won't listen to you tinkle. I have something to tell you."

"Just a minute"

Checo, sweating, cast a glance at Miriam. To his surprise she was not listening. He heard the sound of running water. Unbelievable. Minerva was running water so that he would not hear the sound of her urination.

"Now what? You are glad you married me? Lee is trying to kill you?"

Checo heard the faraway toilet flush and the click as Minerva set the receiver on the back of the toilet. In his mind's eye he could see her pulling up her panties, unrolling her pantihose the rest of the way, kicking them in the corner, and then zipping her skirt.

Minerva sensed his lascivious scrutiny. "Quit it. I should have made you call back."

"Minerva, please. I am in a peasant village. My eardrums are shot. Everybody is drunk. The moon is rising and a tropical storm is rolling in. My shoes are covered with pig-shit and blood. All I can think of is how much I love you. I had a vision of you in the *fiesta castillo*. I am still sorting it out."

"Are you drunk?"

"Maybe so, I don't know. I'm probably the soberest person in the village."

Checo wanted to continue but could not. His heart was pounding, his temples were throbbing, and he had a lump in his throat. He was able to hear the Muppets singing "The Alligator King" in English. Minerva had left the bathroom.

"Said the Alligator King to his seventh son,
All right you get the crown,
You didn't give me diamonds,
And you didn't give me gold,
But you picked me up when I was down."

"Checo," Minerva said, "are you there?"

"Look," he said, "I was just about to beg you to come back to me but . . . I am coming to Ciudad Juárez instead. I will not delay. If I could get on a plane right now, I would do it. They call it 'the milk run' and the plane is probably full of milk cows. Monday I will be on it along with Bossy and Gertie. I can probably get to Mexico City by midday. With a decent connection I'll be there by five."

Once again Checo had astounded himself. The thought of getting on the puddle jumping airplane Rocío had flown in on was terrifying.

"Oh Checo," she said, "thank God. I miss you. I didn't believe you'd really come, that you cared enough. I know how you feel about Cd. Juárez."

"Minerva," he said, "get a sitter for Rudolfo and make us some reservations at a decent restaurant if such a thing exists in Cd. Juárez. We'll take it one step at a time. I need to hang up. I love you."

"Yes my love, my husband, I love you too. Take care and talk sense to poor Lee."

"I'll try."

"Until Sunday, ciao."

"Ciao."

They hung up.

He handed the phone back to Miriam Maldonado. He felt weak in the knees and had no inclination whatsoever to search for the house of *carguero* Don Mateo Carrera. He paid the exorbitant charges for the phone call and asked for another Sidral and a sack of ranch-dressing-flavored corn chips.

€ighteen

As was his unfortunate inclination with his offspring, Lee lectured Courtney and Kevin. "These village *fiestas* mark the end of one cycle and the beginning of another. Pre-Hispanic Indians believed that the world would end at such a moment. You celebrate a *fiesta* as though the nukes had been launched."

They walked along the dark village street. The booze and the encounter with Campos had left Lee a bit garrulous. Rocío tagged along, demanding translations and adding her two cents worth. Dzul, bandaged, limping, and burdened with supplies, brought up the rear. The injured revolutionary could not hold his tongue. "The *fiestas* are reactionary. Poverty drives the men to work like slaves in your country. They come back and lay out thousands for the *fiesta* of the Arrested Carbuncle or *San Büey* or *La Santísima Reina de los Pelados* . . . and nothing is left. Huatepec cannot produce the taxes to afford a decent pump for the village cistern. The village carries those saints on its back."

Campos's half-hearted thugs, Ignacio and Jesús, had broken Jorje Dzul's right thumb and forefinger while leaving the organs of speech intact. Waving his immobilized digits like a banner for the revolution, Dzul continued.

"The entire edifice, the disease that is the Church with its ceaselessly demanding saints, was foisted off on these people to hold them in bondage. And who . . . "

Rocío had enough. She interrupted.

"And whose violated womb did you disgrace?"

Lee had never before heard this astounding insult, but he had to admire the poetics of it. "Mercy . . . Rocío!"

"Excuse me please, sir, but I have something to say to your interviewee here." She bore down on the slight man.

"You stink on the world of stinks," she said. "The only thing that unites these people and gives them dignity is the *fiesta* custom. You come in with some jumped-up ideas out of a book that makes you feel superior to everyone, including your mama, who was obviously an Indian down to the huarache bunions on her Mayateca feet."

Dzul lifted his bandaged hand in an imperious gesture meant to silence Rocío. "I warn you, harlot, leave my mother out of this. How is it that everyone suddenly feels free to speak of my mother?" He shook his head in a gesture of authentic bewilderment, took a breath, and rallied his powers. "I have seen your corrupt films, woman. What makes you the voice of the peasantry? Nothing save hypocrisy."

Rocío interrupted again. She had another surprise. "I apologize, sir, for speaking of your mother, but you are full of shit. It's a poor leader who blames the people he would lead for his failures."

Lee enjoyed translating all this for the edification of Kevin and Courtney. He wondered if Checo appreciated what a tiger he had in Rocío.

Pausing for a moment, she wrinkled her forehead, choked on a sob, and stopped Jorje Dzul, taking his uninjured left hand. "You are right about my movies and I have no excuses. At least no one comes home in drunk despair to beat me with his *machete*. You may wish that your diatribes inspired people, but my big ass is a better draw. She gave herself a slap on the butt and continued. "I've got the history that you claim on my side. *Fiestas* have kept the Indians strong. Every *fiesta* is a fart in the face of the Church and the bosses. Someday, the world will fall to ruin and the strong will survive, the Indians who have persisted and celebrated."

Dzul actually squeezed Rocío's hand. He looked down. "You have no analysis."

"You are right, but anyone can see that the world of greed, of D.F. and the sainted dollar, is doomed. It will burn bright for an instant, like the *castillo,* like my movies, and then it will be gone." Her voice trailed off.

They were stopped in the middle of a muddy rutted road. The band, the dancers, were coming slowly along, followed by a crowd of people who looked forward to food and drink at Don Mateo's. Drunker than Lee's little entourage, the Indian mass moved in slow silence. Rocío Fino, illuminated by moonlight, stood in the ankle deep mud holding Jorje Dzul's hand. Beautiful.

Lee watched in astonished admiration.

What a pistol! Certainly Checo knew! Women of power drew Checo. But Checo could never go all the way with Rocío. He would ultimately hurtle back into the ordered, conventional life that Minerva manufactured in the unseemly chaos of Tenochtitlán. Lee realized that as much as he himself yearned for Minerva, there was no one like her in his life—nothing, in fact, to tie him to convention save his animal need for a sensible daily routine. The only ties he had to the United States were ties of commerce, nostalgia, and a score to settle—a blood feud that dated from Vietnam. With quickening pulse, Lee realized there was nothing to keep him from connecting deeply, authentically, and perhaps permanently with Rocío Fino.

At Don Mateo's house, they ate, drank, listened to the band, danced and watched the *Negritos* dance, drank some more, complimented Don Mateo, the band, the dancers, and the ubiquitous *cuetones*. Susana Güerra, a cousin to Elena, created a stir among the women, flirting demurely with the stunned Jorje Dzul.

Lee always did his best to observe *fiesta* protocol. At this *fiesta* he did a particularly good job. After midnight he walked out of the house across the road and into the banana shrubbery to take a leak. While he was shaking, Rocío surprised him from behind. She put her arms around him and took over the arduous task of shaking his penis. With a mastery of the situation that Lee found impressive and more than a bit daunting, Rocío then used her expert knowledge of the crevices of her clothing to guide Lee's member to the nests of pleasure and intimacy he might otherwise have sought in vain.

Once situated, Lee showed his own mastery of the pertinent landscape. Rocío was impressed but not completely surprised when she found herself gushing with pleasure and juices from the core of her being and his. As is customary, they returned to Don Mateo's house separately and using different routes. Decorum, discretion, and secrecy make the *fiesta* wee hours an unparalleled erotic playground. Later, when Lee's eyes met Rocío's, they regarded one another with a mixture of discretion and satisfaction.

Kevin and Courtney walked Rocío back to Maldonado's store around one A.M. They were pumped, blown away. The *fiesta* was "awesome," " far out," "incredible," etc. Kevin had to carry the equipment, since Dzul was both injured and passed out, sleeping along with a couple of dozen other drunks in Don Mateo's court-yard.

Back at Felipe's house, they zipped their bags together, undressed to the skin, sacked-out beside the sleeping Checo on the floor of the common room, and then spent what seemed like a deliciously ago-nized eternity making love quietly, almost without movement. Checo woke for a moment, smiled in the darkness, and enjoyed the mar-itime smells that engulfed the room.

At five Lee came in and woke everyone. "Get up! This will be worth seeing. For God's sake, Court, get it on film."

He grabbed his new hat. At least he'd be ready for whatever weather the tropical sky threw his way. Courtney shook her head as though the sight of the oversized *chapeau* so early in the morning was too much to bear. "God, you look like a dork in that hat."

Outside, it was first light and everything was enshrouded in a warm, eerie, and beautiful fog that was dense one moment and then thin, nearly limpid, the next.

Lee hurried the group into the hills south of the village, towards the now familiar blare of brass bands and blasts of *cuetones*. The very hills seemed to shake.

Checo was not an early riser. The fog, for him, was oppressive. Where was the civilized breakfast, coffee, and morning copy of *La Jornada*? The path they walked was claustrophobic in the fog, with dense, hanging vegetation seeming to lean in from both sides. Checo hoped that some good photo opportunities emerged.

The conditions made for interesting aural effects. The band music pulled them along, guiding them through the fog more reli-ably than the overgrown, occluded footpath. Suddenly, they were in a clearing. The band, somewhere to their right, quit playing and another band started up, dead ahead. There was other noise like castanets. As they walked toward the music, they saw the four mounted *Santiagos* dancing their horses on the cobbled surface of the clearing. The masked dancers materialized out of the fog, disappeared, and reappeared as their horses danced forward and the fog moved and shifted. Checo felt the hair on the back of his neck rise. The fog revealed, for just an instant, a small but stunning pyramid. People were everywhere, standing back from the dancers, allowing them to march and wheel the horses. The band had climbed the stepped temple.

Don Mateo approached Lee's little cluster. In silence he handed each person a large slab of pink cornbread and a plastic cup. His wife, Dona Carolina followed, filling each cup with a hearty jolt of *ponche*. Kevin and Checo declined without creating offense. Kevin, directed by Courtney, was filming in the poor light. The band was playing "The Isle of Capri." Lee smiled and took a hit of *ponche*.

"Remember the band a couple of nights ago at the funeral in San Lucas?" He asked.

Courtney nodded. She would go to her grave with the memory of THAT band etched in her brain.

Lee bit his lip. "What is this thing, that highland bands have about islands? Probably 90% of the people here know of the ocean only by rumor."

Courtney drank her *ponche* and nibbled at her cornbread. She would never have believed it, but the combination really seemed to hit the spot. The cornbread was almost caramelized with sugar and the *ponche* had an unexpected zip from pineapple juice and *chile*.

The band stopped and the *Santiago* dancers brought their horses abreast in a line at the base of the pyramid. The other band took over, invisible in the fog on top of the pyramid. Felipe and Elena walked up. Elena ladled out heavily sugared coffee from an *olla*, a crockery pot the size and shape of a bowling ball.

The fog was progressively thinning in the growing light. It was a bit warmer, but everyone was sopping from dew. The top of the pyramid was now visible. The band played and the *Negritos* dancers clogged before an improvised altar to Santiago.

Felipe spoke and Lee translated for Courtney.

"This observance concerns the villagers alone. No one has ever told the priest that the *cargueros* do this for Santiago, so he will bring rain. When I was little, the *cargueros* once had to restrain people from attacking Santiago with sticks because of a drought. The Nacotecs built this temple before the days of the Spaniards. We call it a Nacotec name that means 'the stone.'"

Courtney spoke. "The priest spent the night at one of the *cargueros*. Wouldn't he . . . with the bands playing and the *cuetones,* wouldn't he know that something was going on?"

Felipe smiled. "Priests, wise priests, know enough to know what is their business and what is our business. This is between us and Santiago. In Nacotec, our word for Santiago means 'Warrior of the Shaking Earth.' We believe that, rather than rain, Santiago might as easily bring earthquakes to punish people for vanity and arrogance."

Courtney watched the *Negritos* form into groups then break to reform into other groups, while the flirting *Maringuilla* danced here and there. "What does the *Negritos* dance mean?"

"Well," said Felipe, "who knows. Maybe they are the dark skinned people, the Indians that the Spanish whipped in the Conquest."

"And the *Santiagos?*"

"Well, the *Santiagos* are the *Santiagos,* warriors who kill and dominate. They are the champions of the Indians, the humble people."

Courtney spoke to Lee. "What Rocío said makes sense."

"Yes, indeed, Rocío told me that when she was a teenager she danced in the *fiestas* of her village. Her part was 'La Reina Xochtli,' the empress of flowers. She obviously knows what she is talking about."

After an hour or so, people lifted the litter of Santiago and took him back to the church for the first mass of the day. It was not yet seven in the morning and already a good number of people were quite drunk.

Lee was not drunk but churned up. His face moved and shifted. Finally, as the mass of people on the pyramid prepared to make the trek down the mountain to the church, Lee drew Felipe aside. "Do you think you can remember where Kevin buried the gun and bullets? Let's you and me go get them. I'd feel better if I had them."

As Lee's *compadre,* Felipe owed him the support and assistance, even if it killed him, and he knew he could count on Lee. If anything happened to Felipe, Lee would care for Elena and the kids. This had never been articulated but was nonetheless true. Felipe knew it. Lee would help Felipe even if it killed him. Similarly, Felipe knew with certainty that Lee's commitment was more deeply rooted in something more than simple obligation. It came out of respect, regard, and love. This had long given Felipe's existence an unanticipated measure of peace and solidity. Felipe had to indulge his *compadre*. Going to dig up the gun and bullets was an absurd exercise, but Felipe would just have to put up with it. Lee was better than most of his countrymen but he had not completely escaped the *gringo* predilection for absurdity. "How would the gun make you feel better?" He asked.

Lee's face wrinkled into a puzzled expression. He spoke with the forced patience of a man having to explain the obvious. "Sam Cooke is a bully. He can, at any moment, pull out his piece and blow me away. Having a piece will put us on an equal footing."

Felipe found this line of reasoning wanting. "Isn't Sam likely to get angry or threatened if he learns that you have a gun?" Felipe pressed his point.

"Not necessarily," Lee responded. "He will understand my reasons. It's a point of empathy."

Felipe didn't see the point of striving for empathy with Sam Cooke. "Wouldn't it be better to just avoid him for a day or two? The women say that he will leave as soon as he and his men fix the fuel filter. Why not just relax and enjoy the *fiesta?*"

A flush of annoyance colored Lee's cheeks. "I have known bastards like Sam my whole life. I've had it! All my kids are grown and all my ex-wives are married to rich men. I've got a whole butt-load of nothing to lose."

Lee looked weary. Maybe he needed a nap. As far as Felipe knew, Lee had been up dancing and drinking all night.

Lee continued his reluctant explanation. "I'm fixing to write an article about Jorje Dzul for idiots who aren't even aware that people like you are carrying them around on your backs. It leaves me short on patience. Let's go right now. We can be back for the *jaripeo*."

Felipe motioned to Elena, who was doling out coffee at the foot of the pyramid. She hustled over with her *olla*. Felipe told her that he would hook up with her later. Perhaps they'd be back for the mid-afternoon *jaripeo*.

Elena regarded Lee with a skeptical eye. "I don't like the look of our *compadre*." She said, "his face is cloudy under that huge hat! What's wrong with him?"

Lee frowned but Felipe found himself smiling. That hat! Leave it to Elena to point it out. "Nothing, he just thinks he is one of the *Santiagos*."

Elena laughed. "Just as long as you don't start thinking you're his horse!"

"What was that crack about?" Lee snarled at his *compadre* as the two men headed towards the village and the short-cut trail to the marigold fields.

"I was teasing you, *compadre*. You sound like Jorje Dzul. You need to pace yourself or you will foam at the mouth, have spasms, and lose your powers of speech. I don't want my *compadre* to live out his waning years as a mute. If you keep up that Dzul-like line of talk, though, I won't have to worry. This year will be your last.

Lee had to smile but his nose was still wide open.

As they passed Maldonado's store, Rocío walked out. She hailed them. After a short, spirited exchange, the men continued, shaking their heads in resignation. Rocío was going with them.

Nineteen

"So Lee, when you plant guns and bullets, do they grow into bombs and missiles?" Rocío sat on a boulder taunting the men, who were digging yet another hole at the margin of the field of marigolds. It was mid-morning and threatening rain. Patches of fog still hung at the edges of the world and occasional shafts of sunlight broke through everything.

They'd stopped at Felipe's house and grabbed a couple of shovels and a handful of day-old *tortillas*. On the Mictlán road they ran into some luck, Orlando and the Pan Bimbo truck. Orly was on his way to Huatepec to replenish the *fiesta*-depleted shelves of both the Maldonado and Cosme stores. Happy to run into Felipe, Lee, and Rocío, he turned his bread truck around and gave them a ride to the marigold field. As he drove, he looked over at Rocío every few seconds, pulled his hand shakily across his scalp and said "Jeez." When he had mastered himself sufficiently to speak, he said that he recognized Rocío from *"Traileras Sinvergüenzas"* ("Shameless Truckers"), the film that Rocío considered her worst to date. Orlando had loved it. It spoke, somehow, to his condition as a professional driver.

He asked Rocío if she wanted to drive. Rocío declined. She said that she'd not done the driving stunts in the movie. Orlando obviously felt that she was just being modest. It occurred to Lee that there were probably stunts more related to the *"sinvergüenza"* variety that Orlando would like Rocío to show him. Lee smiled with the realization that being with Rocío would mean being constantly in the presence of people, like Orlando, who'd seen her naked or nearly so. This would add an unexpected dimension to his existence. He'd have to ask Checo how he'd coped.

Orlando had found excuses to hang around for several minutes. He did not seem to find it odd that the *gringo* and his friends were digging holes in a remote marigold field. He asked for no explanation. He mooned after Rocío, a task that apparently required his undivided attention.

Lee's and Felipe's shared conviction that they knew exactly where the bullets were buried was short-lived. Lee had found the gun almost immediately, even before Orlando left. Removing it from the camera bag, he gave it a furtive inspection and was pleased to see that it was dry. Hoping Orlando had not seen the gun, Lee wrapped it in his jacket and laid it on a rock near the Twinkie truck. Kevin had buried it just off the road. Lee had watched. He'd paid less attention when Kevin was burying the bullets. Inclement weather since their arrival in Huatepec had destroyed all evidence of the digging Kevin had done. Lee pointed out the fence-corner spot he was certain was "the spot." Felipe said that he'd place the spot some fifteen meters south. They dug hole after hole. Lee sourly suspected that Felipe was purposely digging in the wrong places.

Conversing with Rocío, Orlando was able to point out that the field of marigolds was both beautiful and orange. He spoke of his brake problem. He showed Rocío a picture of his little girl and got her to autograph the dashboard of his truck. The conversation petered out.

Orlando had his deliveries to make. He told Rocío that he would be back "in a flash." Once he was gone, Rocío resumed her running commentary.

Orlando was a nice fellow but his nervousness got old quick. It was more fun teasing Lee. Rocío was excited. Her heart quickened with the notion that there were new possibilities in her life if she could keep Lee out of the clutches of those man-hungry nuns! Checo had been wonderful. He was educated. He knew the arts. He knew culture. She'd felt closer to Checo than she had to anyone since she walked out of her mother's Indian *cabaña*. She was his sideline thing, though, just a centimeter away from being his '*puta.*' Checo's deep affection had always belonged to the Ice Princess, whom Rocío frankly hated.

But Lee was something else. Watching him work the shovel, Rocío noticed how his size attracted her. Everything about him was big. He was a tree, a tower. He looked so handsome in his hat. It took some brass to take on a hat like that one, just like it took brass for a shoeless Indian girl to take on a blond wig and leatherette miniskirt.

Lee was something special. He was someone she could get close to, she knew it! So as Rocío watched the futile earthworks pile up, she teased the men and allowed herself to dream of a life of passion, affection, and mutual regard. The sex would be good too. The little rut in the bushes had been wonderful, juicy, silky. He was so solid, it was like crushing herself against a tree, a deeply rooted tree that could both stand and sway. The silver hair and the spidering wrinkles around his eyes were attractive and full of character, even wisdom. He was old enough to be her father, or even her grandfather . . . but so was Checo and everybody else of any interest. Rocío was simply not able to tolerate the affectations and adolescent vulnerability of the young men she had known.

Lee was getting discouraged. He knew he was not going to find the bullets in the hole he was working on. He was already deeper than he knew the bullets to be. Hearing a vehicle coming down the road from Huatepec, he assumed it was Orlando. Maybe it was time to give up on the bullets and catch a ride back to that shortcut path. It had been crazy to want the gun and bullets. The project proved once and for all that drinking *ponche* for five hours is not a healthy substitute for a good night's sleep. Things had just built up. He looked up to hail the bread truck. The black Cherokee rolled to a stop near the rock where Rocío sat.

Lee strode quickly to Rocío's side. Four men piled out, the "thugs" Elena had said were with Cooke. They had that occluded national identity which enshrouds modern mercenaries. They wore sunglasses, tropical short-sleeved "Hawaiian" shirts, baseball caps, khaki pants and either jungle boots of the Vietnam era or flip-flops. The collective impression was of Papa Doc Duvalier's *Ton-ton Macoutes* gone Hawaiian. They kept their mouths shut so as to seem sinister and deferred to their leader when he emerged. Sam Cooke, dressed in jeans and a windbreaker, got out whistling "Chain Gang."

He smiled, raised his right hand to his cheek and smiled, wiggling his fingers to wave. "Oooh, Aaah! If it isn't the legendary culture worker got on the business end of one 'a them Mexican draglines? I do admire the hat."

He smiled at Rocío and continued.

"You be a gent, now, and introduce your buds. Felipe, I know second hand. My man, *Teniente* Campos, has a considerable opinion of policeman Piñeda after that clinic you all gave him. Your lady friend, though, who she?"

Lee spoke in a flat, bland voice.

"Rocío Fino, a visitor from the capital."

"Row-seeey-oh Feeen-oh, my, my, MY! Now she wouldn't be the type of gal that'd peddle a guy a little, would she?"

Lee ignored the crack "Are these assassins Don Ho and the Royal Hawaiians?" Lee gestured with a nod to the gaggle of thugs.

Sam fixed his eyes on Lee and looked him up and down. "Mr. White, *Señor* Piñeda, and *Señorita* Feeen-oh, meet MY posse. We's the Fort Benning Boyos. This here's Maurice, and that's Emile, our Nawlins contingent. That's Kinshasa Jimmy with the Megadeth tee-shirt, and Roberto 'the donkey' on the end over there. Roberto's a Mexican himself, just like the lady. *Señorita* Feeen-oh may want to know why the boys gave him that nickname."

With a casualness that underlined the habit of command he issued his orders. "Maurice, why don't you just kind of rummage through the portable possessions. The rest of you go catfishin' or somethin', take a leak. We gonna be on our way in a few minutes here. My bud Lee here, the cultural worker . . . he talkin' trash. I think he's about to show me what bad is."

The "posse" did as they were told. Emile got back into the Cherokee. Jimmy and Roberto walked down the road as though sightseeing.

Felipe joined Rocío on the rock. Lee waited while Maurice pawed without interest at the *bolsas* and rain jackets they'd brought. To Sam's delight, he soon found the gun.

"Hey boss! Take a look at this!" Maurice displayed the gun with stunned admiration.

Sam spoke. "Whoa! You all believe in totin' something worth totin,' don't you? Have mercy, let Papa see that puppy."

Maurice handed the gun to Sam, who took the gun with affected delicacy. He closed his eyes and inhaled deeply as though in the raptures of bliss.

" Oh blessed fucking Jesus! Don't leave me alone with this sweet thang. This one a them little wrinkles on the good 'ol MAC-Ten. Man, you must have budget up the wazoo."

The topic apparently bored Maurice, who walked off after his friends.

Lee spoke icily. "We keep ourselves equipped."

Sam caressed the gun. He broke it down in one fluid movement and rebuilt it with another.

"I am in love—I want a date with this little honey dripper. I want to finger her works a little, you know what I'm sayin'? Where'd you get such expensive tastes?"

Lee pressed his lips together. "Aside from the gun, what do you want?"

"Why nothing, good buddy, except your delightful company. You kinda takin' a tone."

"Look, I have got nothing to say to you. What business do you have in these mountains?"

Sam Cooke smiled, not unpleasantly. "Oh, I don't know. 'Plenty' be the short answer. I expect I got as much business as you. Maybe I just be doing a bit of culture work. People here gotta raise they heads outta the mud and piss."

Sam strummed at the gun as though it was a guitar.

"You kinda tense. I think you been getting your panties in a knot ever since I let on about tiddlie-winkin' nuns outta helicopters. You done let it get your goat. I figure you be kinda weak-minded that way."

Rocío and Felipe were sunk in dread, their eyes dull and round as bottle tops. Rocío was understanding about every tenth word. Felipe understood nothing except the sinister feel.

Lee was rigid, his complexion gray. "Just give me the gun, gather up your little *remuda* of cutthroats, and leave us in peace."

"Just hold your horses an' chill. I don't get many opportunities to talk philosophy. You done called your names, 'pimp,' 'sassins,' 'cutthroats,' an' shit. I bein' patient. The 'little sisters of granola,' what business they got in these hills? You asked 'em?"

Lee said nothing. He crossed his arms and endured.

"I figure you and me oughta get on better, Speedo. At day's end we working for the same outfit. I the field niggah an' you the newsboy, Mr. Earl. Take a look-see at who cuts your checks, then go to name-callin. I didn't dig the pool, I just trying to keep my noggin dry."

"You're a living nightmare. Why don't you go pull the wings off flies?"

"Aw shucks, you keep up that line 'a talk and you gonna hurt my feelings. We BROTHERS, you an' me. Why don't we get your buddy with his camera? We two could join hands and sing 'Imagine' together."

This image actually brought a broad smile to Sam's lips.

"My gun?"

"I'm sorry, Mr. Culture Worker, but you got no bullets and I got plenty. You be in deep shit if my man Ezequiel catch you with this baby. I maybe gonna stop down the road here and pop a few caps if the opportunity come up. I gotta be careful, though, this baby easy to bust! I can't go to beating people's brains out an' shit, not with this unit. This a refined kinda weapon."

Lee conceded the point. He felt sick thinking of Sam with the gun. Sam gave him an affectionate tap on the arm.

"Don't let it get to you. You probably developing an unhealthy 'tachment to this little piece. 'Tachments, they'll give a man a spiritual burden, kharma an' shit."

Sam arched his back. It cracked loudly. He yawned, rubbed his face, and surveyed the scene.

"Listen, I gotta make my fond farewell. I got promises to keep and miles to go before I sleep an' all. Little gal there, Row-see-ooh. She look to be a mean piece. She missed herself an opportunity. Remember, forewarned is forefucked and I'll see your sorry ass in hell . . . It's been real, Ace . . . Emile, move your butt. We gonna let the Big Dog hunt."

He gave Lee a sideways look and shook his head. "'Livin nightmare . . .' I gotta kinda admire that. It gives a man something to live up to." He laughed gleefully and gave Emile a head signal to scoot. He wanted to drive.

Emile did as instructed. In a moment, spewing exhaust and mud, and blaring music that Lee recognized as the newly resurrected

Aerosmith CD, they were gone, down the road west . . . and Kevin's gun was gone with them.

Rocío and Felipe were still sitting on the rock by the marigold field. Lee walked up and stood vacantly beside them, too drained to say anything.

Rocío tried to joke. "So that's the harvest of weapons planted in the dark of the moon?" Before anyone could react, however, she moved, almost tackling Lee as she leapt weeping into his arms. "It's a miracle we lived through that," she sobbed, "I was steeling myself for the rape."

Lee held her, smelling the acrid scent of his stress.

"Let's get busy," Felipe urged. "I think those bullets are perhaps a bit further north than we've tried." He stood and picked up one of the shovels. Lee watched with puzzled fascination. Felipe walked to the edge of the field and started digging a hole a few feet north of a previous hole. Rocío held Lee with the grip of a drowning person to a log. Lee stared at Felipe without comprehension. Finally, Lee spoke to Rocío. "Come with me."

He took her hand, she pulled his hand to her, hugged it and kissed it. They walked over to Felipe.

"*Compadre*, why are you doing that?" Lee asked. "The gun is gone. Without the gun it's pointless and absurd."

Felipe smiled. "Ay *compadre*, it was pointless and absurd when we had the gun. If men stopped working at absurd tasks, the world would grind to a halt."

Lee started laughing. He turned to Rocío, who shrugged. "I thought it was foolish to dig for the bullets," she said, "but if you oxen remain determined to find them . . . who am I to interfere in the affairs of men."

Lee closed his eyes and laughed . . . and laughed . . . and laughed. He sat down on the ground and howled with laughter. "So, so Rocío . . . you thought . . . "

She completed his sentence. "It was utter folly, complete madness."

He stepped forward and she again moved to meet him. They embraced and kissed.

Lee held her. Felipe continued to work with the shovel. "Felipe, for God's sake stop digging," Lee shouted. "Let's get back to Huatepec. We've wasted half the day on this caper. It looks like rain."

They walked over to the boulder where they'd left the bolsas and rain gear. From far off, they heard an ominous rumble.

"Thunder?" said Rocío.

Lee raised his hand. The rumble came again, then nothing. They started up the road, east. When they'd walked about 100 meters the rumble came again, louder and more sustained.

A spasm of recognition passed through Felipe's body. He smiled. "By God! It's Orlando and the bread truck. The noise is the brakes."

Sure enough, in just a couple of minutes Orlando pulled up, the brakes sounding like a herd of indignant elephants.

He stuck his head out the door and addressed Felipe.

"Hey ox, what's happening!"

Twenty

At six in the evening the skies opened up and Santiago delivered. It was a fine moment for rain. The *jaripeo* was winding down to a chaotic free-for-all, drunks dancing to the simultaneous music of four or five bands while bulls wandered in the crowd nearly as confused and directionless as the drunken humans. The bulls were more animated, to be sure, and looked better than the humans. The bulls wore their finest—necklaces strung with oranges, grapefruit, and a single pineapple each. The more foolhardy and macho young men had ridden the bulls earlier. The bulls, having injured several young drunks, were a bit friskier than usual and were doing what they could to create excitement.

The arrival of the rain was a huge relief for Checo. He had been standing behind a waist high wall trying to assemble the courage to walk through the crowd, past Maldonado's store, and on to Felipe's house. In spite of Lee's perplexing disappearance, Checo, Kevin, Courtney, and Jorje Dzul had spent the day filming, photographing, and taping the *fiesta*. Now, the *fiesta* had degenerated to utter chaos. Half a dozen fights were going and many of the non-combatants seemed too drunk to even walk. Checo noted that this deterioration of ambulatory capacity did not stop people from accosting him, clawing at his legs, weeping on his shoes, or singing him unintelligible songs. Mounted riders mingled in the milling, lurching crowd . . . and then there were the bulls.

The bulls worried him. Each bull, by coincidence or design, was charging people. They were small by bull standards, and had their horns polled and blunted. They were not able to gore people, but that did not mean that they lacked the ambition to pummel their tormentors with their blunted horns, no doubt breaking ribs. The animals were also stepping on the occasional prone drunk. Mainly, of course, they simply ran through the streets slinging slobber.

Just because a bull was relatively small did not mean that Checo would appreciate the novelty of having one of them step on him or give him a blow to the ribcage. Neither was he in the mood to profit from the addition of a half liter of slobber to his clothing or person. So he whiled away a good half hour, safely ensconced behind his wall, ready to make his exit to Felipe's house. He was willing to wait as long as it took. Surely, the bulls would eventually see the folly of their situation and do the right thing.

The rain came in a sudden fury, preceded by a strong gust of wind out of the west. It came in sheets and ended the disgraceful chaos. The crowd united and reached complete consensus. The time had come to bid a fond farewell to the festivities and find shelter! It seemed to Checo that it took no more than four or five seconds for the streets to clear. Drunks and bulls vanished together, even before the first clap of thunder came to shatter Checo's rising spirits. He was not altogether certain that being hit by lightning was appreciably better than being trampled and gored by bulls. The instant chill and discomfort that came with the innundation mercifully took his mind off lightning, as he hustled through the village to Felipe's house.

Inside, Felipe's kids made the best of the small dimensions of the house. They ran, jumped, and giggled their way from the compound, to the kitchen, to the living area, and back. Felipe had lit a kerosene lantern that hung from the ceiling. Everyone was in the living area, sitting on the floor against the walls while Elena, almost as active as the children, flitted here and there with coffee, fruit, and bread. Kevin and Courtney sat together making as much body contact as they could. Jorje Dzul and Elena's cousin, Susana, sat next to one another maintaining a chaste, peasant distance. Significantly, Elena was not requiring Susana to help with chores. The bandaged Dzul was regarding the girl with a look of longing and admiration. She stole coy glances at him.

Lee had finally shown up. He was sitting cross-legged near the door and, to Checo's slight surprise, Rocío was sitting on his lap caressing his cheek with her fingertips. Felipe, for his part, was giving Elena a quick squeeze and feel whenever she came into range. The odd man out in the little group was Orlando. Felipe told Checo that the brakes of the Pan Bimbo/Twinkie wagon had finally given out completely, with the shoes falling to pieces inside the brake drum. This had caused the wheels to seize up. The truck had come to a profound, ear-splitting halt just outside Maldonado's store. Orlando was stuck in Huatepec overnight and had made the most of the situation by getting into the *fiesta* spirit. He was out, sleeping with his head abjectly in the wood box.

Checo grabbed his little overnighter bag and went into the kitchen to change clothes. He put up with the giggling children, who angled for a naughty gander at his naked behind or, better yet, his penis. When he came back to the main room of the compound, Felipe had gotten down a guitar and was singing, directing his words to Elena, who continued to hustle about.

> "*Este amor apasionado*
> *anda todo alborotado*
> *por volver*
> *Voy camino a la locura*
> *y aunque todo me tortura*
> *sé querer*
> *Nos dejamos hace tiempo*
> *pero ya llegó el momento*
> *de perder*
> *tú tenías mucha razón*
> *y hago caso al corazón*
> *y me muero por volver*
> *y Volver, volver, volver*
> *a tus brazos otra vez*
> *llegaré hasta donde estés*

yo sé perder, yo sé perder,
quiero volver, volver, volver."

Checo thought of Minerva, how he was returning to her arms. His throat tightened and he felt that he could weep. He looked around. What on earth had happened to set off this convulsion of midsummer romance?

Felipe continued to play, lingering over the notes so as to make the sometimes brash song very tender and sentimental. Even The kids quieted for the moment, playing with toy cars. Rocío stood and walked over to Felipe and whispered in his ear. He played on, making a bridge to a song that Checo recognized as another classic, *"Un Rayito de Luna."* Nodding and using her eyes to communicate with Felipe, Rocío struck a *Chanteuse* pose and launched into a spoken introduction to the song in Spanish. Checo was surprised. Rocío had told him she'd worked as a singer in a nightclub before her modeling took off. He hadn't paid a lot of attention.

"I have to say a word before I sing this song, this song that illuminates my life. We are here, protected from the storm. We bring our lives to this moment and all my life I have dreamed and sighed and longed. I am no longer a girl and have chosen with all my heart to live the bohemian life, the life of art and love. I have looked for that something special, that break in the clouds, that shaft of wan light. And now with the rising of the moon, I realize that something has happened to me in these beautiful mountains of despair and marigolds. I dedicate this beautiful song of my lonely soul first to 'Beginning,' to new possibilities, and with humble thanks to Santiago Apóstol. Santiago Apóstol, bohemian warrior saint of justice, art, and love, hear my prayer:

"Como rayito de luna
entre la selva dormida
así la luz de tus ojos
ha iluminado mi pobre vida
Tú diste luz al sendero
de mis noches sin fortuna
iluminando mi cielo
como rayito claro de luna

Rayito de luna blanca
que iluminas mi camino
así es tu amor en mi vida
la verdad y mi destino."

Her voice trailed off and Felipe continued to play the melody. He noodled a couple of improvised runs and then nodded. Rocío made her final run *a capella*. Felipe came in again at the end, using a bridge she made with her voice on the final syllables. Checo could feel his pulse in his throat and the hairs rising on his neck. Rocío's song vaulted him into the storm force winds of long suppressed emotions. He had chills and gooseflesh. It was as though Rocío had sung for him and to Minerva, Checo's *vida*, his *amor, verdad, y destino*. Checo knew he would someday have to find a way to thank Lee, who'd had been truly unflinching in his support of Checo's marriage. Lee knew his heart and pushed him always towards his better nature, even when he fought and equivocated. It was a great comfort to have such a friend. Checo felt tears welling in his eyes.

Elena clapped and everyone followed suit. Even Orlando, who had slept through the performance, woke up and joined the applause. Lee stood and took Rocío's hands. Their eyes met, they moved towards one another, and began to dance among the children and toy cars. Felipe played on, his own eyes drawn to his wife, who watched the dancers with her hands in her apron pockets and one tear making its way down her cheek. "This is the blessing of Santiago, my husband, the fruit of your good works and sacrifice."

Courtney, in a state of drunken and sentimental condescension, told Kevin that her dad and Rocío were "cute." She and Kevin had done a little celebrating. The *jaripeo* was the final event in the *fiesta* and they had it on video. The *fiesta* footage was in the can! Free of the need to maintain professionalism, they ended the *fiesta* with a dedicated assault on the *ponche*. They were bleary from work and drink. They'd enjoyed Rocío's song in a drunken, maudlin way, despite the fact that they did not understand so much as a word. They were just a couple of young puddles on Felipe's floor.

Dzul was so preoccupied that he scarcely noticed Rocío's singing. His left thigh was making contact with Susana's right thigh and all of Jorje's attention was on the electric pulses that emanated from those few square centimeters of ecstatic connection.

Rocío, who'd been drinking steadily with Elena since her return from the marigold field, hung onto Lee. They nuzzled. Rocío's song seemed to have drained the last feeble drops of *fiesta* energy out of the group. The party would not last long.

Sensing this, Checo reassembled his emotional decorum, moved across the room, and joined Lee, who'd slumped back onto the floor with Rocío cuddling against him.

Checo spoke. He had things he needed to discuss with Lee, important things.

"Guess what," he said, "I called Minerva. We are getting back together. I am going to fly out of here Monday on the plane that everybody calls the "milk run." I've got all the stills I need for the magazine articles and I have plenty for Kevin's work on the *fiesta* as well. The images are going to be great, just dynamite."

Lee interrupted, "We need to talk about the article. I figured we'd do it on the drive back to D.F."

"Well, we can't very well do that if I am in Ciudad Juárez."

"How true . . . Talk about the rats leaving the ship."

Checo let it go. Lee told him about his attempt to find the bullets and the confrontation with Sam.

"I hate it that he has the damned gun. I wish to hell I'd found the bullets before he got there. The bastard had the nerve to quote Robert Frost to me. He's a cold killer, Checo. I don't see how I can go back and write that article on Dzul."

"Easy, that's how. You should be able to write the damned thing in your sleep. I got you the photos you need."

"But I don't want to write it."

"What?"

"You heard me. My problem is that I don't have the advance to send back to them."

"So, don't write it. Sell some stock. Or if you need it right away, Rocío will give you the money to send back to the mag. She's making ads for Domeq Brandy and they're paying through the nose."

"No! I've got to write something. You've got to help."

"No! *Cálmate*, Lee!! I CAN'T think. All I want to do is get my wife back to Mexico City where she belongs. I'll help later. I'll even go out to Puebla or Pachuca or San Luis Potosí, whatever wretched backwater you choose."

"Give me a break. You are going to be too busy *schtuping* Minerva."

"Give ME a break. Getting back together is one thing, *"schtuping,"* as you put it, is something else altogether. I hate to spoil your pathetic fantasies about my wife."

"Checo, please spare us the innuendos. You've been moping for weeks about the split-up. Now, I guess you are going to start whining about getting back into Minerva's pants. Your 'Ice Princess' will give you all you can handle once she's sure no one is looking."

Checo smiled. "How'd you know that?" The recollection of Minerva's secretive sensuality was instantly arousing.

Courtney listened to the bilingual banter with a profound sense of unreality. Here she was in a peasant hut, at the ends of the earth, in the central Mexican *Sierra Madre,* with a rainstorm in progress, as well as a beautiful guitar serenade. Meanwhile these two aging jokers were doing the dozens, trading insults, ignoring the fact that despite the departure of Sam Cooke, they were still in a dicey situation.

She looked around the room, unable to assemble the energy to interrupt, to voice her concerns. The entourage was in tatters. Rocío was half asleep and rubbing herself against her dad. Kevin was half asleep and rubbing himself against her. As soon as he quit bickering with Lee, Checo had glazed over; the image of discreetly *schtuping* Minerva was apparently deeply involving. Felipe had quit playing the guitar to give his full attention to copping feels from Elena, who was making every effort to stay in range. Elena made eye contact with Susana, who arose and stood, unsteadily and dreamily swaying, while her aunt told Jorje Dzul that it was time for him to be on his way. He left.

Everyone was fading. There was a small burst of energy as people dragged sleeping bags and *petates,* zipped, walked out to pee, etc. There was another little blip of energy as various couples did some weary, secretive lovemaking in the darkened room. A bit later, Rocío, apparently both sated and unwilling to create a scandal, roused herself and returned alone to Miriam Maldonado's. So ended the *fiesta* of Santiago.

Twenty-One

Elena arrived at the Spring Branch just past sunrise. Her house was bursting at the seams with guests, but they were sure to sleep late. She needed water, had a few things to wash, and did not intend to miss the fresh gossip the *fiesta* was certain to excite.

The crowd at the stream bank was a bit thin. The *fiesta* had dwindled the ranks of gossip *meisters*. Some had stayed home with hangovers. Some had more serious difficulties. Hortensia Ponce, for example, had fallen into a mud puddle, ended up sleeping there, and was now suffering from an *aire*. Other women had broken limbs from falls or fights . . . nothing unusual or unexpected, but the ranks of raconteurs were distinctly depleted. What the gossip lacked, however, in style and breadth of opinion was certain to be more than matched in content.

Elena was able to report to Carolina Carrera regarding the progress of the Jorje Dzul/Susana Güerra project. Carolina gave a detailed account of whose husbands had wandered into the *afueras* coincidentally with whose wives during the course of the *fiesta* wee hours. Lee and Felipe's encounter with Campos and the soldiers was big news up and down the stream, and the women were able to piece together every movement of Rocío Fino's hand and every touch of her shameless breast to Lee's body. Elena enjoyed it all even though the stories about Rocío made her nervous. She did not like any implication that a hint of criticism might apply to Lee.

Time had passed and Elena had finished her bit of washing. She spread the clothes over stream side bushes to dry. She had at least the high points of the *mitote* and was about ready to return to her responsibilities at home. She wiped her hands on her apron and looked for her buckets. Downstream something was up! Carolina seemed to have slumped to the ground. She was weeping!

Elena forgot her buckets and hustled to help her *comadre*. Sure enough, Carolina was in tears. As Elena approached, Carolina looked up and met her gaze. *"Ay comadre,"* she said, "they've killed the little nuns."

Elena went numb. She comforted poor Carolina, who'd always been close with the nuns. While she did so, Concepción Estrada and a couple of other women who'd come in on the red-eye bus from Mictlán told the story.

It'd happened near Las Llagas and the women were certain that witchcraft was involved. No one would miss the Priest and his brutal handshakes, but the nuns. . . . They were nice. They were sweet. They were helpful. They were just the targets for that den of witches, Las Llagas, that open sore of festering envy!

The nuns and priest had been ambushed heading back to San Lucas from the *fiesta*. They'd left a couple of hours before sunset, after the *jaripeo* chaos died down. They left during the rain, wanting to get to San Lucas before the road washed out or darkness fell. The *Combi* was shot full of holes. The priest and two of the three nuns who'd attended the *fiesta* were shot dead inside. Sister Judith had survived because of the fact that she'd come down with food poisoning or something. She was asleep at Carolina Carrera's house where she'd planned to stay until she felt well enough to travel. Sister Remilda and Sister Mary Agnes were dead, along with Father Josef, who'd been driving.

Horrified, yet morbidly greedy for information, the women at the Spring Branch pressed for details and the women who'd been on the bus did their best. The VW had stopped because someone had dragged a felled tree into the road. The blood was three centimeters deep on the floor of the VW. Though riddled with bullets, Sister Remilda had enough life in her young body to haul herself erect in her seat, put her hand against the window, and lay her head on her hand. She died smiling. No one knew who'd done it and no one knew if the dead had been robbed.

At this point the group of women began talking all at once, speculating about the murderers, quick to blame the witches of Las Llagas for the crime. Elena disagreed. It was, perhaps, likely it was that some of the *arrimados* from Las Llagas had robbed the dead *religiosos*. It was very unlikely, however, that the murderers were villagers or that the murderers had killed to rob. The nuns and priest didn't have much and bullets were costly. The murders were expensive, wasteful, surely not the work of the impoverished and penurious half-wits from Las Llagas. Was it witchcraft? Elena thought not. Were the impoverished sorcerers of Las Llagas able to turn goat droppings into bullets? No. The Las Llagas types dwelled on their hatred of those more fortunate than themselves. Witches cause illnesses, small doubt of that, but they do not cause ambushes. Elena shared her theory that the *gringo* Sam and his bunch of cutthroats were responsible. Why would Sam and his thugs kill? No particular reason. It was just the kind of thing that such men did.

Campos, according to the women who'd been on the bus, was at the scene conducting an investigation. Despite her shock and sadness about the poor nuns, Elena almost laughed when Concepción Estrada unburdened herself of *that* little morsel of intelligence. To think of that strutting turkey and his goons! They could investigate until doomsday and not even locate their own assholes. Elena recalled with satisfaction that both she and Lee had run Campos off with his tail between his legs. Now he aired his grandeurs and paraded about, "investigating." What a comedy!

It was sad about the little nuns, though. Elena always thought of them as "the little nuns" even though they were great hulking girls who'd towered over the Nacotec women. They were sweet, smart, useful creatures who were kind, purely kind. They did not profit or attempt to profit from their kind acts. Despite their sporadic Dzul-like attempts to organize, they were mostly levelheaded and practical. Still numb inside, Elena knew she would cry bitter tears over the loss of those innocent girls. She helped Carolina get her things together, got her own buckets, made the appropriate noises to Concepción and the rest of the reduced band of gossips, and rushed home to tell Felipe and the others the news. The Church bell had not yet struck eight. Would anyone be awake?

The morning fog was breaking. Shafts of light broke through, illuminating the whole valley with a lemony yellow light that had a washed out quality. Everybody was up. The adults were drinking the coffee Elena had made earlier. The kids were eating day old *tortillas* and drinking milk.

Without so much as a preamble, Elena marched in and began telling about the murders. She was not prepared for the reaction.

Courtney was feeling cautiously affectionate towards her dad. He'd seemed so cute and vulnerable with Rocío that Courtney forgot to get angry with him. Rocío was only five years older than Courtney and only three years older than her half-sister Marti, who'd have pointed out that Rocío was obviously a slut. Somehow, though, Courtney just couldn't work up any indignation. She liked Rocío. Slut or no, she seemed an obvious good choice for her dad. Maybe Lee still had the capacity to grow, adapt, change for the better. Despite her father's unreasoning attack before they got Kevin back, she had been really liking her dad since they'd arrived at Huatepec. She was beginning to understand what he'd been doing all those times he had been away, in Mexico.

It was frightening for Courtney to see her father react to the murders. Elena had roared into the house talking a mile a minute. Startled, Courtney looked to Lee to translate. He averted his eyes. His skin mottled a purplish red and then seemed to go gray. What on earth could Elena be saying?

Lee looked at Checo. "Shit," he said. He let his head slump into his hand and rubbed his forehead slowly, as though some needed perspective could be coaxed from his brain by physical stimulation.

Checo, like his partner, was ashen, his face bunched with anxiety. He stood, took a deep breath and walked unsteadily towards Lee. "Lee!" he wheezed. He sounded almost asthmatic as he made his best speed to his companion's side.

Lee waved him off, turned slowly towards Courtney, and opened his mouth. The words would not come. He shifted his gaze as though the sight of his daughter was painful to him.

"What did she say?"

Lee took a deep breath and slowly exhaled.

"She just found out that someone killed the priest and nuns yesterday. They were driving back to San Lucas. Someone blocked the road and then just shot them."

Courtney felt a rush of blood to the back of her head. Had she almost fainted? "Sam Cooke?"

"Who the FUCK else?"

"But . . . "

"With our gun, the one Kevin bought. He took it from me. I think I'm going to puke."

Lee stood up and walked out of the courtyard and onto the road. Checo moved to the door as though to follow. Lee waved him away and sat down in the middle of the road shaking his head. Courtney followed Lee outside in spite of the certainty that she should stay put, shut up, and leave her father alone.

"I need to get my shit together," he said.

She took a step towards him.

He stood and slowly turned to face her. "Tell poor Elena it's not her fault. She didn't do anything."

"How can I?"

"Just fucking tell her, Courtney. Figure it the fuck out and stay out of my hair."

Courtney's eyes teared instantly. She turned around and collided with Kevin. Their heads bumped and Courtney saw stars. "God, Kevin!" Her eyes met his. He looked so bewildered that she had to laugh.

"Getting my bearings," he said. "Boy, you sure hit me square."

Lee was gone. He'd disappeared into the jungle-like growth that lined the road.

Kevin and Courtney went back into the courtyard and sat down. Their heads were still ringing a bit from the collision and they sported goofy smiles.

Checo spoke. "So this is a real comedy?"

Kevin and Courtney said nothing, but looked as blank and slack jawed as human beings can look.

"For God's sake close your mouths!" Checo snapped. "Courtney, what will your father do?"

"He said he needed to 'get his shit together.' You know more what he's likely to do than I do."

"Well, I'm concerned. He's been in a funk ever since he took that gun away from Kevin. Maybe this is bringing the war back, pushing some buttons. I guess we have to let him be. This is driving me nuts. I mean, what if he decides to go after Sam?"

"God, I was such an idiot to bring the gun." Kevin sat in one of the hard-backed chairs and stared at the chicken shit bespattered ground between his legs. His nostrils quivered.

Checo watched, his nostrils flared with anger and worry. "That's certainly true. But remember, those guys were already armed to the teeth."

Checo paced around the compound. "Elena says that Campos is investigating the murders. We can probably get out despite the idiotic 'house arrest.' It's going to maybe depend on the two of you . . . what did Lee say to you, Courtney?"

"He told me to apologize to Elena and to leave him alone."

"I wonder if Rocío is up?" Checo continued to pace.

"Shall Kevin and I go see?"

"Yes, good idea."

"Kev?"

Kevin finally looked up. "OK."

Orlando said he would walk with them, he needed to phone Pan Bimbo to let them know that the Twinkie truck was out of commission. Felipe wanted to go as well. He knew Elena's information was good, but wondered if there were nuances or extra information Miriam Maldonado might have picked up. He did not mention this to Elena.

Elena seemed to sense the defection. "Well, don't listen to Miriam Maldonado, who knows what exaggerated crap she'll be spouting? She's the most notorious gossip in all of Huatepec."

Despite the somber mood, Felipe had to suppress a smile at his wife's sudden self-righteousness.

"And take these kids with you," she said. "Get them out of my hair. I'll put together some food while you are gone. Miriam Maldonado will not have given poor *Señorita* Fino enough for a sparrow to live on. People have to eat, whatever else happens. Susana will give me a hand, won't you, girl?"

Susana nodded assent.

Courtney delivered a barrage of orders in English. In a couple of minutes she, Kevin, Orlando, Felipe, and the four kids were gone. Apparently, Courtney did not care if her orders were understood so long as they were carried out.

Elena was impressed. She spoke to Checo "Does she boss her father like that?"

"I don't know. She bossed me like that when I was trying to help her two days ago. I had to lay down for awhile. I hope she starts in on her dad. He could use some supervision. In fact, I'd better find him." Checo walked onto the road and looked around, drawing a deep breath. Damned Lee! Much more of this and Checo was going to end up with gastritis or worse. Checo had long noticed that Americans, even Lee, had exaggerated views of their own importance. It was presumptuous, even arrogant, for Lee and Kevin to feel guilty about the nuns. Pretty soon, Checo thought, the *gringos* would figure out a new Olympic event based on guilt so they could win all the medals.

Lee was sitting on a rock staring out over the valley, watching the eagles and vultures mount the thermals and rise into the stratosphere.

Checo walked up. "So here you are."

"Yup, 'casting my ballot for eternity outside of time.'"

"Feeling sorry for yourself?"

"Feeling sorry for everybody, everything . . . that does include me. It's the shits. We just sit around on the surface of this planet watching people ruin it. God, those poor girls."

"It's not your fault."

"I know, I ran the logic. Sam probably used the little pistol, it would have given him an extra thrill. The son-of-a-bitch quoted Robert Frost to me, the 'promises to keep' line. I guess I told you that."

Checo nodded, even though he'd confused Robert Frost with Jack Frost.

"The hit was planned, one of his 'promises to keep.' I figure, though, he killed those people with a gun I provided. I just know it." Lee felt a heaviness in his chest that he might have compared to an elephant's tread. It was familiar, that leaden footfall at his center.

"I could see it coming, from that first moment when he came out and humiliated Campos. I understood. We're killers, both of us, trained to it and never untrained . . . burdened with ghosts and dangerous to everybody."

Checo sat with his friend and stared out across the valley. He sighed. Lee was OK. He wasn't going after Sam. He wasn't going to fling himself into the *barranca*. It was good for him to talk. The muscles in Checo's neck began to relax and he sprawled on the rock taking in the morning sun.

"I remember Courtney crying when she was a baby. 'Night music,' Hannah called it. I'd lie there shaking in the silences between crying fits. I kept thinking I'd have to make it stop or cut my throat. My wives, I left them with babies, Checo. I couldn't handle the nights, the crying fits." Lee squinted as though the morning light pained him. He took a deep breath.

Checo waited, allowing him to talk.

"Last night," Lee finally continued, "Lilián, Felipe's littlest, cried the way kids do. She woke me up. For a second or two I thought I was in Vietnam. I came down from that and was just lying there on the floor in my sleeping bag thinking that I was never, ever going to get that mess behind me. There was this situation, Checo, me and three others had got our ass in a crack. The Viet Cong had us pinned. We had an exit route but it got too dark to move. They were everywhere, all over us. But . . . we had an excellent hidey hole. They couldn't find us."

Lee gazed into the depths of sky, following an eagle, no, a vulture, tipping and tipping in flight, never achieving the equilibrium eagles take for granted. Checo made a grunting noise he meant to be encouraging.

"Always resourceful, the VC decided to play with our minds. They got a child and tortured him . . . or her. The 'night music' went on for hours. It didn't work. We were too smart, too scared, too disciplined. I hated the kid. I prayed that the brat would just die. We kept our heads down and were able to scoot at first light. We didn't find out what happened . . . to the kid. We didn't have time to think about it. Things were hairy for several endless Goddamned days. By the time I had any breathing room so much had gone down . . . there was nothing to say, nothing to do. I never exactly recalled the incident until last night. At the time it just disappeared. It was like a grain of sand on a beach."

Checo was thinking of Rudolfo and Marisol. He opened his mouth. No sound came.

"Ghost burdens, Sergio, the shit that made Sam Cooke what HE is. Poor Courtney, poor Marti. And now those nuns, those poor dorky girls, killed with a gun I exhumed from the fucking earth. But, 'It's not my fault.'"

Checo did not want to hear any more stories. He remembered how Rudolfo had cried when he fell from a play structure and broke his shoulder. The thought of the child in Lee's story made him feel sick. His guts twisted painfully and his field of vision narrowed in deference to the coming headache. Was Mexico full of *gringos* who carried the burden of such stories?

"No one can blame you. Have you ever written . . . ?"

"Write, Jesus, Checo, I can't write about something I can't face. Shit, you think that story would sell Cutty Sark?"

Checo smiled. Damned straight it would. He wished he had a jolt of Cutty Sark on hand.

"Look," Lee said, pointing with his chin, "there's an eagle there with the vultures. It's lovely how they soar . . . looking for some creature to pounce upon and devour."

Twenty-Two

"We've got to cover it, Lee," Kevin urged. "How can we back away from it? We're journalists."

Checo had a mouth full of Elena's *chilaquiles* with fresh cream. They were heavenly. . . . So why was he listening to this adolescent wannabe talk about their responsibility as journalists? He felt his neck flush. This ox was spoiling his breakfast!

"That's right," Checo agreed, "I'm glad you finally realize that we're reporters rather than arms importers. I only wish your judgment would improve. We're lucky that those assassins didn't murder us. Lee and I are museum and gallery opening journalists, wine and cheese, got it?"

Rocío sat next to Lee and watched him eat while Checo argued with Kevin. She gently massaged the area around his solar plexis.

Enjoying the massage, Lee closed his eyes, took a deep breath and spoke to Kevin. "The problem is we're not set up to cover the situation. We can't even prove that Sam was in the *municipio*. Anyway, Checo is right. We're art and culture journalists."

Courtney flushed, then went pale, and finally had the coughing fit that invariably accompanies attempts to breathe *chilaquiles*, with or without sour cream.

"Spit it out, Towanda, your mama didn't raise you to keep your opinions to yourself."

"We got photos of Sam and his men. Rocío and I got them." she wheezed. "It was the day we got Kevin back." She took a deep breath.

Lee took his own deep breath and smiled broadly. "I always knew you were a resourceful girl and . . . Rocío, well, well." He felt a tingle up his backbone. "Describe these photos and tell me how you got them."

"They were playing basketball."

"Who?"

"Sam, his bunch—Campos' guys too, along with a couple of locals."

"Which camera, which lens?"

"It was a Pentax, one of Checo's," Courtney explained. "The lens I used for the shots of the basketball game was a zoom. We'd just got in trouble with Checo for taking shots of Campos and the Jeep. When he stomped off, we went looking for things he'd told us to not shoot. Rocío would model in the foreground and I'd zoom around her for distance shots. They had their guns in a big pile on the hood of the Cherokee. I know I got the pile of guns and I know I got all of the guys with tattoos. Rocío insisted."

Checo looked at Rocío and shook his head. The woman was a maniac. She might yet get him killed and, sadly enough, he wasn't even fucking her anymore.

Lee pressed his lips together. "Checo, do you know the camera?"

"Of course I know the camera, it's my camera, my favorite camera, the Pentax!"

"Does it date the film?"

"It does if it's been set right and the batteries haven't run down beyond zero."

"Go find out, now. If you keep stuffing your face with all that cream, you won't have to worry about getting murdered. Jesus, you can practically see the plaque forming. You'd better start setting a little aside for your double bypass."

Checo was offended, but let it go. Lee got that way when he was tense. Checo left the table wiping his mouth on his sleeve.

Lee addressed Courtney. "Anything in any of the photographs that'd prove which day it was?"

"Yeah, you'd know it was a day of *fiesta* preparations. I'm sure there were people in the background with flowers and all. Besides that, Rocío got a couple of shots of the guy working on the *castillo* after the basketball game. If you look at the print sequence, you'd know that the basketball game took place a day or so before the *fiesta*, before the *vísperas*, and before the *castillo* event."

Checo came back in with the Pentax. "It's marking the day correctly."

Lee smiled largely.

"So we've got them in town two days before the murders, loaded up with guns, and fraternizing with the people investigating the murder. Are you sure you knew how to use the camera?"

Courtney stifled her annoyance. "Yes, I've got one just like it. Kevin can show it to you. I might be one or two clicks overexposed or underexposed, but . . . "

"Any chance you got the license plate for the Cherokee in any of the shots?"

Courtney didn't know, but didn't rule it out. She estimated that she had at least eight shots of the basketball game. When she and Rocío tired of their sport, there were still seven or eight exposures left on the roll. As far as she knew the roll was still in the camera. Lee eyed Checo, who indicated that he'd been using the Leica for both the article on Dzul and the *fiesta*.

"It looks like the roll Courtney exposed is still in the Pentax, nine exposures left," Checo admitted.

Lee pinned his partner with his eyes. "You see what this does?"

Checo, to his infinite regret, did. "It means that someone could go down there and get some shots of the car and the bodies on the same roll. Just imagine the contact sheet, the sequence of photos. I admit it's tantalizing. But Campos is down there. You think he'll just let us waltz in and photograph the crime scene?"

"No, but let's think about how to do it, not how it's impossible. Come on Checo, there's got to be a way."

"I don't want a way, *büey*, it's too dangerous."

"It's also too good to miss," Lee said. They killed those girls, Checo! I wonder what all Sister Remilda had on them."

Kevin stood to speak. He was so excited that he was practically dancing. "One of them stayed, remember? Let's go ask her. She's at Carolina Carrera's house."

Lee got up and started to pace. He nearly collided with Elena, who was hustling about waiting on everyone. The small courtyard did not accommodate the need for serious pacing. Lee made the best of it.

"Courtney, go talk to her. She'll feel comfortable with you. Take Kevin, he needs to work off some of that excess energy. Her name is Sister Judith. She'll be terribly upset. Don't come on too strong and leave Kevin to drink coffee with Carolina Carrera. Get back right away, though. We don't have much time, and we may want to leave on a moment's notice. Campos is going to be too tied up to worry about us." Lee raised his voice to include Checo. "We could simply get away. All we have to do is to walk away from the story of the murders. Can we do that?"

Checo watched Lee pace.

"Just watch me, Lee. I am in no mood to risk my life to photograph bloody carcasses and a shot-up *Combi*. We really are arts and culture journalists. Face it, Lee. You do amusing, sophisticated pieces, not investigations. Even your thing on smuggled archaeological artifacts was more art history than investigation. We'll end up looking like idiots."

Lee continued to pace. Courtney spoke up as she and Kevin were leaving.

"Honestly, can you just suspend the Lee and Checo show? Have either of you given a minute's genuine thought to the matter of us getting safely out of here?"

"Ah," Lee stopped momentarily to smile at his daughter. "Youth and reason speak with a single voice. . . . As a matter of fact I just mentioned a strategy but I only gave it about thirty seconds of thought. Hannah will murder me if anything happens to you. . . . Checo's solved it as far as he is concerned. He's flying out tomorrow on the milk run."

"Well, Rocío said that she wanted to fly out as well. I don't see why we all couldn't fly out on the plane. Orlando is waiting for the bus to Mictlán. He's got to go there for brake parts. Why don't we get him to drive the van to Mictlán and meet him there?"

Lee looked at Checo. "Didn't I tell you that we'd probably all owe our lives to this young woman before the project was over? It's a brilliant idea. The one problem that occurs to me is that Campos might stop Orlando and confiscate the Dodge."

"So what?" Courtney practically sneered with disdain. "If he does that he'll have the Hertz agency in Mexico City to deal with. It's THEIR car and they deserve whatever trouble it takes them to get it back from Campos. They rented us the van without a spare!"

"Right! Maybe Campos will use the *ley fuga* to execute a few Hertz rental agents. No one can deny that they have it coming. Seriously, let me think about it. You go now and get back just as soon as you can. Flying out might work. We could drive right down to the crime scene, do our thing, come back here, and then split. I wonder what Campos thinks about having to clean up after Sam?"

Leaving the irrelevant question hanging, Lee motioned to Courtney. She walked over. He took her hand.

"Look, I'm sorry. Earlier, I was out of line . . . I'm sorry. You're keeping a clear head and you've done what may be the most important work of all of us. I am so glad you are here with me that it's beyond my ability to even express it. I'm a slow study, but I may yet figure out how to be a decent father to you."

Courtney felt constriction in her throat. Things went wobbly for a minute. She squeezed his hand.

"Here, have a lollipop." He gave her one of the watermelon, chile-lime lollipops he seemed to carry for the express purpose of having them on hand at such moments.

Courtney took the lollipop, gave Lee's hand another squeeze, and motioned to Kevin that she was ready to go.

They left and, after a moment of uncomfortable silence, Checo spoke.

"Lee, this is madness. Are you listening? How do you think you can go down there and get photographs? How?"

"Come on, Checo, let's improvise. It's our best suit. I want to go down to Las Llagas and find Campos. I'm begging you, really. We'll give him and his two soldiers a 'screen test' and let Rocío hang her tits all over the place, while you sneak around and get documentation on the bodies and the *Combi*. We can kiss his ass. Then it's hop on the puddle jumper and 'surprise!' for the good *Teniente*. We can't just let Sam kill those girls like that . . . and the priest."

Checo was tight-lipped as he stared into the indecently naked blue of the morning sky of the highlands. Checo liked a bit of containment, a cloud here and there to remind him that he was not likely to fall into the raw infinity of the sky. He was damned if he was going to speak. What next? The airplane, he supposed, falling into that very raw infinity he found so threatening.

Lee waited in vain for an answer, stretched like a cat, and cracked his back.

"Now . . . what, Checo? Do you want me on my knees? Courtney got all the pre-crime scene photos. Unfortunately, she's no photographer. I want your approach to the images of those dead girls, pictures to play on the emotions of Catholic grandmas in every little ethnic enclave in the U.S. Are you in? I really am begging you."

Checo finally cracked a smile. He'd held out as long as he could. "All right, I'll do it. The plan is insane and dangerous, but it is no more insane and dangerous than riding that damned airplane out of Huatepec. If you are joining me for the suicide junket to Mictlán, then I ought to go take photographs of bullet-riddled corpses. *Ándale, pues.* We've shared everything else . . . " He glanced at Rocío and smiled again. "I guess we'll share the risk."

"*Ándale!* And we'd better get busy or there'll be no risk to share. They'll be moving the bodies as quickly as they can. They'll probably need refrigeration, though, and that'll slow them up. It'd be a shame to get ourselves up to do this and then get there too late. I'll get Elena to send one of the kids to fetch Felipe and Orlando. I want Felipe's take. He'll have an instinct. If Felipe doesn't sign off on the plan, we'll just leave—I'll jump in the van and you can take the blighted milk run. Felipe needs to know what's what and Orlando too, for that matter. We should try to catch Courtney and Kevin. I can't imagine that Sister Judith will have anything anyway."

Lee was wrong. Courtney had already found Sister Judith and Sister Judith had plenty. Sister Remilda had assembled a file of photos, news reports, and witness narratives that documented a legacy of crimes and terror associated with Sam Cooke and his "boyos." The connection with the Mexican Army, however, looked tenuous. Sam was reaching out and apparently had only very recently secured the backing of one of Campos's superiors. That explained the gift holster that Elena claimed Sam had given Campos.

Sister Judith said she was certain that Lee could have the files if he could pick them up at the convent in San Lucas. She was healthy enough to travel and planned to take the milk run to Mictlán the next day and bus from there to San Lucas.

Lieutenant Campos had just about had his fill. Getting passed over earlier in the year for a training slot in the new program at Fort Benning had stung. The work in Huatepec was a weary, tedious business. Working several days at the beck and call of the likes of Sam Cooke had chafed, but this was really the limit. Was he a janitor to have to clean up this *gringo's* messes? It was beyond endurance. Now he was stuck. He'd been with the car and the bodies all morning, waiting for a popsicle truck from Mictlán to show up for the bodies. Eventually, after interminable paperwork, the bodies would be repatriated to the U.S. It was crucial, logistically, to get the bodies on ice immediately.

The hassle he had to go through to get the Yogi Yom Yom *paleta* franchise in Mictlán to part with one of their cursed, dog-sodomizing refrigerator trucks, was beyond belief. Campos had been up all night dealing with the situation. The assassination had been carried out at dusk, about eight in the evening. He had to wait, however, for someone to report the murders. Evidently the morons in Las Llagas (what a name for a town!) walked through massacres without noticing or, at any rate, without bothering to report to authorities. Unbelievable. The bodies sat oozing blood by the light of the waning moon until past midnight. Finally, one of the benighted public buses (four hours late) almost rammed the bullet riddled remains of the *Combi*. Campos had been a wreck, up pacing and chewing his bottom lip when the call came in.

Since then, he'd been back and forth between the crime scene and the ancient, erratic telephone at the las Llagas *Presidencia*. To use the phone at all, he had to have Jesús and Ignacio on hand to relay dialing instructions to the nearly deaf switchboard operator who ran the PBX machine out of her home, some 300 meters from the *Presidencia*. He needed the phone to keep his superiors abreast of the situation and to fight the Yogi Yom Yom dogshit merchants in Mictlán. He had to make what seemed like dozens of calls and never, not once, did he get through without first getting a wrong number and then having Jesús and Ignacio relay instructions for a second try. At length, when he inadvertently reached a beauty shop in Luxembourg, he was beyond anger and frustration and simply had to laugh. It was either laugh or go mad.

The low point came when he had been on the phone for nearly an hour making every effort to give Yogi Yom Yom Army business. He had just agreed to rent their shitting truck at an exorbitant, confiscatory rate when a woman, evidently the franchise owner's wife, cut in on the phone, hysterical and screeching about the damage transporting dead nuns would do to the Yogi Yom Yom reputation. He exploded and told her in plain terms what she could do with the Yogi Yom Yom reputation. Back on the phone later, he had gone through the most humiliating exercise of his adult life, apologizing to the slobbering, bawling, out-of-control bitch whom the owner of the Yogi Yom Yom franchise had the poor taste and worse luck to have married. If Campos had to face anything like that again, he'd just take out his hog-leg and shoot himself.

Jesus, what a couple of days. First, the maniacal wife of the good *Señor* Worm in Huatepec attacks knuckle-headed Jesús with a wooden spoon. But who gets his fingers mashed and ends up on the floor? The officer in command, that's who. What a humiliation! Next, the morons working for him stand around with their thumbs up their asses and allow themselves to be disarmed by Lee White. Next, Sam Cooke, the most arrogant hippy warrior ever hatched out of *Gringolandia*, loses patience and decides to 'send a message' using the medium of dead nuns. Guess which commanding officer is elected to clean up the mess? All of that paled in comparison to the nauseating display of obsequious ass-kissing he'd had to do to get the truck . . . not that he had the truck.

The flesh might well rot off the corpses and the bones bleach white in the summer sun before the bleeding Yogi Yom Yom truck made an appearance. It was a trial to have to sit around while Jesús and Ignacio played with their puddings. He had to wonder how soon the bodies would start stinking. The only thing of even minor interest was the fact that one of the nuns had a piece of paper with an email address: cultwkr@aol.com.

It had to be Lee White, the "culture worker." What truck did he have with the nuns? Campos had gained a measure of respect for the way Lee had handled the Dzul-beating incident. Lee White protected his people and that was the essence of leadership. Campos also half believed the story that Lee was there to document the *fiesta*. The email address in the dead nun's pocket called that into question. He supposed that Lee and the others would take advantage of the fact that he was tied up to conveniently "forget" that they were under "house arrest." They were probably already gone. Oh well.

He had looked forward to scaring the piss out of the *chilango* communist, the half-wit *pocho*, and the sumptuous daughter before letting them all go, but that was a pleasure he was probably going to have to forego. The good *Señor* Worm and his shrew wife merited his attention, but he'd be more or less stuck in Las Llagas for awhile. He would, he supposed, make do by scaring the piss out of the *Presidente Municipal* or some of the other apparently subhuman occupants of Las Llagas. As a last resort, he always had Jesús and Ignacio.

It was an actual relief to Campos when, around midday, Lee and his crew drove up. Unable to go the mountain, the mountain had come to him. His face split with the first real smile of the day.

Twenty-Three

"I hope you remember, Meester White, that you and your associates are under house arrest. You should not leave the vicinity until I have spoken to my superiors and been advised as to whether I should detain you or let you go. I am far from pleased that you are here." Campos was practically beaming. His affect was disconcertingly at odds with both his words and the situation. "This is a crime scene, Meester White, off limits to the public. I urge you to get back in your vehicle and return to Huatepec. We can talk later, when I've finished with my duties here."

Lee, Rocío, and Kevin stood with Campos in the middle of the road at almost exactly the spot, a half mile or so from Las Llagas, where the van had gotten the flat. Fifty yards beyond, almost within sight of the village, was the *Combi*. From where they stood listening to Campos, Lee and the others could see that all the windows had been shot out. There were also obvious blood splatters on the crystalline shards of the windshield safety glass. Trying to avoid showing interest in the *Combi*, Lee was able to see that Campos had the corpses arranged in the shade of a cactus tree, lumps under a tarp, safe from all but the most persistent flies.

A half mile back, as Felipe had suggested, Checo and Courtney left the road and were triangulating into the desert to approach the "crime scene" from the direction of Las Llagas. The desert was a forest of large, tree-like Yucca cacti which offered cover, but also obscured vision. They had to rely on dead reckoning for guidance. Luckily, Courtney had an excellent sense of direction. She always knew where she was. As they approached the "crime scene" and the bodies, they'd have to trust that Lee and the others were creating a diversion.

Courtney was there over Lee's strenuous objections. Checo insisted that he needed another photographer to be certain that they got the documentation. He was not going to risk his life and mental health only to have the enterprise fail because of a camera malfunction. Lee had wanted Kevin to do it.

The problem was the whole artifice of the screen test for Campos. Campos thought that *Kevin* was the filmmaker. Kevin would, therefore, have to preside at the fraudulent "screen tests." That left Courtney and Rocío as the only candidates to operate the second camera. Rocío didn't know anything about cameras except, Checo noted, how to parade her naked butt in front of them.

For his part, Lee knew Courtney's mother. Hannah hated Mexico. She'd urged Courtney to stay away. When that failed, she'd called Lee and exacted a promise. Lee had sworn a solemn oath to his ex-wife that he'd keep their daughter safe. He threatened to scrub the entire plan unless Courtney stayed with Felipe and Elena. It was one thing to take professional risks and quite another to put one's daughter at risk. Courtney, however, had been adamant. She was an adult and a professional, and *she* would decide which risks *she* would take.

Felipe was equally adamant. In his opinion, the plan would not work without Courtney. Checo, he told Lee, was a city boy and could easily get disoriented in the cactus forest. Courtney, he observed, would not get disoriented. It was simply not in her nature. Lee was whipped. He ruefully consoled himself with the thought that Courtney had learned her nature, her relentless intransigence, from her mother and not from him. Anything that happened to Courtney would ultimately be the fault of her mother.

As they made their sojourn through the desert towards Las Llagas, Courtney and Checo were hoping for an opportunity to spend a quick ninety seconds at the "crime scene." They would finish the film in the Pentax and then expose a roll of Ektachrome on each of two other cameras. They would snap like mad, high-tail it back into the desert, and retrace their route. Lee would pick them up in the cover of and arroyo where he'd dropped them.

"This is a incredible, isn't it? Lee's plan . . . I think it's going to work!" Once he'd agreed to help, Checo had lost his reluctance for the gonzo approach. "I love working with your dad, Courtney. There really is no one like him! I mean the connections here are his compadres. Your film, my photos, all of it exists because of the relationship between Lee and the Piñedas. Your dad has dragged me into this peril and into an appreciation of the *campesinos*, the *nacos*. Until this trip, I always feared people like Felipe and Elena. They made me nervous."

Courtney was grateful for the intense dry heat. As frightened as she was, it was a small comfort to finally be warm and dry. Huatepec had been both moist and chilly. The tropical forest was a treat to the senses, but it was also overwhelming and unexpectedly confining. In the desert a person could walk and breathe the stirring, neutral air.

"What are you saying? All I hear the two of you do is gripe at each other."

"Yes, I can imagine how that seems. I irritate him, he irritates me. It's part of our mutual affection." Checo was glad to be talking. It helped him fight down the fear that was rippling up and down his back.

"You didn't want to do this, though. You fought it every step of the way."

"That's because it's so dangerous and ill-advised. But it's also fun, even if Campos ends up shooting us. It is novel to be doing something that may just possibly be consequential."

"So what do you provide for Daddy?"

"I do what his wives would never do. I listen to him. I put up with his eccentricities."

"So you blame his wives? Unbelievable."

"Who said I blamed his wives? No one on the planet has more empathy than I for those poor women."

"I never knew what he did down here. He kept it vague, hedged. He was always guarded, elusive."

"I'd call it reserved, observant, deliberate. In Mexico, understanding *gringo* culture is immensely important. In the U.S., understanding Mexico is irrelevant to the point of being foolhardy. Think of your stepfather, his wealth, his position. . . . While Lee is, what, helping subversive nuns organize crafts cooperatives for Mexican Indians, thus limiting his own profits? Think of the judgments, your mother's, Lee's parent's and sister's. You wonder that he's less than forthcoming? You wonder that he withdraws?"

"Tell me about it."

"I am."

"Checo, you have given me a hard time at least once a day ever since we met. Why?"

"It's partly because you are such a quintessential *gringa*, Courtney. And I am a Mexican. Then too, Lee is my *compadre*. I consider you my goddaughter. Finally, I'm jealous of Kevin and feel that he's beneath you. I make no apologies for my behavior. You have it coming."

"What?"

"Kevin . . . it pains me to admit that he is both talented and energetic. You must realize, though, that you are going to have to wipe his ass for at least ten years."

"You are unbelievable."

"Am I wrong?"

"You are the most arrogant man I ever met. Kev's immaturity wears thin, but he is kind and honest and open. Still, I guess you're right about Daddy. He really does seem at odds with his own people, like me. He does better down here. He's more comfortable and relaxed with Felipe and Elena than I've ever seen him. He relies on them. With them he doesn't have that looking-for-the-exits way about him. He gets annoyed with me because I'm a *gringa* and I remind him of my *gringa* mother. I guess being an American is a big strain on him."

Checo smiled. Courtney had quite a stride. All leg, she was, all breathtaking leg! Since they'd started talking about her father, she'd pushed the pace. Checo was practically running.

She continued to talk. Checo supposed that, like the pace, it helped her to deal with the fear and tension. "It was hard," She said, "to enjoy the *fiesta*. It was so different from anything I'm used to. When we got the shooting done, I was able to loosen up but I know I never understood it."

"We're at opposite poles there. I understood the *fiesta* in my very bones and it filled me with dread and despair."

The cactus forest sloped up to foothills. The alluvial slope, however, was so gradual that it seemed flat. It was impossible to see landmarks. In another forest, Courtney might have climbed a tree to double check her feel for the destination. She did not have the luxury. The conversation with Checo was distracting and upsetting just when she needed to be focused, alert.

"Checo," she raised her voice and clipped her phrases. "We need to keep on task and moving at a good pace."

"Oh, by all means." Checo laughed until he choked, stopped for a moment to compose himself, and spoke. "Listen, this project is dangerous and foolish. I will not walk mutely to my death."

"Why are you laughing like that? Jesus, Checo, get a grip. I think we're getting close to the spot where we'll need to turn east. If you want to talk, then tell me why my dad is so determined to see that Sam Cooke is somehow nailed."

"The truth is that I don't know. I fear it has to do with the madness of the war in Vietnam. Today, for the first time in twenty years, he told me a story from the war."

"What was the story? Protesting the war? Sending back his medals? I've heard all that."

"I won't tell you. It's his business to tell you that horrifying story, not mine."

"Well, fuck you then, Checo. So much for what could be the last conversation of our lives. Just tell me some ball scores. Soccer is what Mexicans are into, isn't it?"

"You know, that crack reminds me of your father. You and he have much in common. Both of you use wisecracks and vulgarity to evade your feelings."

"You're evading my question."

"I suppose I am. Why, by the way, are you doing this rather than staying in Huatepec as your father suggested? Why insist on being at the center of this madness?"

"Two reasons: it's the professional thing to do and it's the right thing to do. It's work in the service of truth."

Checo smiled. They were whispering, he realized, and that was probably smart. They might be getting close to the bullet-riddled *Combi*.

"Just keep in mind," he said, "that the truth is the truth whether we serve it or not. It's arrogant to assume that our acts have importance."

"Checo, you are utterly full of shit," Courtney laughed quietly, stifling the noise.

"I'd be the last to deny it."

They pressed on into the desert. Courtney's dead reckoning brought them to the road about 100 meters west of the bloody, disabled *Combi*. They hid themselves and waited for the distraction Lee and the others would create to allow them to rush in and take their photos.

Campos was immediately suspicious when Lee proposed the screen tests.

"I think you are doing some culture work, here, Meester White. Jesús and Ignacio are *büeyes*. If there are parts for oxen in my brother *Chicano's* movie, then I'm sure you don't need to leave Huatepec to find them. As for me, it is beneath the dignity of my uniform to indulge myself in such a vain exercise. I have this tragic crime to investigate. Now please get into your vehicle and return to Huatepec . . . after you clarify something for me."

Lee was sweating. This was not coming off. "Clarify something?"

"Yes, 'clarify something,' an item of physical evidence. One of the corpses had this piece of paper in her pocket." He showed Lee the note with his email address. "I believe that is your electronic mail address?"

"Yes."

"So what was the nun doing with your address in her pocket when she was killed?"

"I gave it to her."

"Oh, does your 'culture work' involve the Church?"

"Of course not. But I've been coming here for years, I have business concerns, I buy native crafts to import into the U.S. I talked to Sister Remilda at the *fiesta* of Santiago and she took my email address to send me quotes on the crafts that the Maryknoll cooperative sells in San Lucas. It was nothing, pure business."

Lee actually came up with a smile in spite of the stress.

At this point in the discussion, both Lee and Campos noticed a slight Indian man standing between Campos's Jeep and the white van. He had gray hair and a whispy moustache. He was panting, having just dismounted from an ancient, cobbled-together bicycle that he was placing carefully on its kickstand.

Eyeing the old Indian, Campos spoke. "So now it's show business and here's a comedian. Are you here for your screen test, *Señor* Comedian?"

The man smiled at Lee, who recognized him as the person who'd been responsible for guarding the van while they were in Las Llagas getting the tire fixed. He doubtlessly remembered the money and the *ponche.* He took his weathered straw hat, bowed his head, and touched his fist to his forehead. "I am no comedian, sir, just simple Aaron Pombo at your service. If you are Lieutenant Ezequiel Campos, it is my duty to give you an urgent message."

Campos drew a deep breath, directed his eyes upward as though for guidance or succor, and spoke. "So spit it out, Gramps."

"I was bicycling from Las Llagas to San Martín Los Cues to attend the funeral of my *compadre* Don Ramon Feliciano, who was taken by an *aire* and suffered . . ."

"I don't need your life story, ox, just give me the message!"

The old man pressed his lips together, drew a breath, and spoke. "A yellow ice cream truck has broken down. It is seven kilometers on the other side of Las Llagas, just before San Martín. The driver is trying to fix it. Villagers are helping. Who knows if they can fix it? Who knows how long it will take? The driver said he will come when he can, but you may need to make other arrangements. He said you would give me ten *pesos.*"

Campos closed his eyes, took his hat off, and rubbed his head. He took some change out of his pocket and gave the old man five *pesos.* He turned to Lee.

"I do not know what you are up to, Meester Cultural Worker. I am going to see what has happened to this cursed, fucking, violated whore of an ice cream truck. You are going to come with me. We are taking your van. *Señorita* Fino and Meester *Chicano* Power can stay here and have a little picky-nicky with Jesús and Ignacio."

He shouted to his soldiers. "Chuy, Nacho, get your butts over here."

The men responded, almost knocking the old man off his bicycle as he made his shaky way back towards Las Llagas and his disrupted funeral plans.

"OK, listen," Campos said. "Meester White and I are going on a little outing. The ice cream truck has broken down and I need to assess the situation. I want you boys to meet the famous movie star, Rocío Fino. You probably don't recognize her with her clothes on. Keep a close eye on her and also the *pocho*. Keep running villagers off. Got it?"

The men nodded.

No "Sir! Yes Sir!" hypermilitaristic shit from these good boys, Lee noted with pleasure. Lee did have a fond place in his heart for the "apolitical" Mexican Army.

Rocío was wearing a baby blue leatherette mini-skirt and a tight, baby blue and white checkered cotton blouse. Ignacio and Jesús ogled her with unselfconscious dedication.

Lee opened the passenger-side door of the Dodge and went around to drive. "Always pleased to be of service to the Army of the Republic."

Campos did not answer. As they pulled away, Lee gave Rocío a wink. He dangled his left arm out the window, out of Campos's field of vision, and rubbed his thumb against his fingers in the universal sign for "money." Rocío smiled and blew him a kiss.

Standing by himself, abandoned in the dust, Kevin was beside himself with worry. Lee had driven off without translating or giving Kevin a clue as to what was going on. Heartened a bit by Rocío's apparent good cheer, he remembered that she spoke a little English. "What's going on? Where are they going? What happened to the plan?"

"You no preoccupy, Kayban. Campos, Lee, they go for hour. We geebe *soldados* money. Take peectures, do what we want. They don't know nothing. They Indian boys from steecks. I wrap in feengers. You got money? Me no. Miriam has secure."

Kevin did have money. Unfortunately, it was still in large bills, the smallest a hundred *pesos*.

It worried Rocío. "It too much," she said. "Twenny better."

The subjects of this discussion had not moved since their arrival at Campos's jeep. They stared at Rocío, struck dumb by the shamelessness of her miniskirt.

Rocío spoke to them. "Where are you fellows from?" she began. Kevin understood that much, but that was about the limit. Evidently, though, Rocío felt the need to do a very thorough job of chatting the soldiers up before getting down to business. Finally, she had him give each of the men a hundred *peso* bill. Rocío then climbed up on the hood of the jeep, giving the soldiers a bit of a show to go with their hundred *pesos*. Once in position, she stuck her thumb and little finger into her mouth and astonished Kevin (and the soldiers) with a truly ear-piercing whistle. A few minutes later, Courtney and Checo straggled out of a thicket of cactus and sage and onto the road about fifty yards the other side of the bullet riddled Volkswagen.

Kevin explained to Courtney what had happened. He was a little light on details, but was able to communicate the basics. Rocío gave a more extensive explanation to Checo. Under Checo's supervision, they moved quickly. His one extravagance with the extra time was to pose Jesús and Ignacio with the bodies and with the ruined car. He put these on the Pentax. They'd go so nicely with the shots from the basketball game. Checo and Courtney were also able to photograph the wallets, purses, and other pathetic personal effects of the dead priest and nuns. Jesús arranged the stuff on the hood of the jeep. He and Ignacio were a tremendous help. Cash and valuables found with the corpses would establish, for the news services of the world, that the murders were the work of assassins, not bandits.

Checo and Courtney were efficient. Courtney watched Checo and tried to mimic his work. Even with the leisure to work slowly, it took them only ten minutes to shoot all the film they'd want or need. Her professional duty done, Courtney handed her camera to Checo. She then turned and before she could even take one step, she vomited. Kevin, running to lend his support, stepped into the line of fire and got his running shoes spattered with vomit. Rocío took Courtney to sit in the jeep and ordered Jesús to bring some water so she could wash Courtney's face.

Checo smiled when he saw Kevin's shoes.

"Only monsters could do this without getting sick," he said cheerfully.

For insurance, Checo then took ten Polaroid shots. He also took two Polaroid portraits of Ignacio and Jesús standing beside the Army jeep. He knew this was foolish, but the soldiers were so appealing in their brutal innocence that he simply could not resist the impulse. He told them to hide the photos from Campos and send them to their moms.

Their mission accomplished, Checo and the still greenish Courtney departed without fanfare or delay. They walked away from the jeep on the road. They would wait, as planned, at the place Lee had dropped them off.

More than two hours later, around four in the afternoon, the van arrived at the "crime scene," followed by a garish yellow truck festooned with cartoon clowns and the familiar "Yogi Yom Yom" logo. Campos had chosen to ride with Lee rather than the owner of the "Yogi Yom Yom" franchise, who had driven the truck himself and brought his wife. Campos seemed dispirited, listless.

"That woman is a banshee, a buzzard. She is here to feast her shit-colored eyes on the bodies of those communist girls and the fat priest. She's the kind who goes to bull fights hoping for a goring, a disemboweling."

He was mainly silent on the way back to the jeep, which suited Lee fine. Before the sight of the wife of the "Yogi Yom Yom" franchise had cast him into gloom, Campos had gotten quite chummy. Lee had gotten correspondingly anxious. Chums like Lieutenant Ezequiel Campos he could do without. At the crime scene, Lee did not even stop the engine. Campos got out, downcast at the weary prospect of dealing with the corpses. Rocío and Kevin hopped in. Campos came around to the driver's side and spoke to Lee.

"Remember, Meester Culture Worker, you should not leave this *municipio* before you check with me. Your help today will be duly noted." He slapped the van and waved Lee on. Jesús and Ignacio, their faces alight with big fruity grins, gave Rocío and Kevin a big wave. Campos looked surprised.

"Uh-oh," Lee spoke to Kevin, "those meat-headed soldiers have Campos wondering. Well, can't be helped. How did the photo session go? Jesus, what's that smell? You haven't soiled your trousers, I hope.

Twenty-Four

"The milk run arrives around seven every second morning and leaves around eight."

Felipe was noodling on his guitar and the fried onion smell of Elena's *enchiladas* wafted through the compound. Lee hated waiting. It made him feel superstitious. He and Checo sat outside watching the sun sink red and molten behind the cloud enshrouded mountains to the west.

When he spoke, Lee's voice was pinched, anxious. "I'm just counting the minutes until that plane takes off. When those clowns try to break those bills, the whole western drainage of the Sierra Nacoteca will know about it."

"I just hope Campos doesn't find the little portrait Polaroids I made them."

The sun was gone and the light effects in the western sky were dramatic, eternal. Lee was beginning, by small degrees and against all reason, to relax. Could he possibly have heard Checo say something about portrait Polaroids?

As Checo apologized, Lee smiled. There was no use getting mad. It was touching that Checo still had the innocence to do something so stupid. If Campos found those photographs, he would flip. Checo felt that Campos would not learn of the bribes or the photos for "a while." This was not entirely reassuring. Lee'd observed that such projections, more hope than substance, are forged on the anvil of denial.

Checo had other worries. "What about Felipe? Will Campos try something nasty with Felipe if all of us disappear?"

"I notice you weren't concerned about Felipe when you took your goon portraits."

Lee cast a glance at Checo that made him wince. "But yes, I thought of that. Think what we owe them. We're ephemeral, Checo. We'd wash away in a strong shower. Felipe and Elena gave us the solidity and stability to do our work. Kevin may well owe his life to the Piñedas . . . and the rest of us too, for that matter."

Checo nodded in agreement. The strength and solidity of Felipe's quiet reserve was matched only by Elena's indomitable dynamism and cheerfulness. He spoke. "You've got a plan?"

"Yes and I hope it isn't too disruptive for them. I figure we should take Felipe along with Elena and the kids. They can stay with the relatives they're bound to have in Mictlán or San Lucas until Campos leaves. They could call Miriam Maldonado every day or so to check. He probably won't hang around more than a day or two. Yup, the Piñedas can now make that long overdue visit to Auntie Hortensia. Felipe's got about a zillion *compadres* to see to his crops and animals."

Hearing his name bandied about, Felipe stopped playing, looked at Lee, and arched his eyebrows. Lee wearily translated. Rocío clapped her hands together as did Elena, but Felipe's face clouded. Elena seldom got to go anywhere and would want to go visit an aunt (not Hortensia but Remedios), who lived in Mictlán.

Remedios was a widow. Everyday she would wake up from twelve or fourteen hours snoring on the *petate* and tell the first person she saw that she had not slept a wink. She would then say that she did not know why God had chosen to torture her by keeping her alive in such a state. Thus warmed up, she could devote her waking hours to her art and avocation. She would complain for the entire day. Felipe particularly disliked the way she served meals. "Here," she would say, "it's a poor meal, but I can't afford to keep food in the house. You go ahead and eat it, and I'll go hungry. It doesn't matter, I ought to be dead anyway." The potential menace that Campos posed could not be much worse than three or four days with Aunt Remedios. He supposed, though, that in Mictlán he could hang out with Orlando. That made him feel a bit better. He could see the merits of leaving Huatepec for a few days. "So we'd fly to Ixtlán and take the bus to Mictlán so you could pick up the Dodge from Orlando?"

"That would be the plan, *compadre.*"

Lieutenant Ezequiel Campos piloted the jeep through the dark, silent village. At ten P.M. everything was wet, dripping, cold, and smelling of death. He missed Hermosillo, the pleasant desert oven of Sonora, with it's clean creosote smells and far shimmering horizons. The business with the corpses had been horrible. It'd shaken him to oversee Jesús and Ignacio loading the shredded remains into the refrigerated truck. Now more than before, he bitterly resented being the one to clean up the mess for Sam Cooke. What was the point? It was beyond the simple pleasures of petty cruelty he so enjoyed. It lacked the brisk utility of *ley fuga* executions that cleansed the world and preserved decency. If shredding the bodies of old fat men and gawky girls was the future of military enterprise in Mexico, Campos was not sure he had the stomach for it. He'd faced the blank page for almost an hour and not been able to make a start on his report. Perhaps the drive would clear his head.

It was no wonder that Jesús and Ignacio, louts that they were, had run off to spend the evening drinking. They walked the four kilometers from the checkpoint to the Cosme store in drizzling rain. The Maldonado store was closer, but the soldiers had noticed a frostiness in the demeanor of Miriam Maldonado.

Contrary to his usual custom, Campos decided to go get his men and give them a ride back to the checkpoint. Lee White stood up for his men and no one could say that Ezequiel Campos did not do likewise.

As he pulled up to the Cosme store, Campos could hear the raised voices of discord. He smiled indulgently, turned off the motor and stepped into the store to get "his boys." The situation inside was chaotic. Mauricio Cosme was making a drunken attempt to total a bill. He was upset.

"Seventeen *pesos* and sixty-five *centavos,* that's what they owe.

Sir, your men are drunk. They refuse to pay. Cheats! Drunks! Losers! Bastards!"

The man, overwrought, lapsed into indignant mumbling. He was waving a hundred *peso* bill at Campos.

María Concepción Cosme was standing with Jesús directly under the Coleman lantern that lit the store to a midday intensity of brilliance. Ignoring Mauricio, Campos, and Ignacio, they were admiring a Polaroid photograph of Jesús standing beside the Army jeep that Campos had just parked outside the store. When Jesús noticed Campos, he grabbed at the photo, obviously intending to hide it.

"What is this?" Campos asked mildly, snagging the photo.

Jesús moaned and Mauricio piped up with an answer.

"It's for his unfortunate mother. He is an animal with no respect. They come here, keep us awake with their drinking, and have the nerve to flaunt their money and puff themselves with their photos. Then, at the end, they try a hustle. Look Sir, at this . . . they drank up seventeen *pesos* and sixty-five *centavos*. I asked my payment. . . . They handed me these." He held up two fresh, new, hundred *peso* bills.

"I'll take those."

Campos took the bills. From his wallet he counted out eighteen *pesos* and told Mauricio to keep the change. He then put the hundred *peso* bills into his wallet and walked towards the Coleman lantern. "This is a fine photograph," he said pleasantly.

Concepción agreed. Ignacio, resigned, handed Campos his photograph. Campos took a breath to compose himself, looking around at the pathetic, understocked store. Handing each of them a *peso*, he mildly asked Mauricio and Concepción to leave him alone with his men.

"Listen, boss," Ignacio began, "we weren't going to stiff you on the money. We were sick because of the corpses and it slipped our minds."

"SILENCE!"

At about one, a smiling Campos stepped smartly out the door of Cosme store. He carried Jesús and Ignacio's clothing. He also had all of the information on the afternoon's photo session at the "crime scene." Things had gotten interesting! Campos's face burned with excitement as he drove back to the checkpoint. The information was windfall, like unexpected wealth. He wondered how he should spend it.

His mood ebullient, Lt. Campos's fury against his *"büeyes"* cooled. He considered the impulse to take a bribe as so fundamental to human nature that he could hardly blame the boys on that account. Perhaps the cold, wet walk back to the checkpoint in their shorts and tee shirts would be punishment enough. He was, after all, a generous commander. The effrontery, however, of the *gringo* was insupportable. Did Lee White think he could secretly bribe his men, coddle them with portrait photos, and not suffer consequences?

When he arrived at the checkpoint, he decided to take a late-night ramble to enjoy the new possibilities and stimulate his creativity. As he walked west, down the road, away from the checkpoint, however, his chest tightened, his mood sank. Despite the amusements to be had at the expense of Lee White and his entourage, there would almost certainly be a shit storm. If the *gringos* had any ingenuity at all, then Campos was plucked and parboiled from the get-go. Prints and negatives could be duplicated and transported out of the village in some peasant's *naco* fucking plastic *bolsa.* digital images could be scanned and faxed or scanned and sent with email. The possibilities were practically limitless in terms of breaking his balls and showing his still unwritten report to be a pathetic lie. All it'd take would be one image from that crime scene . . . and then the authorities would have to have a scapegoat, but who?

The Lieutenant smiled bitterly recalling what his father had taught him about gambling. In every game there's a patsy, a turkey being plucked. Anytime you have to wonder just who it is, it's you. Sam Cooke had sure given him a screwing. Why hadn't the bastard made the effort to make the massacre look like a robbery gone bad? The Dzul types and their worm followers would have gotten the message along with the lesbo communist nuns. It'd be almost impossible, now, to write a credible report that'd square with the images that were sure to emerge. At the very best, Campos would be in the Sierra Nacoteca for months "investigating" the murders and catching flack from all quarters.

God, how he hated those mountains. Now that the rain had stopped, the insects had started up. The insects, when they were not swarming to bite, filled the world with such a racket that he could barely think. The madcap pilots who flew the milk run liked to buzz the checkpoint, flying at treetop level. The insects were often loud enough to drown out the noise of the engines. The sudden appearance of the planes was often unpleasantly startling. Campos stopped, drew a breath, and turned his head back to consider the clearing sky and the multitude of stars. How nice it would be to board the milk run and fly out of those hateful mountains and away from the report he had to write and file.

The next morning at nine, the elderly DC-9 that provided the remote villages of the Sierra Nacoteca with dirt cheap transportation arrived at Huatepec from San Anselmo Amacatl. As usual, the plane was two hours late. Flying conditions were perfect; the rain had cleared and it was sunny with almost no wind. The next stop was Ixtlán, thirty-one air kilometers or one-hundred and thirty two kilometers on the dirt road that linked the towns.

Elena had been too excited to sleep and had spent the entire night cleaning house around the sleeping visitors. Rocío had made her tearful farewell to Miriam Maldonado, who congratulated her on her "new possibility" with Lee White.

When Lee and his expanded entourage boarded the plane, it was already loaded down with people and animals on their way to Monday market in Ixtlán. Sister Judith, a tall, thick-ankled young woman with a shell-shocked look had already boarded. She greeted Courtney and met the others. Carolina Carrera was there to see her off. Carolina thanked Lee one last time for the pump and left the cabin. Checo boarded the plane with a sigh of resignation. Jorje Dzul helped to load Kevin's equipment and flirted with Susana, who was helping Elena with the kids and parcels.

At nine fifteen the plane rolled away from the shack that served as the staging arena. It lumbered its ponderous way towards the edge of a sheer precipice that dropped a thousand meters to the valley floor. Checo closed his eyes and was making supplications to his creator when the plane suddenly ceased it's bone-jarring revving and rolled to a clumsy stop three hundred meters from the ledge of the canyon.

Opening his eyes, he was perplexed and then horrified. A familiar Army Jeep pulled up next to the shuddering DC-9. Campos jumped out, followed by Jesús and Ignacio. A couple of confused minutes passed as the pilot and Campos shouted amiably at one another.

At length, the pilot walked into the passenger compartment to inform the passengers that he was going return briefly to the loading area. There'd be a short delay. People could leave the plane if they wanted, but for no more than a couple of minutes.

As the plane made a graceless turn and waddled towards the loading area, Lee came alive with energy. He crackled, rubbing his hands together and smiling, as he gathered his entourage together.

"OK," he said, "the important thing is to keep our perspective. This is not the same as getting caught in the *afueras*. It's going to be miserable, but the threat will be to our financial rather than our physical well being."

He went on to explain that he'd given Miriam Maldonado a package, Checo's exposed film, to mail. It was addressed to Checo at his parent's address in San Angel.

"So don't despair. We'll have something when we get to D.F. whatever happens here. We can expect histrionics and threats. We've got to allow him to slowly convince us to give up the photos of the crime scene along with a big bribe. The price of poker just went up. Kevin, Courtney, for God's sake don't say a word about your rights as Americans and don't ask to talk to anyone up the chain of command. Campos is probably angry, but count on avarice to prevail. We have access to more money than he could strip off our dead corpses. We deal with HIM, got it?"

They all nodded. Rocío, who'd wiggled her way to Lee's side laid her left breast with seeming innocence against his arm. Lee smiled and shifted his weight almost imperceptibly against her. Danger and adrenaline made the moment all the more delicious. It pained him, on the other hand, to see poor Courtney's shaky hands, tight lips, blanched face, and terrified expression. He had to note, however, that fear sure made some people look silly.

"We act casual," he continued. "We leave the plane, stretch our legs, go pee, whatever. Just dummy-up, keep your mouths shut. I'll be explaining to Campos that we're flying out for the sake of speed and convenience; that I misunderstood the terms of the house arrest;

and that the bribes to the soldiers were simply tips in gratitude for their help. I'll claim that the photos were tourist *'recuerdos.'* Tourists, after all, take photos of everything. The lies are transparent, but they will give me a place to stand in negotiations. Checo, you stay close, he may come on pretty strong, so you pick up the slack if I go blank."

They left the plane via the very basic, very shaky, moving stairway which was constructed of pipe. Campos and the soldiers waited at the bottom. He spoke to Lee as Lee descended the steep stairway.

"Ah, Meester White, what a surprise to see you here. I am pleased that I've found you. My compliments on the hat. Your efforts to support Mexican craftsmen are nothing short of heroic. Could I prevail upon you to step aside for a moment? We must talk."

Looking down on Campos, Lee felt loathe to move. He had the crazy feeling that if he could continue to tower over Campos, he would prevail, dominating the ensuing confrontation. He also annoyed himself with a fleeting wish that he'd been able to keep the gun. He nodded.

At the bottom, Campos led Lee and Checo a discreet distance from the plane and its rag-tag gaggle of passengers and their animals. Lee raised his eyebrows, met Campos's gaze. Campos shifted his gaze to the horizon.

"I was not aware, Meester Cultural Worker, that you had psychic powers."

Lee nodded, indicating that Campos should continue.

"Here I was, looking high and low, the bearer of good news, I thought that the house arrest is suspended. Now I find you ready to depart, obviously informed of your happy situation. Perhaps too, then, you know that startling evidence has emerged in my investigation of the murders near Las Llagas."

Lee, usually responsive if not glib, was having difficulty. He glanced at Checo and saw that no aid was likely from that quarter. Campos looked rested, happy, and relaxed. He was holding an expensive looking cordovan leather folder.

"I know nothing. How could I know anything?"

"Don't be modest, Meester White, you have your ways. At any rate, you'll agree that the crime scene at Las Llagas had the appearance of a botched robbery?"

"From my limited knowledge, I would say so."

"Well, that's what I thought too. The lesson of this is that first impressions can be very wrong."

"Which is why I qualified myself."

"Yes, I fully understand your caution. Now, as I proceeded with my investigations, I ultimately came to a startling conclusion: the victims were murdered. And not simply murdered, they were assassinated for political reasons. Your countryman, Sam Cooke, whom you so aptly characterized as a 'pimp,' is my prime suspect in the case." Showing a flare for dramatic timing, Campos paused to let the information sink in. He lit a small cigar and called for Ignacio, who ambled over. "Nacho, find *Señor* Worm and his harridan wife. Search their belongings. I do not care to have that woman wielding her spoon and menacing passengers in flight."

Ignacio, sniffling, shuffled unhappily off towards Felipe and Elena, who stood nearby.

Campos turned to Lee with a pleasant smile.

"Investigations often produce unexpected results. Since the breakthrough last night, I have been an insomniac, on the phone constantly. I nearly missed the plane for that reason. I am now on my way to the state capital to brief my superiors, who will be answering questions at an international press conference that is scheduled at eight tonight at Judicial Police headquarters. As a journalist, you are, of course, welcome to attend. Forgive me, can I offer you a small cigar? These are from the San Andrés Valley and stand up with any cigar in the world."

Lee took one and accepted a light. Checo declined.

"It's probably good," Campos continued, "that you've finished your work. Official protests of U.S. adventurism (involving both the nuns and Sam Cooke) in Mexican internal affairs are forthcoming from the highest levels of government. The sovereignty issue will play well in the upcoming elections. Heads, too, are sure to roll at the American Embassy, and we must endure a period of strained relations between our countries. The situation might well have affected your work here."

Lee was not a smoker, but he accepted Campos's assessment of the cigar. It was mild yet rich, calming somehow. So when would the boot fall? Campos's eyes scanned the horizon.

"I absolutely must fly out of here today. That's why I had to take the unfortunate step of stopping the plane. It looks like we are going to be fellow passengers, Meester Culture Worker, at least as far as Ixtlán."

Lee had to check to see that he was not allowing his mouth to hang open. He gave the baffled Checo a wary glance that Campos noticed and acknowledged with a wink.

"I am hoping you can help me, Meester White. Chuy and Nacho tell me that during the time you so graciously drove me to see about the refrigerated vehicle, your daughter and your Mexican associate," he nodded at Checo, "profusely photographed the crime scene. Is that the case?"

"Yes," Lee drew a breath. Now the boot would surely fall. He was almost relieved.

"Well, first, I want to emphasize that Mexican soldiers require no payment when they provide assistance. Such gifts are, in fact, against federal regulations. I naturally understand that your daughter and her filmmaker friend, the young *Chicano,* would not necessarily know of this law. I am inclined, therefore, to look with indulgence on the gifts they made to my soldiers. Unless circumstances change, I do not feel inclined to misconstrue the generosity of your young associates nor report them to the authorities."

"I was not aware . . . " Lee's voice trailed off.

Campos raised a hand and smiled, shaking his head. "Don't concern yourself further with the issue of the gifts. It is forgotten. I do, however, have a small favor to ask. The shift in the focus of the investigation was unexpected. At present, I lack photographs of the crime scene, photographs that would enhance my report and satisfy the press. I am wondering, then, if you would be willing to allow me to use your photographs in my report. I would provide a receipt, arrange for speedy processing in the state capital, and, of course, forward the negatives to you."

Lee spoke to Checo who looked as though someone had hit him between the eyes with a mallet. "Let's use English here. He has every conceivable advantage."

"No shit. He's saving his ass by going after Sam! It's brilliant!"

"So we give him Courtney's film to develop?"

"Absolutely. We might as well give him my Polaroids too. He

obviously has us by the short and curlies. But how did he . . . "

"Who knows? Whatever's going on is wicked clever, certainly beyond our poor skills. We never wanted to do a murder expose anyway. If he does it, fine. If our photos help, fine—especially since we don't have any choice. You did pick up on the threat to arrest Kevin and Courtney? It's lucky all he wants is the film. Basically, what we can do is declare victory and get the fuck out of Dodge."

"No, Lee, you get the Dodge the fuck out of here if you feel you must. I have summoned my courage and boarded that soul-destroying airplane. You can get the van, or Orlando can drive it as planned, or it can stay here until doomsday for all I care."

Lee laughed.

"'Get out of Dodge,' is a *modismo* Checo. I mean we make our exit . . . listen, Campos is going to think we are imbeciles yammering on like this. Let's just 'get out of Dodge'."

Checo shook his head in disgust. Learning English was apparently a lifelong process. "Jesus, what a language. Forget the *modismos,* I don't want to hear about 'inside straights,' 'necks of the woods,' 'moving the goal posts,' or 'getting out of Dodge.' I don't have the stamina for it. He wants to hear from you, so I beg you for the love of God, just tell him in simple, unambiguous terms that the exposed film is his. It's good that, in spite of your colloquial speech, you had the foresight to mail the roll I shot to Mexico City. We may yet use them. Now, speak to Lieutenant Campos."

Switching to Spanish, Lee addressed Campos.

"Yes, we do have photographs—exposed film, that is—and a few polaroids. You are welcome to them. I will see that you get everything and I will also introduce you to Sister Judith, who would have been murdered along with the others had she not been too sick to travel. She has access to a wealth of information on Sam Cooke, his men, and their 'activities.' It's gratifying, after our strained relations, to be in accord at last."

Campos, his star obviously on the rise, smiled warmly.

"Yes, and I'm also most appreciative of the opportunity to meet Sister Judith. Sam Cooke's espionage, terrorism, and attempts to use the Army of the Republic to legitimize his activities have failed. The hunter has now become the hunted. Roadblocks are in place at the foot of the mountain and I expect news of his arrest at any moment."

Luckily, during the short stop, the engine had not died. Checo had spent a night almost as ridden with insomnia as Elena. After all the mental gymnastics of preparation for the worst, it felt like a real luxury to fall into the abyss in an airplane that actually had it's engines running. There was a slight dip, but the roaring engines intercepted the scarcely perceptible fall and the plane began to heavily gain altitude.

Sitting Campos with Sister Judith, Lee gave Courtney a chile-lime watermelon flavored lollipop and the window seat. When the plane shuddered in a pocket of turbulence, Courtney took her father's hand. She held it all the way to Ixtlán.